Damn him!

How could he do this to her? She didn't want to be attracted to him. He stood for everything she didn't want in a man. Why wouldn't he leave her alone?

"Please," she whispered, her mouth dry. "I think you'd better leave."

He didn't speak; he came closer, stopping in front of her, a hairsbreadth away. "Don't send me away." His voice was a husky, seductive lure.

A sense of absolute finality overcame Raine as she looked up at Ashe, making her ache with a strange excitement mixed with fear. A current was flowing between them, without words and without touch. Her nerves tightened in unwelcome awareness. It was the most powerful experience of her life....

Dear Reader,

When two people fall in love, the world is suddenly new and exciting, and it's that same excitement we bring to you in Silhouette Intimate Moments. These are stories with scope, with grandeur. These characters lead the lives we all dream of, and everything they do reflects the wonder of being in love.

Longer and more sensuous than most romances, Silhouette Intimate Moments novels take you away from everyday life and let you share the magic of love. Adventure, glamour, drama, even suspense— these are the passwords that let you into a world where love has a power beyond the ordinary, where the best authors in the field today create stories of love and commitment that will stay with you always.

In coming months look for novels by your favorite authors: Maura Seger, Parris Afton Bonds, Elizabeth Lowell and Erin St. Claire, to name just a few. And whenever you buy books, look for all the Silhouette Intimate Moments, love stories *for* today's women *by* today's women.

Leslie J. Wainger
Senior Editor
Silhouette Books

IMRL-7/85

A Handful Of Heaven

Mary Lynn Baxter

Silhouette Intimate Moments

Published by Silhouette Books New York

America's Publisher of Contemporary Romance

SILHOUETTE BOOKS
300 E. 42nd St., New York, N.Y. 10017

ISBN: 0-373-07117-5

First Silhouette Books printing November 1985

10 9 8 7 6 5 4 3 2 1

MARY LYNN BAXTER

owns and manages the D & B Book Store in Lufkin, Texas. Romances have been her favorite books for years, and she sells more romances in her store than any other kind of book.

To my son, Jody.

With special thanks to William Maxey
for his aeronautical expertise

and

David Goza for keeping both me
and my computer together.

Prologue

Panic coursed through Ashe Elliot's veins like sharp, cold chips of ice.

"Dammit it, Todd! Slow her down!" he shouted. But his words fell on deaf ears as the man flying the navy attack plane could not hear his agonized cry.

Gut instinct told him that something was wrong, terribly wrong, but there was not one damned thing he could do about it on the ground. Simulated carrier landings were difficult to do at best. However, he had been so sure Todd could handle it. But he wasn't sure about that now. His approach was all wrong; he was too high and too fast.

Perspiration dotted Ashe's forehead and upper lip as he kept his face turned toward the sky, oblivious to the blazing east Texas sun bearing down on him, scalding his head. Frustration held him rooted to the spot, chewing his lower lip, his fingers digging into the palm of his hand, watching, waiting, and praying. The noise around him was deafening, but he felt totally alienated. The ground crew was scurrying around and someone was yelling orders as the crew anticipated disaster.

Suddenly, and without warning, it happened. Just as the plane's tires made screeching contact with the hot asphalt of the runway, the landing gear folded under the belly of the sleek bird of prey like a priest kneeling at the altar. As though in slow motion, the plane began to skid down the runway, showering sparks into the dead grass alongside the runway. Ashe's frantic "God, Almighty!" was lost in the grinding sound of metal as the plane ground its inexorable way down the six thousand feet of runway before veering off to the left and flipping over on its top.

Ashe managed somehow to free his frozen muscles and join the others as they began running toward the plane, only to come to an abrupt halt, as though he had slammed into a brick wall, watching in horror as fuel spilled on the ground, coloring it dark and dingy.

Then suddenly the tanks burst into flames, spreading like wildfire throughout the fuselage.

"Todd!" Ashe yelled as he ran toward the flaming inferno.

Chapter 1

Raine Michaels glared down at the folder in front of her as though it were poison.

"Stop frowning. You should know better than anyone that it causes wrinkles."

Raine's head popped up and a halfhearted smile softened her lips as she eyed her assistant, Valarie Holland. "It's this account that's causing the wrinkles."

Val gave an unladylike snort, the cap of carrot-colored curls matching the fire in her eyes. "Even with a magnifying glass, I couldn't find a wrinkle anywhere on your face if my life depended on it."

"Well, it's only because you haven't looked close enough," Raine said. "And I'm going to have a lot more wrinkles if I can't get out of carrying the Mosby line of sportswear in the new boutique."

Valarie frowned. "What's the deal? I thought that had already been settled."

"I thought so, too, but..."

Valarie's eyes narrowed. "Don't tell me she's on your case again? If I'd known that, I wouldn't have buzzed you. Of course, when she asked for you—said it was terribly important—sugar wouldn't have melted in the ole biddy's mouth."

Valarie's quip, so aptly phrased, brought another smile to Raine's lips. "It's not your fault; you did exactly right by putting the call through. After all, she's an important designer as well as a client. I hate to offend her, but with money being so tight I can't stock every line, even though I might want to. I have to be practical and selective."

Suddenly, Val scooted off the desk and began pacing across the carpeted floor, tapping her pencil in the palm of her hand with every step she took. "And of course she's being pushy and, if I had to guess, rather nasty. I wish you'd tell her to go take a flying leap. New Image doesn't need the kind of grief she dishes out, especially when there are so many other lines that will fit the needs of our women much better than hers."

Raine sighed. "I know, if only I could afford to stock them. The boutique is costing so much more than I thought. Money is getting to be a real problem." She paused momentarily, focusing her attention on her assistant's nervous pacing. "For heaven's sake, will you stop that? If you don't, I'll be joining you, and then where would we be? Two crazies wearing a hole in the carpet, that's where."

Valarie stopped pacing and turned to stare at Raine with slightly raised eyebrows. "What about your banker, Ed Giles? Won't he loan you the extra cash?"

"Oh, I'm sure he would, but I've already had to put New Image up as collateral, and at this point I'd hate to go any further into debt."

Valarie hesitated, then asked, "You could always ask Ross Thomas for the money, couldn't you?"

"You already know the answer to that question," Raine replied crossly, then got up wearily from her chair and made her way to the window and stared out into the bright sunlight. Although she watched the activities on the streets of downtown Dallas, she was scarcely aware of what was happening

"But what I don't understand is why," Valerie said, forcing Raine to collect her thoughts.

Raine turned around with a sigh. "Because I don't want to be obligated to Ross in anyway, that's why. So he has the largest chain of clothing boutiques in Dallas and is capable of loaning me all kinds of money. So what? I want to do this all on my own, without Ross's influence or his money."

Valarie gave another unladylike sound and followed it with a full-fledged grin. "Whatever makes you happy. But it's beyond me how you could turn down someone like that who's so rich, so good-looking, and so crazy about you."

"Forget it, my friend," Raine responded quickly, putting a damper on the bright light that had suddenly sprung into Val's eyes. "You know I don't have time for a man in my life. And even if I did, I don't want one. Not now, anyway. I'm finally getting what I want out of life, and nothing is going to stop me now."

And it was true. Raine's life was indeed full of promise. As the owner and manager of a consulting firm, New Image, she worked with three or four hundred clients a year, from fashion editors and television personalities to women executives, putting together their personal wardrobes. Often she built around clothing in her client's closet, taking into account the woman's personality, body flaws, budget, and life-style.

However, Raine was not satisfied with what she had accomplished. She wanted more. She wanted to expand her business, branch out into women's apparel, and eventually add her own line of clothing that she herself had designed.

Soon the first part of that dream, her boutique, would be complete. At last she would be able to clothe her clients in their seasonal colors on the spot. It was a dream come true and she was resentful of anything or anyone who tried to interfere with her project.

Valarie's expression softened as her gaze remained on Raine. "Why don't you let me have the Mosby folder? I'll see what I can do to soothe her ruffled feathers. And I promise I'll be very diplomatic," she added with a wicked grin.

Smiling, Raine quickly reached for the folder and held it out to her assistant. "Have I told you lately how much I appreciate you?"

Valarie waved her hand absently before grasping the thick manila folder. "That's what I'm here for," she said airily, heading for the door and closing it behind her. Valarie adored Raine and would do anything she could to make life easier for her. Raine had given her a chance to prove that she could make it in the competitive world of glamor and fashion when no one else would even talk to her because she'd had no experience behind her.

Now alone, Raine felt the need for a cup of coffee before tackling the folders of two of New Image's latest clients. What a day, she thought. But she had so much to be thankful for, she quickly reminded herself. With the phones continually ringing, business was booming. And in the coming months she would be moving to her new building and opening the boutique.

It wasn't like her to overreact to anything. Usually she was a pro at dealing with the Sharon Mosbys of the world. She guessed she was tired. Bone-weary. But it was all worth it.

She had just poured herself a steaming cup of black coffee and was carefully making her way back to her desk when she looked up and saw Valarie standing in the doorway. So deep was she in thought that she hadn't heard Valarie open the door.

"What on earth is wrong, Val? You look like you've just seen a ghost."

Valarie's face bore testimony to Raine's statement. Her usually mischievous features were pinched and devoid of color, her eyes subdued. Raine felt a sudden uneasiness climb up her spine and knew an immediate premonition of disaster.

"Val?" Raine said again, trying to keep the tone of her voice even. What had happened? When the phone had rung only moments before, she had paid no attention to it. After all, if the phone didn't ring, then it meant no new business. But the ominous feeling persisted as she raised questioning eyes to her assistant.

"You...have a phone call on line one." Valarie's voice was low, anxious.

Raine made a face, then laughed. "Don't tell me. Let me guess! It's Sharon Mosby and she wants another pound of flesh!"

Valarie shook her head. "I'm...I'm afraid it's much more serious than that."

"Well, come on, Val, out with it. It couldn't be all that bad." Yet Raine couldn't deny the feeling of apprehension that was making itself felt in the pit of her stomach.

"It's...it's the hospital in Tyler!" Val stammered, licking her lips nervously. "It's about your brother..."

"Oh, my God!" Raine whispered, her face paling visibly. Then, with trembling fingers, she groped for the phone and lifted the receiver slowly to her ear, fear churning within her.

"Raine Michaels speaking." It took every ounce of willpower she possessed to keep from shouting her terror into the phone.

"Ms. Michaels, my name is Harry Townsend, a spokesman for Elliot Aircraft. I'm afraid I have bad news for you. A Mr. Todd Michaels, who listed you as his next of kin, has been injured in a crash."

Raine heard herself gasp.

Harry Townsend went on in his flat professional tone. "But let me assure you that everything possible is being done for him."

Gripping the instrument so tightly that she was sure the bones in her hand would shatter, she whispered, "Which...which hospital?"

"Medical Center," Townsend replied, his voice softer, more comforting.

"How...how bad is he?" Raine's cheeks hollowed as she sucked in her breath and held it, struggling to keep herself from falling apart.

"We're not sure, Ms. Michaels. It's too soon to tell, I'm afraid."

"I'll be there as soon as I can make connections out of Dallas." Now her voice was devoid of emotion as she felt Val's hovering presence behind her, a comforting hand squeezing her shoulder.

"There will be a car waiting for you at the airport."

Too frightened and numb with grief at the sudden turn of events even to say "thank you," Raine lowered the receiver back onto its cradle and doubled over, sobs racking her slender body.

"Oh, Val, how am I going to stand it?"

The next few hours were a living nightmare for Raine. Without Valarie's competent help, she could not have made it. Val hustled Raine home and helped her throw a few items in a travel bag and drove her to the Dallas-Fort Worth airport. Luckily, Raine had to wait only half an hour for a flight to Tyler.

During the hour-long trip to the small county airport on the outskirts of Tyler, Raine tried to empty her mind of all thoughts, hoping to hold on to her sanity. But no matter how hard she tried, she could not block out the mental image of her brother's body lying broken and mangled in the hospital bed. Oh, God! What if she was too late? What if... No! Don't think like that, she chided herself. He was going to be all right. He just had to be.

If Raine had a weakness, it was her brother, Todd. She doted on him and always had. With only two years separating them, they had always been close. Now with their parents both dead, she and Todd depended on each other. That dependence stemmed from having been reared as air force brats, dragged from pillar to post, left in the care of one housekeeper after another.

When Todd decided to follow in his father's footsteps and became a pilot, Raine had been devastated. She had begged him to change his mind, but her pleas had fallen on deaf ears, just as her father had ignored her mother's pleas. Raine's mother believed to her dying day that her husband cared more for flying than he did for his family.

Not only did Raine remember the numerous times her mother had drunk herself to sleep, but she also remembered the shock of having to uproot, leave friends, and move to another place, having to start over and over again. But most of all, Raine remembered the fateful day her father's lifeless body had been pulled from the charred wreckage of a plane.

Now she was experiencing the same shocking horror all over again. Only this time it was her beloved brother.

Once the plane had landed and Raine was on solid ground, she was taken immediately to the small compact car made ready for her. A short time later, she parked the car in the visitors' lot before making her way across the hot pavement to the side door of the hospital. The moment the automatic doors swished open, the sterile smell slapped her in the face.

Taking a deep breath, Raine squared her shoulders and approached a young woman dressed in a candy-striped uniform sitting behind the desk at the emergency room entrance.

"Please, can you tell me where they have taken Todd Michaels?" Now that she was here and about to see her brother, she felt herself unraveling on the inside. She stilled the trembling of her bottom lip by sinking her teeth into it. The taste of blood was salty on her tongue.

The woman spoke without hesitation, "Fifth floor. Room 507. Elevator to your right."

With a murmured thanks, Raine made a dash in the appointed direction.

The door to room 507 was slightly ajar. With her heart in her throat, she paused momentarily in the hallway, preparing herself for the worst.

It was then that she heard the voices. One had to be her brother's. It sounded weak, raspy. But the other was strong and well modulated. At first she could not make out what was being said, so she took a tentative step closer and opened the door wider. She froze in her tracks just inside the dimly lit room. A strange man was leaning over Todd's bed. This time there was no mistaking his words.

"Todd...about the plane," he was saying. "I want you to—"

Raine didn't bother to listen to the rest of his sentence. Rage suddenly swept through her like an out-of-control forest fire. "Just what do you think you're doing?" She was like a woman possessed as she stormed into the room and crossed to the bed.

God! She couldn't believe it. The military. Did they have to do everything by the book? Couldn't they have waited until later to investigate?

The stranger opened his mouth to speak, obviously hoping to defend himself, but Raine didn't give him a chance. Suddenly, she vented her thoughts aloud, her attack vicious. "How dare you question him at a time like this? Leave him alone!"

The man's head reeled back as though he'd been struck, before focusing startled eyes on Raine. But nothing about the intruder registered. The fact that he appeared both puzzled and more than a little perturbed by her hostile attack was completely lost on her. All that was important to her was that he was no longer looming over her brother's bed and hurling questions at him.

Raine eased herself down on the edge of the bed and reached out and very gently clasped one of Todd's limp hands in hers. Tears were saturating her face.

"Oh, Todd, darling," she cried softly, "what have you done to yourself?"

Todd's eyes, completely devoid of eyelashes, fluttered once or twice before he was able to hold them open. His words were barely audible. "Sis...please...please...don't wor-worry. I'll...be fine."

Swallowing the huge lump in the back of her throat, Raine whispered, "You bet you'll be, you big brute. Because I'm going to see to it. Do you hear me?"

His eyes fluttered once, twice. It was obvious he was not up to talking anymore, that one sentence having exhausted him. But he did manage to put a gentle pressure on Raine's hand before drifting into what she prayed was only a deep sleep. She peered at his chest, waiting for the thin sheet covering him to move, indicating that he was indeed breathing.

"I promise I won't leave you," she whispered to his sleeping form, feeling as though her heart was breaking.

The man, leaning against the window ledge of the hospital room, shifted his position and stretched his left arm, daring it not to go to sleep again. His incredibly broad shoulders served as a backdrop for a mass of dark unruly hair that made him seem as tall as a giant, and curiously light eyes that were neither gray nor blue, but a combination of both. However, when one color predominated, which was often the case, either the gray of gunmetal or the icy blue of a sapphire, they were both piercing and cold.

There had been a time when his eyes had actually danced and grown warm with passion, but that was long ago. So very long ago.

At this moment they were blue and watching the woman who had come barging into the room, jumping down his throat for being there. He had to admit, though, the woman had spunk. No one else he knew would have gotten away with talking to him like that. But it was understandable that she was upset. He shifted again, this time positioning himself so that he had a clearer view of her. Damn, but she was a knockout.

Who was she?

To his recollection, he had never heard Todd talk about any woman other than Heather. But then he had to admit he rarely heard his men discuss their personal lives, mainly because of the danger they lived with on a day-to-day basis, where, more often than not, tomorrow was a forbidden topic.

Again he asked himself, who was she? Ex-wife? Possible, but doubtful. Sister? Could be. But whoever she was, it was obvious she felt she had the right to counter his presence in the room.

He could not take his eyes off her, nor could he bring himself to intrude upon her genuine grief. The light from the lamp above Todd's bed allowed him a free perusal of her.

She was lovely as well as intriguing, he thought. Hard to pinpoint her age. About thirty or so, he decided. Slender, but not too slender, projecting an aura of strength. His lips twisted sardonically. Hadn't he been the victim of that strength? Hand free of rings. Yes, she was breathtaking. Caramel-colored hair that caressed her shoulders like a silk curtain, flawless skin, small narrow nose, appealingly wide mouth, soft brown eyes, lovely long neck. Perfect. A complete whole. Not like many of the women he took out on occasion. The edges of those women seemed to him in comparison to be all runny, blurred like unclear pictures taken with a bad camera. She had the sophistication of a woman who had beauty, brains, and class all in the same package.

He admired her carriage, the suggestion of voluptuous breasts, long thighs. Her figure was the kind that made men's throats get a little thick. She was wearing a loosely tailored skirt, but he could make out the flat stomach and the swell of her hips. And even from where he stood, he could see the way her firm breasts pushed against the material of her blouse.

Standing perfectly still, his long body rigid with tension, something stirred within him. He felt the sudden heat of desire surge through his veins, setting his whole body on fire.

Damn!

He stifled a cough while shifting his position yet again. Then suddenly deciding this fiasco had gone on long enough, he moved out of the shadows.

"It's all right, you know. He's just asleep."

Raine did not try to stop the flow of tears as they continued to trickle unheeded down her face, making a tiny splash on her hand that was still wrapped around Todd's. He looked dreadful, she thought, as her eyes roamed covetously over him. His leg was broken, molded in a cast and raised slightly in traction. A bandage was secured tightly around his forehead, covering every square inch of his head. The entire left side of his body also appeared to be bandaged. There were lacerations on his arms, neck, and face. He was a mess. And even though he hadn't been severely burned, it was still a miracle he was alive.

And to think someone had the unmitigated gall to question him about the condition of the plane.

Then it dawned on her. Dear Lord, the man! She had forgotten all about him! Her hand flew to her mouth to stifle her cry. Was he still in the room?

Then, as though on cue, the sound of his voice drew him to her at the same time his tall silhouette appeared out of the shadows.

He was looking at her with an air of private concentration, almost as if he were meditating. The space between them was suddenly charged with electricity; it made her eardrums hum, her skin crawl.

It was the most unbelievable sensation. Her hands were starting to shake. Time became strangely suspended in the sterile room.

His eyes continued to stare into hers.

Fighting against the chaos this man had stirred within her, she lashed out at him in an unsteady whisper. "Who are you? What gives you the right to be here?"

Raine knew she was behaving irrationally, but she could not control her tongue any more than she could control the pounding of her heart.

"I could ask you the same question," he countered coolly.

Raine's mouth compressed. "I don't—"

"Please..." he cut in, his tone soft, yet effectively silencing her. "How about if we continue this conversation outside in the waiting room? We don't want to disturb Todd."

Raine once again swung her eyes toward the bed. Had their voices disturbed him? With a sick feeling washing over her, Raine turned around, hoping against hope that the stranger had disappeared.

No such luck!

He was standing as though glued to the floor, watching her every movement. Bristling, Raine pivoted and, in a jerking motion, made her way out the door. Would this nightmare ever end? First Todd's accident, and now this overbearing, arrogant stranger to contend with. What next?

Upon entering the deserted waiting room, Raine took a stance in the middle of the room and turned around, wrapping her arms around her.

The man pushed his hands into his pants pockets as he halted in front of her. "I'm sorry about Todd. Is he a friend of yours?" he asked, his voice guarded.

"You could say that," she said waspishly. What was there about this man that both attracted her and repulsed her at the same time?

"Care to be more specific?" Although the thin lips below narrow cheekbones twisted mockingly, his tone didn't leave room for argument. His clipped tone told her that he was used to having his own way, that he wasn't used to having his demands thwarted. And that authority was impressive and formidable. She could not imagine how she had ever thought she could elude him.

Determined to disregard his question, she countered with another of her own. "Are...you investigating the accident?" Raine's tone remained hostile. She was afraid for Todd. It was a fear that was becoming more intense as the minutes ticked by. Had the accident been Todd's fault? Pilot error? Had he been drinking? No! How could she even think such a thing? But, then, everything was out of whack, warped, distorted.

"Yes, I'm investigating," he said lightly, "but not in the way you think." Then he smiled, and it transformed his face. He held out his hand. I'm Ashe Elliot, owner of Elliott Aircraft. And in spite of what you thought, I was not harassing the patient."

Her brother's boss! Oh, Lord! For the second time in one day, Raine found herself at a loss for words, and not because she had made a fool of herself, but because for the first time in her life, she was completely caught off guard by the way a man looked at her. Even with the gravity of the situation, she could not help but see the glint of desire that leaped into Ashe Elliot's eyes as they dwelled on her.

But, then, he was not just any man, she reminded herself. Oh, God, when he smiled, it made everything inside her race around like a mouse in a cage. He was beautiful. In fact, he was like no other man she had ever met. If there was a single word that described Ashe Elliot, it was *magnetism*. She had never met anyone who possessed it to such a degree.

Raine felt the heat rush to her cheeks as she forced herself back to reality and placed an unsteady hand into his outstretched one.

"Sorry..." She had to force the apology from her lips. "It's...it's just that I'm upset, worried," she added haltingly, trying desperately to keep her mind on Todd. But she was distracted by this man who suddenly seemed larger than life. Was he a friend? An enemy? Then she felt his large hand close around hers and underwent a spasm of self-disgust for caring either way and for responding to this good-looking stranger at so inappropriate a time.

As discreetly as possible, she removed her hand and stepped back, shifting rather uncomfortably beneath his appraising gaze.

"Would you like to sit down?" he offered. She'd turned pale, and small pinpoints of perspiration were gathering on her forehead, dotting her upper lip like a string of white pearls. His eyes darkened with concern.

"No...no, thank you," she said, her eyes darting toward the door, looking for a way to escape. "I must get back to Todd. He... he may need me."

For a moment, there was a silence as he kept his gaze on her. For a reason she could not identify, she was eager to put a safe distance between them. It was when she turned her back on him that she felt his hand on her arm.

"One moment," he demanded, detaining her.

Raine turned and looked at him more coolly than she felt, irritatingly aware that her pulse rate had quickened.

"You haven't told me your name." He was smiling and his voice was almost hypnotic; it seemed to caress her.

God! Was she losing her mind? "It's Raine, Raine Michaels. Todd is my brother."

Ashe could not ignore the feeling of relief that surged through him, leaving him feeling weak. Already the thought of her being personally involved with Todd was abhorrent to him. From the first moment he had laid eyes on this woman, he knew he wanted her. And that had not changed.

"Again, let me tell you how sorry I am this happened." The corners of his attractive mouth lifted. "But I give you my word he'll have the best of care."

Raine moved her shoulders. "Thank you." Her eyes sought the security of the door. "I have to go." He was close enough for her to smell the tantalizing scent of the cologne that clung to him, and to feel the heat of his body.

"Until later, then," he murmured, the fresh odor of his breath stirring the hair on her forehead and making her overwhelmingly aware of his alien attraction. "Because I'm sure our paths will cross again, Ms. Michaels."

Not if I can help it! Raine thought as she walked with her back rigid out the door, her heart beating abnormally.

Todd was still sleeping. A nurse was adjusting the intravenous bottle and gave her a small smile as Raine sat down in the chair next to the bed.

Once the nurse was gone and Raine was alone, she glanced down at her watch, hoping she hadn't missed the doctor. Five o'clock. God, it seemed as if it should be twelve o'clock instead. At least she hadn't missed the doctor; it was still too early for his evening rounds. But she couldn't thank Ashe Elliott for that piece of luck.

After caressing Todd's limp hand, she sank farther down in the cushion and laid her head back and closed her eyes.

Ashe Elliot. Just thinking his name sent a tremor of fright through her. Ridiculous as it seemed, she was instinctively aware that this man meant trouble, and although she had no reason to be alarmed, she was.

"Ms. Michaels?"

The sound of the gruff voice gave Raine a start. "Yes, I'm Raine Michaels," she said, making an attempt to stand up.

A gentle pressure on her shoulder stopped her. "Don't, keep your seat. I'm Dr. Anders. I've come to check on our boy, here."

Raine tracked him with anxious eyes. "How is he, Doctor, really?"

The doctor looked bleak. His white coat was crumpled, giving him a disheveled look. Apparently, it had been a long day for him, too. "We've done all we can. Our main concern now is that infection doesn't set in."

"What are the chances of that happening?"

"Right now, a good chance," he replied honestly.

Raine steadied her voice. "Exactly what is the extent of his injuries, other than the obvious facial and body lacerations?"

Dr. Anders sighed heavily. "Aside from several broken ribs, one extremely close to a lung, there are internal injuries."

"I see." She began twisting the damp tissue in her hand until it was in shreds.

Sympathy deepened the grooves around the doctor's eyes. She looked so feminine, so fragile, and so tired. "Try not to lose faith," he said consolingly. "Let's just take one day at a time. He's tough and he's a fighter. Considering what he's been through, he's in remarkably good shape. Stable enough, in fact, to have been moved out of intensive care, for the time being, anyway." He paused, looking as though he just remembered something important. "By the way, a special nurse will be here shortly, or so I understand. Orders from Mr. Elliot."

Raine shuddered. The mere mention of his name made her insides go haywire. "But...but that's not necessary," she said defensively. "I don't intend to leave him."

"That's no problem, you'll be needed, too." His eyes had grown soft. "Why don't you get away and rest for a while? There's nothing you can do now except worry, and that won't do either of you any good." Still seeing her hesitation, he pressed, "Promise?"

Raine nodded. "Thanks, Doctor, I promise."

But she could not make herself leave. How long she sat beside her brother's bed, watching and grieving, she did not know. Finally, she made her tired limbs unwind, and after leaning over and kissing Todd, she crossed the room to the door and opened it.

She heard his voice before she saw him. "How about letting me buy you a cup of coffee?"

Chapter 2

Raine's heart almost stopped beating when she saw *him*, leaning negligently against the wall. Seen in the brighter light, he was definitely more disturbing. His eyes. He had the most unusual eyes. Why hadn't she noticed them before? Blue? No, gray, she corrected herself quickly. Oh, God! She was indeed losing her mind. Here she was, thinking about his eyes at a time like this!

She expelled her breath raggedly as her nails pressed into her palms. The last thing she needed or wanted was to see Ashe Elliot again this evening. She was simply not up to coping with his overbearing personality.

But should she refuse him?

Even though she might not want to admit it, Ashe Elliot intrigued her.

He was now standing in front of her, blocking her path. When she made a deliberate attempt to get around him, for the second time that day, Ashe's fingers curled around her bare arm. This time he was acutely aware of the feel of her skin. Against his callused hand, it reminded him of smooth satin.

"Well?"

Raine shifted her gaze, unwilling to look him in the face. "I don't think so. I really should be getting back," she said, tensing beneath his touch.

Her uneasy movement made Ashe aware of her fragility. Her arm felt insubstantial in his grasp, the bones thin and delicate.

"Why?"

His bluntness caught her off guard, and it took her a moment to collect herself. "It's been a long day, that's why." Had she actually replied in that cool, touch-me-not tone, she wondered. She felt proud of herself.

"I've had a long day, too," he persisted, holding on to her arm and continuing to hold his firm stance in front of her. Her eyes were round and perfect, he thought. If he wasn't careful, he could lose himself in them.

When she did not answer him, he continued, smiling, stopping short of pleading. "What do you say? A cup of hot coffee is just what you need to relax."

Raine shivered, feeling herself beginning to weaken. Yet she was determined not to give in. It was an uncomfortable moment. But when it came down to it, wasn't she being foolish, she asked herself impatiently. Here was the chance to find out the details of Todd's accident. This might be her only chance. Yet, an inner voice warned her to decline, to find an excuse to get away.

Ashe looked at the pulsing whiteness of her throat and wondered if she was cold. "Please."

It was becoming harder and harder to refuse. "Look, Mr. Elliot, I—"

"Call me Ashe."

Raine opened her mouth to argue, but then she closed it just as abruptly. She was overreacting, she knew. It was perfectly reasonable that Ashe Elliot should ask her to join him for coffee. After all, he was Todd's boss. He was probably just being hospitable. And for heaven's sake, the invitation was only for a cup of coffee, not to share his bed!

As though their thoughts were on the same wavelength, Ashe said, his smile widening into a mocking grin, "Hey, I'm harmless, I promise. You don't have to worry; anything permanent scares the hell out of me. I'm immune to entanglements."

He was laughing at her openly now, but Raine didn't care. And even though his words were lightly spoken, meant to tease, she knew better. He was serious, and because of that she felt a crazy sense of relief.

In spite of herself, her lips tilted into a smile. "All right," she capitulated, ignoring the trembling deep inside her.

He finally withdrew his fingers from her arm with some reluctance. "Now, that wasn't so painful after all, was it?" Receiving no immediate answer, he went on, a twist of mockery still in his tone. "Are you always this uptight? Or does it have something to do with me?"

God, what arrogance! "You flatter yourself, Mr. Elliot," Raine said flatly, wishing now she'd told him to go to hell.

Raine had no idea what reaction she was expecting from her blunt comeback, but laughter was certainly not one of them. When he threw back his head and laughed, she was more than a little disconcerted.

"Chalk that one up to you," he said, his grin still intact as he guided her firmly but gently out the side door of the hospital. Then on a more serious note, he added, "There's a quiet restaurant a few blocks away. We'll take my car and then I'll bring you back here."

Taking for granted Raine would not argue, Ashe nodded toward the car, a sleek maroon Lincoln Continental. After seeing Raine comfortably settled in the plush seat, Ashe coiled himself behind the wheel and pointed the front of the powerful vehicle out of the parking lot and into a busy intersection.

Raine sat rigidly erect, forcing her eyes off the strong, competent hands grasping the steering wheel. She turned her attention out the window, concentrating on her surroundings. The small east Texas town was lovely. Just the right size. She had envied Todd his move to this quaint city. It was the ideal place to live, but with her work, it just wasn't possible. She needed to be in a metropolitan area, though at times she had to admit the people and the traffic got to her.

About the only criticism she had of Tyler was the humidity. At times it was unbearable, such as now. Even though it was getting late, the sun was still bright, intensifying the heat and humidity. And it promised to get worse, as it was only the middle of June.

After a few minutes every bone in Raine's body was stretched to its limit. She was trying so hard to keep her thoughts from dwelling on the man next to her, fighting to ignore the heated scent of his body that was drifting to her nostrils.

But it was impossible to keep from inhaling the fresh, clean smell of him. For a sudden moment, she felt suspended, disoriented.

What was happening to her? The heat in her cheeks intensified and she twisted uncomfortably in the cushioned seat. She wished she could stop her heart from beating irregularly, stopping and starting and fluttering in her chest. She wished she could get things under control. Damn! Was she really losing her mind?

"Feeling any better?" Ashe asked, slicing into the silence.

Suddenly the tears were dangerously close. Raine was unable to utter a word, her throat was so tight. Her face melted into a spasm of grief, which she kept from his view by keeping her head glued toward the window.

Finally, after a moment, she found her voice. "I'm...I'm fine, thank you, " she whispered.

But she hadn't succeeded in fooling Ashe. He was aware of every breath she took and his gut instinct told him that she was close to the breaking point.

Minutes later a hostess showed them to a quiet table in the corner. As soon as they were seated, Ashe ordered two cups of coffee. After leaving a menu with them, the waitress took her leave.

"Would you care for anything to eat?" Ashe asked softly, gazing at Raine, absorbing the full impact of her beauty. He knew it was not a trick of the lighting, nor something in the muted atmosphere that gave her that aura of ethereal fragility and innocence. The dark circles beneath were permanently etched into the delicate skin. Suddenly, he questioned his good judgment in bringing her here.

Raine shuddered. "No...no, I couldn't eat a thing."

Still concerned about the pallor of her face, Ashe grasped the pitcher of ice water that was within easy reach and poured a glassful. "Drink this," he demanded, handing her the glass.

Her fingertips brushed his hand as she reached for the water. The immediacy of his reaction surprised him, causing him to turn away, but not before their eyes met and held, a mysterious current crackling between them.

Suddenly, Raine had to fight the urge to lean against him and have him put his arms around her. She could almost feel the warmth of the skin under the shirt, could almost sense the comfort in being held. She wanted to say, "Hold me. I'm afraid." Once she realized how her feelings were betraying her, sanity returned with a jolting force. God forbid! How could she even think such a thing! But again she was experiencing that lack of control, her world collapsing around her, and she didn't know what to do about it.

"I'm better," she said. "I thought for a moment I was going to be sick, but I'm all right now."

"Good." He was glad to see the color returning. But he couldn't stop picturing her naked on the carpet. Sweet Jesus! He quickly turned away and gave his attention to the waitress, busy filling their coffee cups. After informing her in a rough voice that coffee was all they wanted, he took a gulp of his steaming brew.

While his attention was focused elsewhere, Raine felt free to look at him. He was even better looking than she'd first thought—if that was possible. The navy-blue slacks he wore with a light blue shirt emphasized the long, muscular power of his body. The light, hitting his head just right, showed to perfection his dark brown hair. Judging from his tan, it was safe to surmise he spent a great deal of time outdoors.

It was hard to tell how old he was. On close observation she could see the tiny lines around his eyes and mouth. She guessed his age to be somewhere between thirty-five and forty.

What type of man was he? Stubborn. She had learned that from firsthand experience. And hadn't she also learned that he was used to having his own way? And arrogant, as well. At present his face revealed very little. Yet there seemed to be no room for compromise in the granitelike hardness of his jawline, no margin at all. He appeared primarily intelligent and effective.

He glanced up then and caught her examining him. Raine blushed furiously, and he laughed, suddenly looking much younger and less severe.

"Don't worry, there's no charge," he teased. "Although I can think of better things to look at."

Covering her embarrassment, Raine blurted out the first thing that floated into her head. "Do you test planes, or do you just sit behind a desk?"

He smiled at her choice of words. "Both. And I guess you could say I'm a frustrated farmer, to boot. I own a hundred-fifty-acre spread just north of here," he volunteered. "And every chance I get, I hightail it up there."

"Oh." At least now she knew where he got his beautiful tan.

"You say 'oh' as if you're surprised."

"I'll admit I am."

"Satisfy my curiosity. Why?"

"Well, let's just say I've learned the hard way that pilots aren't interested in anything other than flying." She didn't bother to keep the bitterness out of her voice.

"You're speaking of your brother, of course?"

"And...and my father." This time the bitterness was more pronounced.

Ashe waited for her to expand on the subject of her father, but when she didn't, he spoke again, filling the uneasy silence. "I'll have to admit that ranching will never take the place of flying with me." He shrugged. "It's in my blood and always will be. It's a feeling that can't be explained unless you've experienced it."

Typical test pilot, Raine thought bitterly. They were a breed all their own, cut from the same bolt of cloth. "It was in my father's blood, too, and he paid for it with his life," she lashed out. "And now...my brother..."

"God, Raine, I'm sorry," Ashe said sincerely.

It was the first time he'd said her name. It sounded strange, yet right, on his lips. Then, realizing that her thoughts were still heading down a dangerous path, she rebelled silently. Back off, Raine! This man is trouble spelled with capital letters.

Struggling for control, she whispered at last, "That's all right. It's been a long time now."

"You have to believe that Todd's going to pull through."

She experienced another twist of panic. "I have to think that or...or I wouldn't be able to hold on to my sanity." She paused, looking down at her cup, moving it around in the saucer. "But, then, I think about how badly he's...he's hurt..." Her voice broke, while her eyes darkened with pain. Then after a moment, she added, "Forgive me, I'm not usually this teary-eyed, this emotional." And what she didn't say was that she didn't usually confide in someone she had just met, whom she did not trust.

Ashe was having trouble thinking clearly. All he could see were the glimmerings of tears trapped in her eyelashes. "Shh! Don't apologize. Todd's a fighter. He'll make it." He couldn't take his eyes off her.

This woman affected him as no other ever had, Ashe realized. Maybe it was the standoffish attitude that she wore like a second skin. Maybe because she was a challenge? But there was no room in his life for such complications, he reminded himself harshly. It had been a long time since he'd felt more than a mild interest in a woman. The ones he took out on occasion were for a good time and nothing more.

For the longest time, he'd worried about that flaw within himself—the inability to form ties. He'd thought that a switch had been disconnected, that his feelings, responses, and desires had quietly gone dead.

And now, of all times, when he had more on his plate than he could digest, this woman appeared and they all came to life again to plague him. It was so unexpected and so unfair. Yet he burned every time he looked at her.

It was Raine's softly spoken voice asking the waitress for a refill of her now tepid coffee that forced him away from his chaotic thoughts.

While sipping her coffee, Raine finally got up the courage to ask the dreaded question. "Please tell me how it happened—the crash, I mean."

Ashe sighed, taking a hefty swallow of his coffee, stalling. He hated giving her the details, knowing it was going to intensify her pain. But he had no choice; it was a matter of either hearing it from him or someone else. It was his responsibility.

"Your brother and I go back a long way," he began by way of explanation. "Vietnam, to be exact. Todd saved my life."

"Go on."

"So when Todd came to me asking for a job, I gave him one. I felt I owed him. It was that simple."

"I wish you hadn't," Raine responded, a slight tremor in her voice.

Although his eyes narrowed, his tone was even. "I can understand that." He shrugged. "Most women feel that way."

"Well, this one certainly does," she said with emphasis, her eyes flashing. "I would've given anything for Todd to have found something else to do. I pleaded with him not to go back into flying, but he wouldn't listen." Her voice held a desperate note.

"As I pointed out before," Ashe said soberly, "it's in our blood. We can't help it. It's like an addiction—once you've tried it, you can't seem to get enough."

Raine shuddered, the excitement in his eyes and voice turning her stomach. "Well, as I pointed out before, I for one have always abhorred that type of life and still do."

Guess that tells you what she thinks of you, old boy. "That's your perrogative, of course." Though his response was quiet, he might as well have been shouting.

Silence.

He feels nothing but contempt for me, Raine thought. Well, that's just great. Now we know where we stand.

At last he asked, "Did you know that at one time Todd had a...drinking problem?"

His carefully worded question sent her heart skidding to her toes. "Yes, of course I was aware of it," she answered savagely. "But why are you asking? What does his past have to do with all of this?" Her voice was steadily rising.

He averted his eyes. "Probably nothing. Oh, hell, just forget it. I shouldn't have even asked you that."

"No, damn you, we won't forget it!" she said tersely.

Her outburst was met with another long bout of silence.

Suddenly, she couldn't stand not knowing. She had to ask. Her tongue circled her dry lips. "He...he hadn't by any chance..." She paused. God, this was harder than she expected. But she had to be sure. "He hadn't by any chance been drinking when—?"

She hated herself for doubting Todd's innocence. But when her brother had come home from Vietnam, he hadn't been the same. He began drinking and had recklessly zipped through his trust fund. As a result, Raine was forever having to dole out money to him. Nothing she said or did had any influence on him. But that had been a long time ago. He had changed.

Ashe's features softened momentarily, when he saw the fear and frustration mirrored on her face. "I was aware of Todd's bout with the bottle a few years back; Nam had a tendency to do that to a person. But, no, you can put your mind to rest on that score; he was definitely not drinking."

Raine gave a heartfelt sigh. "Thank God," she breathed, more to herself than to him.

Ashe lit a cigarette and drew on it. "There may be questions you'll have to answer, such as the one I just asked you. And Colonel Jackson of the air force's investigating board will more than likely be the one to question you."

"But why?"

Ashe's lips thinned. "The board won't leave a stone unturned. That's the way they operate. So be prepared just in case I can't keep Jackson sidetracked."

She smiled. "Thanks for the warning, but I think I can handle anything now that I know Todd wasn't drinking, even though deep down I knew he hadn't been." Then, more clearly, she added, "But I had to know that the crash wasn't his fault."

She paused, noticing the look of frustration that suddenly covered Ashe's face, but thinking nothing of it, she continued, "For the past two years, Todd's been happier than I've seen him. Although it kills me that he decided to fly again, he seems to have made peace with himself. And because of his diligence in his work, I know he would never bounce back if the accident was his fault. Even now I can't believe it happened."

"Forget the drinking." His tone was short, clipped. "That's not the issue here, anyway." He paused, shifting his gaze. "Oh, hell, what I should have said was that you shouldn't jump to conclusions."

Raine shook her head as if to clear it. Had she celebrated prematurely? Another cold knot of dread formed in her stomach. "Exactly what do you mean?"

"I don't know any other way to break this to you, except just to come out and say it." He stopped just long enough to watch what little color she had left in her face completely recede. Damn it to hell, he cursed silently. "The consensus is that an error in judgment not only caused Todd's injury, but the loss of a valuable plane as well."

"But, but I thought..." Raine's heart was hammering so loudly in her chest she was certain he could hear it.

Continuing as though she hadn't interrupted, Ashe said, "It was a technical error. Todd was attempting a similar landing, which, at the best of times, is difficult to do. He hit the tarmac too hard, causing the landing gears to fail. If he'd handled the machine as he'd been trained to, we're sure the crash could have been avoided."

"Who is 'we'?" Her voice was low and vibrating with pain.

Ashe sighed, finding this whole mess worse than he'd expected. "Me and the air force investigating board. Todd was testing an A-7 attack plane built for the air force. Any time there's a crash involving one of their planes, they step in and more or less take over."

"How can you be sure that Todd was at fault?" She didn't even recognize her own voice.

"I saw the crash; I lived through it with him." He sighed, combing his fingers roughly through his thick mane of dark hair. "I watched as he came down and just managed to escape with his life." His voice was flat, emotionless.

Her lashes swept up. "Are you saying you agree with the judgment?"

He paused as if weighing his next words carefully. "Remember, I was there, Raine. The way it looks as of now, the crash could have been avoided."

Raine kept her lips from quivering by sheer force of will. "I don't believe you. Todd was an excellent pilot, conscientious to the point of being obsessive. He would never have gone against orders. You're wrong; he's not to blame."

"If he's innocent, he'll be vindicated."

"And what if he isn't?"

"If negligence is proved, Todd will probably never fly again."

Suddenly, it seemed as if all the air had gone out of the room and she couldn't catch her breath. "Oh, God," she whimpered, battling the urge to get up and outrun the pain his words had inflicted.

Ashe watched the play of emotions cross Raine's face, watched as she began to tremble. He longed to hold her face between his hands and say, "Everything's going to be all right," because she seemed, at this moment, as if she were on the verge of disintegrating.

"Raine." Somehow he had to make her understand that his hands were tied, that he was only doing his job. But following on the heels of that thought came another one equally as troubling. Hellfire, he thought. Why should he have to defend himself to this woman? You know why, you ass? You're besotted, letting a pair of beautiful breasts and a set of good-looking legs color your sound judgment. No strings, no promises, no tomorrows—hadn't that always been his motto? Why was Raine Michaels any different?

Raine blinked, willing away the tears. "Please don't say any more. I've heard enough." She looked him straight in the face, her eyes bright with anger. "I have faith in my brother's ability, as well as his innocence. And in the end, you'll see that I'm right." Her gaze still unflinching, she said, "Now, if you don't mind, I'd like to go back to the hospital."

Both mentally and physically exhausted, Raine plopped down on the spacious but cluttered couch in her brother's apartment. From the moment she and Ashe had left the restaurant, not one word had passed between them. It was only after they had pulled up in the hospital parking lot that she spoke, and that was to formally thank him for the coffee.

Ashe had looked as though he would try to reason with her, but she had coldly rebuffed him. As far as she was concerned, the battle lines had been drawn, regardless of the fact that she was being grossly unfair and unreasonable. But she could not help herself. She was making no excuses; it was simply the way she felt.

But, dammit, why did he have to be so attractive?

Suddenly pushing all thoughts of Ashe Elliot aside, Raine looked around the apartment. What a God-awful mess, she thought with a grimace. From the looks of things, Todd had not straightened out—much less cleaned—this place in no telling how long. Ashtrays filled with cigarette butts, newspapers and glasses were strewn everywhere. If this was what the living area looked like, she shuddered to think about what shape the rest of the apartment was in.

On shaky legs, Raine got up and trudged into the guest room, dragging her travel bag with her. Thank goodness, she noted, it looked halfway decent. Hoisting the bag onto the bed, she rummaged through it and took out her robe. It took only a matter of seconds to discard her rumpled clothing and slip into it. Then, padding barefoot into the kitchen, prepared for the worst, she was again shocked that it was also presentable.

It didn't take long to prepare a pot of coffee and wander back to the couch with a cup brimming full. She had just gotten settled when the loud jangle of the phone next to her elbow caused her to slosh the hot liquid on her hand.

"Damnation!" she yelped aloud, raising the burned hand to her lips. Then, with her heart in her throat, she very gingerly set the cup down on the coffee table. Todd. Oh, God!

"Hello," she whispered, maintaining a death grip on the phone.

"Where the hell have you been?"

Relieved, she sighed, relaxing somewhat. "I'm sorry, Ross, but it's a long story. It's been a hectic, exhausting day," she explained.

"I didn't wake you up, did I?"

"No, as a matter of fact, I just got in."

"I wanted to call during the day, but I didn't get a chance. I've been calling every half hour for the past few hours. I'm still at the office and have been thinking about you ever since Val phoned."

Raine could picture Ross Thomas as he sat at his desk, more than likely sipping on his favorite, Scotch-and-water, and working, trying to do ten things at once. But she knew that was why, at age fifty, he was the owner of a successful chain of department stores that catered to the rich, and was now himself a millionaire. He never seemed to run out of energy.

"Todd's seriously ill, Ross," she whispered, shattering the silence.

"What are his chances?"

Raine rubbed her burning eyes; they felt as if they were filled with sand. "The doctor thinks his chances are good if infection doesn't set in. Oh, Ross, he's a mess."

"Shh! Take it easy," he replied gruffly. "You've got to keep your spirits up, think on the bright side.

"I...I know, but it's so hard."

"How long do you plan to stay?"

Although quietly spoken, it was a loaded question, and she'd been expecting it. "As long as I'm needed," she replied without hesitation.

"I see."

But Ross didn't see, she knew. With him, business always came first. He didn't understand how she could just walk off and leave her responsibilities, even for an emergency. And the fact that he had been her mentor all these years and was instrumental in helping her get where she was today didn't help matters. And because he cared for her, he never seemed to know when to back off. Such as now.

He greeted her silence with another question. "Have you forgotten our meeting the day after tomorrow with Jules Burns? Remember, I had the devil of a time getting him to agree to see you and look at your designs." He paused. "Without your thinking that I'm an insensitive brute, would you—?

"No, Ross," she said tightly, cutting him off in midsentence. "I can't leave. Not now. Not until Todd's out of danger. Please, make my apologies to Jules."

"Always Todd." He sighed bitterly.

"Please, Ross, not now. Don't you think I'm sick that I can't meet with Jules. I know how important he is, and if I could get him to work with me on my designs, I'd have it made, but, God, Ross, not at the expense of Todd. I could never live with myself..."

Suddenly changing his tactics, Ross asked, his tone more understanding, "What about New Image?"

"Val can handle things for a while."

"And the boutique?"

Raine was hanging on to her patience by a thread. "She can handle that, too," she said evenly.

For a moment the crackling on the line was the only sound between them.

Finally, Ross asked, "Do you need me, want me to come?"

"Thanks, but, no, thanks," she answered coolly.

"I'm sorry, I didn't mean to upset you."

"That's all right. I understand."

"Do you? I wonder."

Silence.

"We'll talk soon," he said at last.

"Thanks for calling, Ross."

"I'll be in touch."

Raine let her head rest against the back of the couch and sipped her coffee, feeling as though she had the weight of the world on her shoulders. Ross couldn't have called at a worse time. She had too much on her mind as it was to add him to her list. If only she loved Ross and was willing to let him take over, how much simpler her life would be. But she could never do that. She valued her independence too much. And she'd meant it when she told Val that there was no room for a man in her life.

Suddenly feeling the need for something more than just plain coffee to relax her, Raine set her cup aside and got up and crossed the room to Todd's makeshift bar. After rattling around through the cabinet, she found a bottle of Irish cream liqueur. Pouring herself a fresh cup of coffee, she added a small amount of the creamy liquid to it. Now maybe she would be able to relax.

Unfortunately, she found it impossible to do so. Her mind was wound as tight as an automatic tape. She couldn't seem to shut it off no matter how much she tried.

Todd's listless body kept jumping in front of her vision every time she closed her eyes. Her heart ached from him and his plight. And she was feeling sorry for herself.

Deciding a hot shower was the panacea for her ills, she hauled herself to the bathroom. But she was unable to escape her thoughts there, either. This time it was Ashe Elliot's face that haunted her. What was there about that man that held such fascination for her, she wondered. The truth was she'd found Ashe attractive. More than that, she'd found him desirable. For the first time in her life, she'd met a man who stimulated not her brain, but her nerve endings.

Raine stepped out of the shower and dried herself vigorously in an effort to distract her thoughts from Ashe. Securing her robe around herself, she slowly walked into the bedroom and lay down on the bed, wondering how she could be attracted to him when he stood for everything she loathed in a man. He was egotistical and brash and took great pride in flaunting his psychological attitude toward life: live for today and to hell with tomorrow. It seemed dangerous, as if by admitting to more than a passing interest in a man, she was revealing a treacherous vein of weakness in her nature.

Because she had been determined to avoid the pitfall of her mother's unhappiness, it was extremely difficult for her to form a lasting relationship with a man. Any man. Instead, she had fled to her work, where she was in control. And if at times the loneliness became almost unbearable—

well, she just buried it deeper inside her, nearly denying it altogether, like a secret, shameful illness.

Though she hadn't given it much thought, she realized she had concluded that no man was a match for her as long as she kept her guard up. Now she wasn't so sure. About anything. Everything seemed to be coming apart, just spinning out of control. Flopping over and burying her face in the pillow, she let the tears flow.

Chapter 3

Ashe awoke feeling as though his head had been used as a punching bag. He yawned and sat up slowly, stretching every weary muscle in his body. Then, naked, he got up and crossed the hall into the bathroom and stepped into the shower, hoping it would revive him, make up for the lost hours of sleep.

Minutes later, hair still glistening with drops of water, he made his way into the kitchen and plugged in the coffeepot. While he waited, he dug into pants pocket and pulled out a cigarette and, after lighting it, took several deep puffs. The shower hadn't helped, he thought. He still felt like hell.

He'd had to get out of town. After he'd left Raine Michaels at the hospital, he'd headed straight for his condo, changed his clothes, and headed north. He'd needed the time to think, to get his head on straight. But nothing he had done thus far had helped; his thoughts were just as jumbled and chaotic as they had been when he wheeled out of his driveway. He had been up half the night, staring out into he darkness, smoking. And now within a matter of a few hours, he would have to head back toward Tyler, and the plant, and his responsibilities. God!

A groan escaped through his taut lips as he took another drag on his cigarette, then let it dangle from the corner of his mouth while he replenished his coffee. The ash dropped from the forgotten cigarette, leaving a sloppy silver trail down his denim jeans before exploding softly over a solid portion of his upper thigh.

"Damn!" he muttered, taking the cigarette from his mouth and blowing sharply to send the ash tumbling to the floor. He drew on it again, then stubbed the butt out in the ashtray.

Thoroughly disgusted, he jumped up, his action sending the chair crashing to the floor. It sounded like the echo of a gunshot exploding in the silence of the early morning. Another expletive followed as he stomped across the room and out the door, convinced that a change of scenery would act as a soothing balm to his frayed nerves. *What the bloody hell was wrong with him?* His insides, even before a dangerous flight, hadn't been this scrambled.

But he knew what was wrong. Raine Michaels, for starters. Todd and the accident, for another. The safety board hanging around, for yet another. The last two he no longer had control over, but Raine Michaels was a different ball of wax. He was forced to admit that she had totally captivated him.

He shook his head as he stepped off the porch and walked briskly across the yard, stopping only when he came to a barbed-wire fence. He paused, leaning his arm on a fence post and propping his booted foot on the bottom rung of the wire, and looked around him. A feeling of pride swept over him as he surveyed the herd of cattle grazing peacefully in the distance. The erratic pounding of his heart began to slow considerably.

The sun had broken through the haze, but the damp morning air still felt cool as it whipped across his skin. He drew a deep breath, pulling the clear air through his lungs. This was home. It served as his retreat, his hideaway when the going got tough, when he needed to think.

He turned his attention back to the scene before him. Several yards behind the house was his vegetable garden. He sauntered toward it, through the morning dew, and paused at the edge of a row that in the spring would be heavy with stalks of sweet corn. He squatted down and scooped up a handful of the rich earth and watched as it sifted through his fingers like sand through an hourglass.

"When everything else fails, you'll always be here," he said aloud, his hand now stained a charcoal gray as he continued to pilfer through the dirt. And it was true. Harvesting this land—an acre in all, the rows of corn, tomatoes, peas, and countless other vegetables—was his salvation.

After a grueling week of work, he couldn't imagine not being able to slip into a pair of old jeans and toil long hours over a grubbing hoe until every muscle in his body cried out for relief. But then later, after a hot shower, his body never felt better, his mind never more free.

Suddenly feeling foolish for playing in the dirt, he jumped up and kicked the loose particles back in place. Then with only a cursory glance over his shoulder, his eyes touching on the shed that housed his personal airplane, a single-engine Cherokee, he headed toward the house.

But after a moment, he stopped in his tracks, the tantalizing aroma of bacon teasing his nostrils. His steps faltered. "What the hell?" he cursed aloud. It was too early for his housekeeper, he mused; she never showed up till midmorning. Stretching his gait, Ashe took the last two remaining yards as one, entering the back door of the house with a loud bang.

"Oh, good morning, Ashe," a bright, chirpy voice greeted him.

Ashe almost let loose another string of curses before he clamped his jaws together, forcing him to swallow the vile language.

"Leigh," he said instead, controlled anger in his voice, "just what do you think you're doing?"

She laughed, though a trifle uneasily. "What does it look like I'm doing? Why, Ashe, honey, I'm cooking your breakfast."

Ashe hugged the doorjamb and continued to stare at her. "How did you know I was here?"

The woman raised rounded shoulders in a careless shrug before turning her back to him and lifting the bacon out of the sizzling grease with a pair of tongs.

Ashe watched her, a dark frown flickering over his face. Leigh Hardy was a good-looking woman by anyone's standards. She lived on a twenty-acre spread bordering his. He had met her at a get-acquainted barbecue at a neighbor's house two years ago. She had been left the responsibility of taking care of her ranch following the untimely death of her father. Ashe had felt sorry for her and had taken her out. But she was a friend and nothing more.

He knew she'd fallen in love with him. However, he wanted no part of ties that bind. Not to anything or anyone. He'd told her this, determined to set the record straight from the start.

For a while things had been fine. But lately when he'd had time to see her, she'd been possessive, demanding. And now here she was at his house without so much as his knowledge, much less an invitation.

Having completed her task, she slowly turned around. The silence was smothering.

"Leigh, answer my question. How did you know I was here?" he repeated.

Uncertainty laced her tanned features. "I...I didn't," she stammered. Then she went on hurriedly when she saw the menacing look on Ashe's face. "What I meant was that I passed this way coming home last night and saw your car." She shifted, a tentative smile crossing her face once again. "Thought I'd surprise you with breakfast and a visit." She paused. "Why are you looking at me like I've committed the crime of the century?"

"Dammit, Leigh! I value my privacy, that's why. If I'd wanted..." His voice trailed away at Leigh's look. "Oh, to hell with it," he said harshly, turning away from her tear-filled eyes.

"What's wrong, Ashe?" Her voice was low, but on the defensive. "You never used to mind my surprise visits. Any other time you would have already wolfed down the food and hauled me toward the bedroom." She sniffed back the tears. "I don't understand..."

Ashe understood, only too well. And it was eating away at his insides. With a sigh, he covered the distance from the door to the table and lowered his frame heavily into the chair.

"It's not you, Leigh. It's me."

Her chin began to quiver. You mean...you don't want me anymore?"

"Leigh, don't. Not now."

"What's the matter? Aren't I good enough for the high-and-mighty test pilot all of a sudden? Not pretty enough?"

"For God's sake, Leigh, that has nothing to do with it." And it hadn't. He still respected her and admired her. That hadn't changed. But, dammit, she wasn't Raine Michaels!

"Well, at least let me finish breakfast before I leave."

"No." His tone was short and to the point. Then, forcing a gentleness into his voice, he added, "Thanks, anyway. But I've got to shower and get back to the plant. I'm late as it is."

"I could wash your back for you," she offered seductively, stopping short of pleading.

Ashe's patience snapped. "Dammit, I don't want anything from you! Not now. Not ever. Will you just please go home!"

Leigh Hardy's eyes narrowed into tiny slits and her shoulders bowed back as though she was preparing herself for battle. "I'm no imbecile," she spat. "You don't have to draw me a picture. It's obvious you have someone else warming your bed. God," she added contemptuously, "I don't have anyone to blame but myself. I should have listened to the rumors and to the advice I was given about you."

"Leigh..."

"I was warned that women never said no to you—that all you have to do is lift your little finger and they stumble over themselves running." She lifted her head defiantly as though daring Ashe to rebuke her statement.

"That may very well be true, but it has nothing to do with you. We're friends, Leigh, and that's all we've ever been." His expression relented somewhat, hoping to take some of the sting out of his words. "And that's all we'll ever be."

"You're a bastard, Ashe Elliot!" she cried hotly. "You—" Her voice broke as she frantically groped to untie the apron that hugged her waist.

Not bothering to defend himself one way or the other, Ashe got up and strode to the side door. "Leigh, before we both say anything else we'll be sorry for, why don't you go home? We'll talk later."

"No, we won't talk later. I don't care if I ever see you again." With those choice words, she all but ran across the room and out the door, slamming it behind her.

After making sure she got to her car safely and was headed down the driveway, Ashe trudged slowly back to the table and sat down. With a bitter twist to his lips, he automatically reached for another cigarette. It tasted foul, and knowing he was smoking too much, he crushed it out and got up and strode toward the bedroom.

He had taken only a few short steps when the phone rang, stopping him cold in his tracks. With a mumbled curse, he swung around on the ball of his foot and headed back to the den.

Lifting the receiver, he barked, "Yes."

The words "Whoa, I surrender" came over the wire, followed by a laugh that filled his ears.

Ashe laughed in return, feeling himself relax.

It was his friend Mickey McAdams, known as Mac to his friends. They'd gone through Nam together and had been friends ever since. Tall and lanky, with red hair and freckles, he was a crackerjack mechanic and pilot who hauled cargo for a company to and from any place regardless of the risks. Ashe had told him more times than one that he took too many chances in the air and that one day he was going to get his tail in a crack so tight he couldn't get out of it.

He was always jabbing Ashe about something. Today was no exception.

"Hell, old buddy, things aren't so swell, huh?"

"You got it."

"What's up?"

"An A-7 crashed and burned. It's been hell."

"Goddamn!"

"That's what I said, only worse."

"First one you've lost, isn't it?"

"Yep."

"Did you lose the pilot?"

Ashe's deep sigh filtered through the line. "No, thank God. Not yet, anyway. He's pretty banged up, but he's hanging in there."

"Anyone I know?"

"Yeah. It's Todd Michaels."

"Well, I'll be damned. Who'd ever have thought it? Isn't he one of the best? Saved your ass in Nam, if I remember correctly."

"One and the same."

"Guess you got the safety board crawling all over the place."

"You got it."

"What a friggin' mess. Who's to blame?

Ashe shifted the receiver to the other ear. "From the way it looks, Michaels is, but the investigation has just gotten under way."

"Anything I can do?"

"No, not a thing, except to save me a cold beer."

"Sure thing. But that goes without saying, and you know it."

Changing the subject, Ashe asked, "How about you? How are things?"

Mac chuckled softly. "Same old one and two. Nothing ever changes."

"Wish my life was that tranquil."

Mac laughed again. "What you need is some R and R, my friend. Why don't you bring what's-her-hame—Leigh, isn't it?—to visit and see how the other half lives?"

"No can do," Ashe drawled.

"What do you mean, 'No can do'?"

"Leigh and I are no more."

"Mmm, that surprises me. Kinda thought she might be around for a while. Seemed like the marrying type."

"Huh! You know me better than that, Mac. Or you should."

"Well, I keep hopin'."

"Well, do me a favor and bury your hopes."

"Seein' anyone else? I've never known you to be without a woman for long."

Ashe laughed. "Hell, man, did I ever tell you you're too damned nosy?"

"Bull!"

"Now, Mac..."

"Don't you 'now, Mac' me. I know there's something you're not telling me."

"Oh, no, I'm not falling into the same old hole. Quit trying to play Cupid, will you?"

"All right. I don't know why I try. You're hopeless when it comes to settling down with a home and family."

"That's right. My home is the sky."

"Well, when you get this mess straightened out, we'll be expecting you."

"You got a date," Ashe said, hanging up.

Then his eyes dipped to his watch. It was getting late. If he planned to get to work by noon today, he had to get the lead out of his pants and get ready to leave.

As he shaved, his thoughts wandered back to Leigh Hardy. It had been a terrible scene, and he wished it hadn't happened. But it couldn't be helped. It was long overdue. He had been the marriage route. Once, but never again. His ex had tried to make him into something he was not, and the results had been fatal. Marriage meant commitment and making sacrifices, and he was just not interested. Not anymore.

However, if there was a woman who could make him change his mind, it would be a woman like Raine Michaels, he added jokingly to himself. Her cool beauty certainly represented a challenge to him. He wanted her; she stirred his blood as no other woman ever had. Yet he found this disturbing.

He wanted nothing to interfere with his flying. It was the most important thing in his life. The only rival to that passion was his ranch, and even it came in a distant second.

But the moment he had met Raine Michaels, he sensed she was different. He had never had such an instant and strong reaction to a woman. But the fact remained he had no intention of becoming involved. He was used to his life, to being alone. In his line of work, it was better that way.

Hadn't he learned that the hard way?

An hour later, he steered his Lincoln onto the hospital parking lot. God, he hoped Todd was better this morning. Suddenly he wondered if he would see Raine. And if he did, how would she react? Then realizing how crazy his thoughts were, he swung out of the car, slamming the door violently behind him. He was behaving like a besotted teenager, mooning over his first and only girl friend. More to the point, he was behaving like a fool.

Raine felt wretched. Her head was throbbing dreadfully and her stomach was revolting, threatening to empty its contents. God, what a way to start the day, she thought dejectedly. She was living on nerves and she didn't know how much longer she could hold up. She hadn't slept a wink the night before. When she hadn't been dreaming about Todd, she was dreaming about Ashe Elliot. His eyes haunted her all night.

Now she counted to ten, trying to relax while she waited for Val to answer the phone. Earlier she had called the hospital and was told there was no change in her brother's condition. Everything remained status quo. But as soon as she talked to Val, she planned to spend the day with Todd. Suddenly, Raine heard the click of the receiver.

"New Image. Valarie speaking."

"Val, it's me, Raine."

"Thank goodness. I've been out of my mind with worry."

"Well, I wish I had good news to report, but unfortunately I don't. He's about the same."

"Oh, Raine, hon, I'm sorry."

"Me, too. But I refuse to give up."

"Of course, you can't give up." Valarie responded softly. "How are things at the office?"

There was a brief moment of silence. Then Val spoke. "Hectic. But don't you worry about a thing here. We'll survive." She paused. "If only..."

A smile touched Raine's lips. "I know, if only Sharon Mosby would drop from the face of the world." Val could always make her smile.

Val giggled. "Not a bad idea. Surely there's a way we can bring that about." Then suddenly her tone became serious again. "But it's not Sharon I was referring to this time." The sigh that followed was deep and profound.

"Don't tell me another catastrophe has occurred." Just let her be gone for one day and all hell breaks loose. It's just not fair, she fumed inwardly. She was beginning to feel more and more like a sitting duck with everyone taking potshots at her.

Val began to hedge. "Well, it's nothing, really. I'm sure I'm just making a mountain out of a molehill."

Raine swallowed her irritation. "Come on, Val. You know me better than that. If it has to do with the business, and I assume it does, then of course I have to know about it."

"It's Mr. Thomas."

"Ross?" Raine was surprised, and it showed in her voice. "None other."

Raine was puzzled. "But I just talked with him last night. Although he wasn't overjoyed that I planned to stay with Todd, he seemed to take it in stride."

"Well, he may have taken it in stride, but he has a strange way of showing it." Even through the static of the phone lines her agitated sigh couldn't be missed.

"What's the matter now?"

"I'm not sure you're ready for this in light of everything else that's happened."

"Valarie," Raine warned, "quit stalling. Out with it."

"He called my apartment early this morning and asked me to get together all the sketches and swatches of your materials. He said that since you couldn't make the meeting with Jules, he'd surprise you and take them himself."

"What!"

"I knew you'd be upset, because my gut instinct warned me you hadn't given him permission to take the sketches or you would have told me." There was slight quiver in Val's usually calm voice. "I...didn't know what to do. I was toying with the idea of calling the hospital, but truthfully I didn't know what to do."

Raine wasn't just upset; she was livid. "I told him to make my apologies to Jules."

"I might have overstepped my authority, but I told him outright that I was going to call you. He said he understood, but that you'd worked too long and hard to throw this golden opportunity away, and he aimed to see that you didn't."

"I can't believe his nerve. What a mess." And he professed to care about her. Men!

But if she were honest, she would admit that Ross was right. She did want to see her designs become a line of clothing. She wanted that almost as much as she wanted the boutique. That was the problem. She wanted it too much, and Ross knew it. Damn him! But she didn't want it at the expense of sacrificing her brother. She had to keep her priorities straight, didn't she?

Ross was also right about Jules Burns, the famous designer. He was extremely volatile and temperamental. It was only because of Ross that he had agreed to look at her designs in the first place. But those ideas were hers, her baby, her dream, and she didn't want anyone horning in on the deal. And that included Ross. On the other hand, how could she be in two places at one time? She was damned if she did and damned if she didn't. God, how much more mixed up could things get?

"Raine, are you all right?"

The husky, concerned note in Val's voice snapped Raine's mind back on track. "I'll take care of it. Don't worry. As soon as I get to the hospital and check on Todd, I'll call Ross."

"Are you sure you're all right? I mean..."

"I'm fine."

"If only I could do more," Val cried. "I feel so helpless."

"You've done more than enough already. Now, is there anything else we need to discuss?" Raine had become all business now. Even though Todd needed her, and she had no intention of letting him down, she still had an obligation to herself and her business. It was because of this business that she would be able to give Todd the special care he was more than likely going to need. She had no intention of taking anything personally from Ashe Elliot.

"Yes, actually there is," Val said in answer to the long silence.

"Let's have it."

Raine forced herself to pay attention while Val went over a few points that needed taking care of, but her mind kept straying to Ross and what she would say to him.

At last Val said, "A woman by the name of Catherine Cole called late yesterday afternoon." She paused. "Does that name ring a bell with you?"

Raine thought for a moment, her brows furrowed together in concentration. "No, can't say that it does. Yet there is something about it that sounds familiar. Why?"

"I didn't know the name, either. But she's an author and has supposedly written a blockbuster titled *If Tomorrow Comes*. According to her it has just made *The New York*

Times best-seller list." Valarie laughed. "Seems it's a steamy novel about a Texas family."

"Now I know!" Raine exclaimed excitedly. "There's a display in the window of the bookstore down the street from the office. They have a mountain of her books stacked up with streamers surrounding them."

"Well, she wants us to take her on as a client. Her publisher is sending her on a promotional tour to several states, plus she's been asked to be on 'Good Morning America' and the 'Today' shows. Of course, she wants to look her best."

"Mmm," Raine commented, suddenly experiencing an uplift to her sagging spirits. "Sounds better by the second."

"I'm excited, too, but wait till you hear this. Ms. Cole lives in Tyler, actually a few miles out, but close enough that if Todd should improve in the next few days, you might be able to go see her."

"I'd love to, if I can. After I get to the hospital, I'll call and let you know about Todd. Then we'll go from there."

"Talk to you later, then."

"Right. Oh, by the way, don't worry, I'll handle Ross."

"Good luck."

The second Raine hung up the phone, she hurriedly slapped on her makeup and threw on a beige cotton skirt and blouse. After stepping into a pair of red sandals and adding a wide red belt and chunky red necklace and matching earrings, she was ready to go. She should have been at the hospital an hour ago, she thought as she drove her rental car into the street.

The hospital seemed quiet for a change as she made her way down the hall and to the elevator. Oh, God, please let Todd be better this morning, she prayed as the elevator whizzed up to the fifth floor.

She was upon them before she realized it. Two men were standing outside Todd's room, their voices a low rumble.

Raine froze. The man facing her was a stranger. But the other one she would have known anywhere. Ashe Elliot.

When the man saw her pause and then continue toward them, he broke off his speech. Ashe turned around.

For a brief moment, they simply stared at one another. Ashe was furious, Raine thought. It was almost as though she could see the muscles bunching with tension in the back of his neck. Then his face changed as quickly as an artist would dispose of a dirty canvas, leaving it devoid of all expression. He stepped aside and made room for Raine to stand between him and the stranger.

"Raine Michaels, meet Colonel Tom Jackson from the air force investigating board."

Chapter 4

Colonel Jackson extended his hand before Raine could get her bearings. She had no choice but to accept his firm grasp, though every muscle in her body rebelled. He was a tall man in his early sixties with a narrow tanned face that was stern in repose, and a well-conditioned body clearly emphasized by the impeccable fit of his uniform.

"It's a pleasure, Ms. Michaels, though I wish it could've been under different circumstances."

Raine forced herself to remain calm. "So do I, Colonel, so do I," she said, withdrawing her hand. What was going on, she asked herself apprehensively. The air was thick with suppressed emotion and for several seconds no one spoke.

"I'm sorry about your brother," he added sincerely, taking the edge off the silence.

"Thank you, Colonel."

Then, removing her gaze from the colonel, Raine looked at Ashe. Thank goodness his face no longer reminded her of a thundercloud about to erupt, though it appeared as if he was holding himself in check. She was aware of a muscle twitching in his cheek.

Yet she couldn't find fault with his appearance. Under the close-fitting navy slacks and blue pin-striped shirt he wore, hard muscles rippled as he crossed his arms.

For the longest moment, Raine's eyes involuntarily clung to his, uneasily, helplessly. Then, suddenly, she shook herself mentally, deciding that whatever they had to say to her, if anything, would just have to wait. She had to see her brother. Now. Without further hesitation, Raine made a move to open the door to Todd's room.

"If you'll excuse me," she said, making a point not to look in Ashe's direction again. "I must—"

"Raine, wait. Please." This time it was Ashe who spoke. "A team of doctors is with Todd now. They asked us to wait outside."

Raine tried to push aside the mounting sense of fear. *Had Todd taken a turn for the worse?* Her troubled eyes strayed toward the closed door and unconsciously she moved closer to it. Forgotten was the ominous presence of Colonel Jackson. Right now all she had on her mind was bursting through the door. "I'm sure they'll want to talk to me. After all, I'm his closest relative."

Colonel Jackson shifted his weight, his sudden movement claiming Raine's attention. "I know this is a bad time," he said, his voice edged with an apology, "but when it's convenient, I would like to talk to you."

"Dammit, Jackson!" Ashe chimed in hotly. "I told you…"

He got no further. The door opened and at the threshold stood Dr. Anders with two other doctors standing in his wake.

Dr. Anders's eyes pinpointed Raine. "Good morning, Ms. Michaels," he said gravely, stepping aside so that his colleagues could get by him. With courteous nods in Raine's direction, the two men made their way down the hall.

"How...how is my brother this morning, Doctor?" Raine asked faintly.

Dr. Anders frowned. "He had a good night, but early this morning he showed signs of developing new complications, mainly a problem with his lungs." The panicked look that crossed Raine's face didn't go unnoticed, but he continued, his tone soft as well as comforting. "I don't want you to go borrowing unnecessary trouble just yet, my dear. My two colleagues have looked at him, and on their recommendation I've started him on a new medication. We're very optimistic." He reached out and took Raine's hand in his and squeezed it reassuringly before he let it go.

Tears glistened on the edge of Raine's lashes. "Thank you," she whispered. "I know you're doing your best and I appreciate it."

Dr. Anders shook his head. "Don't thank me yet," he cautioned. "Let's just hope my best is good enough. Now, why don't you go and sit with him a while? He was asking for you earlier." Then, turning to Ashe, who was now standing within breathing distance of Raine, he added, "I'd like to see you in my office a moment, Ashe, if you have the time."

"Of course," Ashe answered respectfully. "I'll be right there."

It was while Ashe and Dr. Anders were exchanging words that Raine noticed Colonel Jackson was gone. She breathed a sigh of relief. At least for now she had drawn a respite. But there was still Ashe. She could feel his warm breath as it grazed her cheek. She felt herself tense.

"Raine." His voice was guarded.

"Yes?" she said sharply, staring straight ahead, daring herself not to look at him, while clutching the doorknob for dear life.

She heard his sharp indrawn breath, but still she refused to look at him. "I'll be in touch," he said at last. Then he turned and walked away. But Raine knew that wasn't what he had wanted to say. His sense of frustration was almost tangible.

With a heavy heart, Raine tiptoed silently into the room and closed the door softly behind her.

Ashe found Raine's image interfering with his concentration. Her face interposed itself between his eyes and the mountain of paperwork on his desk. He sat, staring at the rubble, unable to stop thinking about Raine; going back over every remembered aspect of her face and body, the sound of her voice, the misery in her eyes. He had to see her again, to find out what it was about her that kept his mind from letting her go.

From the office door, his assistant, Jake Everette, commented, "You seem out of it, Ashe. Anything else happen with the Michaels case that I need to know about?"

"Without going into the details, it's been a bitch of a morning," Ashe said.

"Anything I can do?"

Ashe grimaced. "No, there's nothing anybody can do."

Everette stared at his boss privately for a moment. He had never seen him in this kind of mood before; he was certain it was the flak from the investigating board that had him so uptight. The military hated losing a plane. But Ashe was right; there wasn't a thing anyone could do until the investigation was completed.

"Well, if you've got a minute to spare, Winston needs you in the engine room." Everette moved away from the doorway. "There's a problem with the engine on the C-3. Take your time, though. There's no hurry."

"Tell him I'll be there shortly," Ashe said, thinking.

Nothing he seemed to do could erase Raine from his thoughts. She had looked absolutely shattered yesterday when the doctor had told her that Todd had developed complications.

He would have traded almost anything, except his freedom, for the privilege of reaching across and hauling her close against him, to have her share his embrace, to be glad he was there. Fat chance, he'd told himself. But he hadn't been able to banish the fantasy. He'd wanted nothing more, as he'd stood there silently, unbending, avoiding the smallest contact, he'd wanted it so much that his whole body had screamed with the effort of not touching her.

And he still felt that gut-wrenching tension. Elliot! That woman is driving you out of your mind!

Suddenly he made a decision. Now all he had to do was to make it work....

Raine had always considered herself practical, possessed of a fairly logical mind, an independent person. She thought she knew herself well. But Todd's accident seemed to have invalidated all her personal assessments. It shook her to the very depths of her soul to think that her brother, whose life she valued as equally as her own, might still die.

Why did this have to happen, she asked again and again as she continued to sit beside Todd's bed, attentive to his every move, his every breath. The private-duty nurse Ashe had hired had not shown up, so wild horses couldn't have dragged Raine away from his bedside.

Thank goodness, she thought, Todd had a suite. Courtesy of Ashe Elliot, no doubt. But she had no intention of letting Ashe assume the responsibility for Todd. Ashe. Just thinking about him caused her heart to skip a beat. Absurd! Pushing visions of his image aside, she settled down at the small table in the corner to the sitting room. She then edged the lamp closer to the table and lowered the shade, angling it so that the light would not disturb Todd.

Opening her briefcase, she rummaged through it until she located a specific manila folder. Once she had spread the contents in front of her, she just sat and stared at it. Was she too tired to work? Or was she too disheartened?

Lowering her eyes, Raine forced herself to study the photograph in front of her. This particular client had come to New Image last week wanting a complete makeover, the works: face, hair, and wardrobe. She had told Raine shyly that she needed self-confidence to meet the public.

Raine recalled her exact words, bringing a smile to her lips. "What I need is an overhaul," she'd said. "That may sound like a joke to some, but if you'll notice, I'm not laughing." Then she'd gone on to say, this time with a laugh and her head cocked sideways, "Are you sure you can perform miracles?"

Now as Raine studied her measurements, trying to figure out the type of clothes that would be exactly right for her, she chewed on her lower lip, thoroughly engrossed in her work. And so it went for hours. The only time Raine broke her concentration was to check on Todd, to make sure he was still resting as comfortably as possible.

When she heard the door open, she didn't bother to look up.

"Don't you think you've been here long enough for one day?"

The rich tone of Ashe Elliot's voice roused her thoroughly and effectively. It was as though someone had suddenly flung a glass of ice water in her face. The pen slipped out of her hand, making a loud sound on the Formica-topped table before falling to the floor. Damn, she thought recklessly as she leaned over and scooped it up in her hand.

"How's Todd?" Ashe asked when Raine remained silent.

"He seems to be better, thank God." She had regained her composure and had answered without a tremor in her voice.

His strange-looking eyes were shadowed in the muted light. "Did you know that it's after six o'clock?"

Raine's eyes dipped to the gold watch circling her arm. God, he wasn't lying; it was six-thirty, to be exact. Where had the time gone?

"I hadn't realized it was so late," she said after a moment. "I was able to lose myself in my work after Todd quieted down." She moved her shoulders, feeling the kinks loosen up. "The time just flew by," she added, her eyes following his movements to the side of the bed. He appeared stern and foreboding as he stared down at her brother.

The room was silent, though the sounds from the corridor seeped through the closed doors. Vaguely, Raine was aware of the clanging of the doctor's page system, the clanking of the water carts, and dozens of other sounds that she had come to associate with the hospital.

"His breathing does seemed to have eased," Ashe said, his eyes lingering on Todd as though he was seaching for signs of improvement.

Raine crossed to the foot of the bed and for a moment joined Ashe in watching her brother as Todd's chest rose and fell in an uneasy pattern.

"I hope the medication they're giving him continues to work," she whispered, turning to meet Ashe's brooding gaze. "If...if his lung fills up with fluid again—" She paused, swallowing hard. "They will have to go in and drain it."

"Try not to think about that," Ashe cautioned gently.

Raine touched Todd's hand. "That's what Dr. Anders told me, but it's so hard—" Again her voice broke. She looked away, fighting for control. Why didn't he go away and leave her alone? She didn't want him here. His presence was unsettling. What did he want from her, anyway? Was he hoping to absolve his conscience?

"How long has it been since you've eaten?" he asked, moving away from the bed, clearing the path for the nurse who had just entered the room. She was carrying a new I.V. bottle.

"I haven't." Unconsciously, she raised her hand and began massaging the back of her neck. She was exhausted. Suddenly, the thought of going to Todd's apartment and indulging herself in a tub of hot water seemed like heaven.

After the nurse had exited with a nod in Raine's direction, she turned to Ashe. "I think I'm...I'm going to call it a day," she said haltingly.

Ashe noticed the pinched, worried look on her face and did not like it. He knew she was once again close to collapsing. The signs were there: the bruised circles under her eyes, the tired droop of her mouth, and the defeated set to her shoulders.

His gut instinct had been correct after all. He had made the right decision in coming here, and if she would only agree to the rest of his plan, he would have it made.

"I want you to have dinner with me." They were now standing outside the door of Todd's room.

Raine lifted widened eyes to his. "What!" Were her ears playing tricks on her?

"You heard me," he answered patiently.

Her next breath was a short sigh. "I—"

"Good, I'm glad it didn't take you long to say yes."

She couldn't help but smile. "This conversation is beginning to sound familiar."

He chuckled, leaning his arm against the wall. "My thoughts exactly. So why put us through another hassle? You're exhausted and hungry; I'm exhausted and hungry. So why shouldn't we share a meal?"

Raine could think of a thousand reasons, the main one being that it was dangerous to become involved with this man on any level. But she held her silence.

"Besides that, you've never tasted anything as good as one of my steaks."

An incredulous expression crossed Raine's face. "You mean have dinner at your place?"

His chuckle deepened, making him appear more attractive than ever. She stilled herself against the tide of emotion that swept through her.

"Why not?" he asked, his drawl deepening, becoming more pronounced. "I guarantee I can best any restaurant in this city. Come on, it'll do you good not to go home and brood."

Suddenly the fight went out of her. She was too tired to argue any longer. And what harm could come from sharing one simple dinner with him? After all, hadn't he told her that he was immune to entanglements? Yet...

She liked his condo. It was neat. Cluttered, but neat. There were shelves and shelves of books lining one complete wall. And an elaborate multi-speakered stereo system dominated all four corners of the living area.

Raine stood in the middle of the room, her teeth chattering, trying to concentrate on the luxurious surroundings. But she couldn't seem to stop shaking. It must be the dampness, she reminded herself. Just as they had left the hospital, the rain had suddenly begun to fall. Not in sheets as she had expected, having watched the lightning dance in the sky, but in a slow, steady drizzle. She had gotten wet enough, however, to cause sharp chills to shoot through her. And it didn't help that his house was as cold as an iceberg. Or was she having an attack of nerves and blaming it on the cold? Suddenly, she felt uncomfortable, wishing she hadn't come.

While Ashe flipped on more of the lamps, plunging the room into a soft glow, Raine slipped out of her soggy sandals and walked over to look at the books.

"I gather you like to read," she observed aloud, noting the majority of the books were mysteries—a row of Ross MacDonald's Mickey Spillane, Agatha Christie by the bucketful, a dash of James Clavell just for flavor, plus numerous others. His choice of reading material surprised her. She would have thought his shelves would have contained more nonfiction, facts on aircrafts, the techniques of flying. Where were the best-sellers such as *Space?* and *The Right Stuff?* This man was becoming more of an enigma with each passing second.

"I read every chance I get," he agreed, watching her. "Coffee?"

"I don't think so," she said dryly, her heart starting to pound. Then suddenly changing her mind she said, "Yes, I believe I will, after all." She couldn't think what to do. She was as nervous as a kid in a candy store.

"Make yourself comfortable, why don't you." He leaned in the doorway, smiling at her, trying to put her at ease. If only he could ease that haunted, painful look she wore like a veil. "I'll get your coffee, and then I'll get the steaks ready to throw on the grill."

Raine shivered again as her eyes collided with his. "Let me help. There's bound to be something I can do."

Ashe pushed away from the door and approached her. "You're trembling," he said huskily. "And you're cold. God, what an insensitive brute you must think me."

Raine stood still, frightened all over again, positive that he was going to touch her.

She looked up at him, feeling the heat of her body rising up in waves, replacing the numbing chill. The air around them was smothering in its intensity. "I'll...be fine," she stammered, moving back, "especially when I get some hot coffee in me."

For a long moment, an eternity, Ashe did not move. Then reluctantly he, too, stepped back, shattering the moment into a thousand pieces.

"Come on, I'll get you that coffee," he murmured brusquely.

Breathing deeply, Raine nodded.

The kitchen was compact, but extremely functional, equipped with the latest gadgets and appliances. The cabinets were filled with brightly colored canisters, and a microwave oven occupied the space adjacent to them. The colors were muted oranges and yellows, and they blended perfectly with the paneled cabinets. She liked it. But again she was surprised that his home was so organized. It just didn't seem to fit the type of personality he had or the type of life he led. She was expecting it to be more like Todd's— everything in complete disarray. But then maybe she was giving him too much credit—maybe he just had a good maid.

"Would you be more comfortable if I got you one of my sweaters to throw around your shoulders?" he asked, gesturing for Raine to sit down at the table in a corner of the kitchen. There was a floor-to-ceiling window beside it, looking onto a deck and terraced yard. "I've already turned off the air-conditioning, but it may take it a while to warm up."

"I'm fine." She forced her eyes away from the urns of plants lining the edge of the deck and turned back to him. "Don't make yourself uncomfortable just because of me. I'm always cold when everyone else is hot."

Ashe grinned. "In other words, I'm wasting my time and good energy trying to please you."

A tiny smile touched her lips. She suddenly felt her insides begin to unwind. Maybe she hadn't made a mistake in coming here—if she kept in mind that a meal was all it was. An escape. Things must be kept in their right perspective, she warned herself.

"Exactly," she answered at length, watching him as he measured the coffee and then dumped it in the filter. Shortly, the smell and the gurgling sound of fresh coffee permeated the room.

"How do you like your steak?" Opening the refrigerator, Ashe brought out two huge cuts of meat wrapped in Saran Wrap and plunked them down on the counter. They were so heavy they landed with a thud.

Raine's eyes widened. "Surely you don't expect me to eat a steak *that* big? One that size would last me a week."

Ashe turned around, his eyes taking in the stunning picture she made sitting by the window, the late-evening sunlight dancing around her, calling attention to her fragile beauty, to the odd color of her hair. It shone like satin in the sunlight, and he wondered how it would feel to run his hands through it.

He cleared his throat. "You're right," he said, forcing his mind back on track. "There's no way you could consume even half of this."

"Are you sure that isn't half a cow on that plate? She laughed, the sound caressing his ears like sweet music. *Dammit, Elliot, at this rate, you'll never get the meal cooked!*

He turned his back to her and began stabbing the slab of meat with a fork. "One steak will be enough for both of us," he flung over his shoulder. He then grabbed the salt and pepper shakers and saturated the holes generously with each, trying desperately to ignore his shaking hand.

"Is there anything I can do to help?" Raine asked after a moment.

He smiled. "Nope. Not a thing. Salad's all made and waiting in the fridge."

Raine scrutinized him from under heavy lashes as he rimmed excess fat off the outer edge of the meat, mesmerized by the way the muscles in his arms tightened as he manipulated the knife. He looked sharp in a pale green, custom-made silk body shirt, tucked into spotless, perfectly pressed light tan pants, secured with a woven belt.

For a breathless moment her gaze concentrated on his broad shoulders. Suddenly, she remembered something her grandmother told her a long time ago. "Honey, beware of narrow-shouldered men. You can't rely on them, can't trust them to be there when you need them. I've always been leery of men with narrow shoulders; it's like a visible character flaw." Ross Thomas has narrow shoulders. Funny, she'd never thought about that before.

Finished with his task, Ashe swung around, catching Raine in the act of staring at him. He grinned knowingly.

Damn him, she thought. The charm was explosive; he was using it deliberately like someone displaying a talent. She could feel the flush as it crept up her face, beginning with her neck.

As though he could read the defiance on her face, he said casually, "If you're ready, let's head for the deck and I'll put my culinary expertise to work." The corners of his mouth were tilted in a mocking grin.

Again Raine found herself suddenly short-winded, as if she'd been climbing up a Down escalator. Realizing that Ashe was waiting for her with his hands loaded down with the steak and tongs, she scooted past him with an apologetic nod.

The deck was lovely. Plants and flowers surrounded it, teasing her senses, making her dizzy. She plopped down on the heavily padded porch swing and watched while Ashe poured charcoal down into the bottom of the smoker, to the right of which was a freestanding gas grill.

Her curiosity was piqued. "Is there a difference?" she asked, covering the small silence.

Ashe turned to face her, thinking once again how lovely she was. He blinked several times to clear his head. Raine was eyeing him strangely. "Difference?"

She gestured to her right. "You know. In the gas grill and the smoker?"

"Oh," he said inanely, then regrouped. "The grill is quicker, but the smoker adds the flavor through and through. Besides that, I can add several hickory limbs to this baby." He paused and patted the lid of the smoker. "That, too, enhances the taste."

"Sounds good to me. I didn't realize I was so hungry until you mentioned food." Then suddenly her expression changed.

"What's wrong?" Ashe inquired, tuned in to her every move.

She hesitated and then said faintly, "I was just thinking about Todd. He's lying in the hospital while I'm..." *While I'm cavorting with the enemy,* she added silently. Such a cold man one minute and yet so warm the next; so familiar and easy, yet so unapproachable. There were so many contradictions about him that she felt herself swept away in confusion. At the moment, she was less sure of herself than at any time in her life.

He was standing close to her now. Though he was not touching her, she actually felt as though he was. The effect this man had on her was uncanny. She hated herself for this weakness.

"There's nothing more you can do for Todd this evening," he responded softly, peering down into her upturned face.

Raine gnawed at her lower lip. "I know."

He regarded her a moment longer, then said, "I'll be right back. I'm going after your coffee and my beer. And the sauce for the steak.'' Making an effort to lighten the mood, he added with a grin, ''I make a mean sauce, called Elliot's brew. But don't ask me for the recipe, because that's top secret.'' He threw that last sentence over his shoulder as he made his way back into the house.

Raine signed and changed her position in the swing, once again breathing deeply of the plants and sweet-smelling flowers. However, her respite from his powerful personality was short-lived.

Ashe came through the door carrying a tray. After setting her coffee on the table beside her, he heaped a generous amount of sauce on the steak. Then he dropped two plump, foil-wrapped potatoes on the grill before placing the lid over it.

''Now, all we have to do is wait with our mouths watering.'' He sat down opposite Raine, watching her. Suddenly, he felt compelled to find out all about her: everything she'd done, everything she'd known. Everything.

''Do you realize I don't even know where you work? Or even *if* you work,'' he clarified lightly as he lit a cigarette, then took a sip of beer.

Raine lowered the coffee cup and stared at him over the rim. ''Of course I work,'' she said bitingly. ''If there's a way to get around it these days, I don't know about it.''

He shrugged, realizing he'd apparently hit a raw nerve.

''Don't mind me,'' she added suddenly. ''I own a consulting firm called New Image. I love my work; actually, it's my life.''

''Sounds interesting.''

Her face brightened. She could talk about her work for hours and never get tired. ''Oh, it is. I have about four hundred women who depend on me to look their very best before tackling their respective jobs.''

''And how do you accomplish that miracle?'' he asked, genuinely interested.

"Well, to make a long story short, we do a color analysis on each one to determine what season she is." When he looked completely lost, she smiled patiently. "Colors are divided into the four seasons and they fall into two families of color; one with blue, or cool, undertones, and one with golden, warm undertones. The winter and summer seasons belong to the same family of cool colors. Autumn and spring seasons belong to the same family." She paused. "Now, aren't you sorry you asked?"

He scratched the top of his head and grinned before getting up and strolling over to the smoker. Lifting the lid, he then flipped the steak and potatoes. "You're right. All that's about as clear as mud. But it does seem as though it's more play than work."

Was he making fun of her work? "Huh, that's what you think," she replied, eyeing him as he sat back down, stretching his legs out in front of him and taking another drink of his beer. "I work as hard or harder than you do. Just because it isn't dangerous..." She was piqued and it showed.

"Point taken," he drawled with raised eyebrows and a mocking slant to his lips, "but at least mine's meaningful."

Raine bristled. "Meaning mine isn't?"

"Hey." He laughed. "Lighten up. Give me a break. I was only teasing."

"Maybe so, but I'd still like an answer."

He shrugged, taking another sip of beer, his grin still intact. "Well, for starters, I'm making a valuable contribution to our country."

"How? By making planes that are used as weapons, that destroy people's lives?"

"I have to look at it philosophically; if I didn't, someone else would," he said lightly.

She shuddered. "I hate anything to do with war. It's such a waste."

"And you think I like it?" His eyes sparked dangerously.

She was quick to respond. "Well, don't you? Your company builds war planes and you test them. Isn't that right?"

"Yes, but..."

"But what?" Raine sensed she had him backed into a corner and was enjoying it to the hilt.

He studied her for a moment. "I know what you're trying to do, but it won't work." She flushed and he went on. "But I will say this in defense of myself, and then we'll let the matter rest. You're right, I am proud of what I do, especially my latest endeavor, which is a special prototype plane for the military, code name Black Cobra. The Cobra is my design, and if it turns out like I hope it does, then we'll be years ahead of the Russians. And to me, that's important," he added flatly.

While battling the silence, Raine felt like a fool.

"Sorry," she apologized after a moment, "I overstepped my bounds. It's none of my business how you choose to live your life or—"

Ashe leaned over with a grin and ran his fingers slowly across her lips. "Shh!" he whispered. "Everything about me is your business, but for now I want to get back to what you do."

He was watching her with a smoldering gaze that shattered her already shaken composure. "I just told you," she said, swallowing hard, unable to look away.

"I'm sure there's something you haven't told me."

Raine forced her eyes away from his powerful limbs and got up, strolled to the edge of the deck, and leaned over the rail, her back to him. "Well, I'm in the process of branching out, opening a clothing boutique. Hopefully, soon, I'll be able to market a new line of clothing for the working woman that I've designed myself." She paused. "But now that Todd's so ill, things—"

"May not work out like you planned. Is that it?"

She nodded, turning to face him. "That's right."

"Look, Raine," he said, his voice warm and engaging, "we need to talk. I want to help—"

"No!" she ground out suddenly, overreacting, fear spinning a web inside her. "What...what I mean is that I don't want to discuss Todd or...the accident." *I just want to go home,* she cried silently. What was she doing here in the first place with her brother in the hospital? God!

Ashe's face hardened at her stiff rebuke, though his voice remained light. "All right, Raine. I won't press you now." He swung his gaze toward the smoker. "Elliot's special is coming right up," he added lightly, striving to recapture the moments of tranquility.

His efforts were futile. Dinner was not a success. The thin thread of civility that had once held them together was broken. Although the food could have been delicious, it tasted like cardboard to Raine. She was conscious of his every movement, as he of was hers. They were both glad when they could push their plates aside and get up and make their way into the den. But over coffee, it was no better. Ashe lit a cigarette and watched her through the haze of blue smoke.

Suddenly a wave of exhaustion from two sleepless nights engulfed her and she closed her eyes for a moment.

"Raine."

Her eyes flew back open and he was standing up, watching her, the bones of his face sharply shadowed in the light from the fringed lamp. "For God's sake, don't shut me out!"

She clambered to her feet, though her legs threatened to buckle beneath her. "No, please...I'd like to go home."

"I'm not your enemy, you know," he said quietly, steadily closing the distance between them. "You're driving me crazy, you know that. I can't think of anything but you. I want to help, to be with you." His voice was soft, seductive.

Panic welled up inside Raine. She took a step backward, but there was nowhere to go. She suddenly felt sick. And afraid. She had been fooling herself that Ashe's interest was platonic, ignoring the way he watched her, the sensuous touch of his hand on her bare arm. She was frightened, frightened of the desire that flickered around her like fire. And like fire, it burned.

She fought back. "No...I, we don't need your help."

Ashe went on as though she hadn't spoken. "I'll take full responsibility for all Todd's medical bills and see that he wants for nothing."

"Why? So you can ease your conscience?" Raine didn't take the time to weigh her words; she said the first thing that came to mind.

His sharp intake of breath was the only sound in the room. "Just what the hell is that supposed to mean?"

She raised her head defiantly, though she was quaking on the inside. "You're blaming Todd—"

"No, dammit! I'm not. I just have to report the facts!"

"You can swear at me all you want, but I know better. You and Colonel Jackson—"

"Jackson's an ass! He takes pleasure in bullying all parties concerned."

Raine had gone too far; she wasn't about to back down now. "Well, it doesn't matter," she hammered on. "I'm perfectly capable of taking care of my brother, and I don't need you. You just go ahead and play your dangerous games in the sky and forget about me, about us."

It was not so much what she said as how she'd said it that rankled Ashe.

His light voice, almost a monotone, was a thin blade, cutting through the silence, sliding coldly into Raine. "You're a liar."

"Get out of my way," she cried, her fear deepening.

His eyes narrowed and turned icy blue. "You may not need me, but you want me just as much as I want you. And I intend to prove it."

No! She shook her head from side to side, strands of silk slapping him in the face. "How dare you say that to me...you arrogant brute!"

That was the proverbial straw that broke the camel's back. His hand shot out like an arrow and clamped around her upper arm and spun her around. This time there was no tenderness.

His action brought her paralyzed limbs to life and she twisted, struggled, with violent motion, but to no avail. He pinned her arms behind her, and for a brief moment they faced each other. Raine felt the impact of his body.

"If that's how you think of me, then I'll just have to live up to your expectations, won't I?" Touching this woman had been uppermost in Ashe's mind from the moment she set foot in his house. He would deny himself no longer.

The kiss was intended to punish, to bring pain, determined to prove she ached for him as much as he did for her. But the moment his lips tasted the trembling softness of hers, punishment changed to sensuous persuasion.

His lips melted into hers, drowning in their sweetness. Even with her resentment, anger, and humiliation, Raine was aware of the surge of emotion that drowned out all other feelings. The contemptuous caress deepened and lengthened, her response causing Ashe to groan deep in his throat as her lissome body arched against him, seeking an unknown intimacy.

"God, Raine," he whispered into her mouth, "what am I doing?"

And then it was over. When he let her go and looked away, Raine supported herself against the wall, her face turned against it. Tears spilled onto her swollen, trembling mouth.

She could see him out of the corner of her eye. He was standing near the kitchen door, his eyes tracking her every movement. His eyes spoke of fresh wounds and recently drawn blood. He looked battle-fatigued.

"I'll take you home," he said.

She crossed wordlessly to the door, hating herself. For, in spite of everything, she ached for him to touch her again.

Chapter 5

His days became fragmented, like shards of pottery. He had worked in his office, going over the report on the crash a thousand times, and had put up with Colonel Jackson and his team until he was sick to death of them. And still the report wasn't complete.

Since Michaels's plane had crashed, several other A-7's had been flown, and to date, nothing out of the ordinary had happened. They had breezed through the test with flying colors. Because of that, it wasn't looking good for Todd. Yet, Ashe was determined to keep searching for mechanical failures.

Each morning, sometimes before dawn, and late every evening, Ashe would go by the hospital. On his visits he noted very little change in Todd. His condition vacillated between serious and guarded.

At night, Ashe sat in his den with piles of work he had brought home. However, he spent most of his time trying to think logically, knowing that he should have nothing on his mind but the Cobra project. The success of this project was the culmination of years of hard work and turning his dream into reality. Nothing, he kept telling himself, must hamper its completion.

Of course he hadn't counted on the plane crash and the investigation. Nor had he counted on the unsettling presence of Raine Michaels.

What the hell was wrong with him, anyway? Was it because he hadn't had a woman in several months? Maybe if he'd taken Leigh up on her offer... No. He could never have used her like that. For pity's sake, Raine Michaels wasn't the only good-looking female left in the whole world, was she? Why couldn't he simply face the fact that she didn't want him around, that she didn't trust him as far as she could throw, that she hated test pilots and everything they stood for?

He hadn't laid eyes on Raine after the disastrous evening at his house. Several times he had picked up the phone to call her, but then had slammed it down in disgust, chastising himself for running after a woman who didn't want to be chased. But he couldn't relieve his mind of the way she had felt in his arms, her softness, the way she smelled, sweet like honeysuckle that grew wild around the ranch, the way she tasted....

But now, he was determined not to waste the only Saturday he'd had off from the plant in Lord knows how long brooding. He jackknifed out of the chair and in a jerking movement strode outside. As he walked toward the hangar, the clear, clean morning air surrounded him like a hypnotic drug, soothing his troubled mind.

When he reached the hangar, he opened the door to his plane, then, attaching the tow bar to the nose of the airplane, pulled it out of the hangar.

Taking his favorite toy, his Cherokee, out for a joyride always made him feel better, put things back in their right perspective. Maybe he'd even fly down to the border, re-membering Mac was working on a job down there. Who knows, he thought, if he could find old Mac they could share a beer.

After kicking the chocks from under the wheels, he checked the fuel, making sure the tanks had been topped off and were free of contaminants. Then one fluid motion took him up to the wing and into the seat. After following through with other preliminary checks, he taxied to the end of the runway and was soon airborne.

Up, up and away, into the wide blue yonder, he mused, the gauges telling him all was well, that he was on course. Now, to settle back and enjoy. No matter how often he went up, the thrill was always there—just like sex, he thought— it always got better with practice and patience.

Suddenly Raine popped into his mind. It was too bad he could never convey these feelings to her. She despised flying and all it stood for. He could understand that, even though he couldn't accept it. She had lost a father to the sky and damn near a brother as well. But he could never change; he was what he was and made no apologies for it.

His life had never been a bowl of cherries. He had worked his way out of more than one pit to reach the current pla-teau in his life, beginning with his stint in the navy as a pilot and then on to Pax River, where he'd trained to become a test pilot. It hadn't been easy. In fact, a number of people had accused him of being "snake-bit." His whole life had been a risk, beginning with the way he'd lucked himself out of the beatings his drunken father had tried to give him.

Then after Vietnam, he had gone from bad to worse. His wife, Laura, had found other "amusements" while he was busting his buns for his country. After she had admitted that she had indeed found grass greener on the other side of the fence, he'd told her to get the hell out of his life and stay out.

Following his divorce, he'd done free-lance flying for several air-freight companies, and then he got his first break.

He began testing planes again by what he deemed a sheer stroke of luck, being in the right place at the right time. It was Mac who had gotten him the job. After finally tracking down Ashe, he'd told him that Bell Aircraft was looking for just the right pilot to test a special plane for the air force, and that his name had been mentioned. Mac had promised to find Ashe and see if he was interested.

He was interested. From then on he never looked back. His career was off and running. Using the experience he'd gained in the navy and Nam, he worked for both government and private industry on a contractual basis by testing planes for them. His outward appearance of having a happy-go-lucky, don't-give-a-damn attitude, his daredevil feats in the sky, and his unmatched skill with a plane kept him in constant demand as a pilot.

It was this dangerous but lucrative work that enabled him eventually to buy his aircraft company, and from that moment on nothing had stopped him from rising above the squalor of his past and amassing a fortune.

From then on, everything had gone according to plan. Until now. The loss of the plane and the near death of a pilot had shaken him to the core. And it wasn't because he feared that he would eventually meet the same fate himself; that had never worried him, and still didn't.

"We all have to die sometime," was his favorite quote when questioned about the danger connected with his job. No. It was because he felt responsible. Responsible in that the flight was under his direct supervision and it had failed. To his way of thinking, the accident was a direct reflection on him, his company. He demanded the same perfection in his men as he did in himself. He would tolerate nothing less.

And then there was Raine Michaels.

Ashe's fingers tightened spasmodically around the wheel as the Cherokee soared through the azure sky. Frowning, he berated himself for once again becoming a slave to his own emotions.

Against all rationale, Ashe wanted to possess Raine Michaels with an intensity that shook his well-ordered existence. And he damned well didn't know what to do about it. As far as she was concerned, he could go hang himself, he thought savagely.

Suddenly, losing interest in flying to the border, he made a course correction and was headed back toward the ranch.

After that, there was nothing left to do except flick on the automatic pilot, light a cigarette, and damn himself all the way back to the ranch.

"You're a goddamned fool, Ashe Elliot!" he shouted into the clouds.

Ashe.

Twisting and turning, Raine groaned aloud in protest, willing his intrusive image to disappear. For no sane reason, she could feel his hands digging into her shoulders, the smell of his potent cologne, the feel of his lips on hers.

"Oh, hell!"

With the muttered curse, Raine rolled onto her side, pounding the pillow, venting her frustration. She wished she could stop her heart from pounding irregularly, stopping and starting and fluttering in her chest. She wished she could get things back in their right perspective. Clutching the pillow close to her body, she shut her eyes tightly, praying that this time the image of Ashe Elliot's face would have faded away.

Nothing doing.

Exactly one hour later when the alarm buzzed insistently in her ear, her thoughts were just as muddled. Glad to have an excuse to get up finally, she flung back the sheet and hit the floor with a bounce. After checking on Todd, and if his condition permitted, she was to meet with the new client and author, Catherine Cole.

Raine dressed quickly in a slim, sky-blue linen dress belted in white. A short time later she sailed into the hospital, only to find Todd's improved condition was short-lived. Dr. Anders was concerned now with the overall damage due to internal injuries. But at the same time, he assured Raine that there was nothing to be accomplished by staying in the room and wringing her hands.

"We'll be running tests all morning," he said, "and maybe into the afternoon as well. Just leave a message as to where you'll be at the nurse's station, and if there's any significant change, we'll call."

Raine frowned, her eyes deeply troubled. "I...I don't know. I should cancel my appointment."

"Don't."

She spread her hands. "But, Doctor..."

"I'll call you," he stressed again. "Now, go. You need a break. Doing nothing but sitting day after day will drive you insane."

Finally, Raine acquiesced, but none too eagerly. But she trusted Dr. Anders implicitly and knew that he would indeed call if Todd's condition worsened. Still, her mind was in turmoil as she steered the car onto the loop, following the directions that Catherine had given her yesterday on the phone.

Yesterday. What a day that had been. Discounting Todd's signs of improvement, the day could have been labeled a disaster. With an impatient twist to her mouth, she recalled in detail her phone conversation with Ross.

She had called him early, at the office, determined to catch him before his mind splintered in several different directions at once. In her most authoritative tone of voice, though careful not to let the anger seething within her bubble to the surface, she'd told him that under no circumstances was he to show her sketches to Jules Burns.

"Ah," he'd said, "Val was indeed good for her word, I see."

Her chin jutted out. "Let's not play games, Ross. You knew Val would call me; that's why you told her what you did."

Then completely and smoothly changing the subject, he asked, "How's Todd?"

Raine managed to curb her impatience, though it was difficult. "About the same, though I haven't been to the hospital this morning."

"I tried to call you several times yesterday, but received no answer at the apartment, and I hated to call the hospital."

"Had you wanted to tell me what you planned to do?" she inquired innocently.

There was a slight hesitation. "Raine, honey, I'm sorry, but if you don't get Jules when he's in the mood, we may never get him at all. Anyway, what's the big deal, for heaven's sake? We've slaved over those designs together, and I know what you want—I'm familiar with the sketches, the notes." He paused. "Of course, I'm sure Jules will want to get together with you later, but by then, hopefully, you'll have a commitment from him."

"No, Ross, I don't see," she answered irritably. "This is my deal with Jules, and I don't want you or anyone else substituting for me. Is that understood?" She had never used that tone of voice with him, had never had to, she quickly reminded herself. But she was fighting for her future and maybe Todd's as well.

"Are you saying you don't need me anymore, Raine?"

Tears were threatening, but she forced them back, refusing to give in to the chaos that was churning within her. Ross could very well axe the deal with Jules for good, if he so desired. Was she a fool to gamble her future by not giving in to Ross? Well, maybe she was, but she had to do what she thought best for her.

"No, that's not what I'm saying, but if that's the way you want to interpret it, then..." Her voice trailed off.

Silence.

"All right," Ross replied heavily, "you win. I'll tell Jules you'll be in touch. I just hope you don't regret your hard-headedness and are prepared to pay the consequences."

She wasn't, but she had no intention of admitting that to Ross. A feeling of relief made her weak. She might not have won the fight, but she had at least won a round.

"Please call me as soon as you've talked to him."

"All right," Ross said, before the buzz sounded in her ear.

Now as Raine spotted the brick house that was her destination, she realized that, with each passing day, she was being pulled in two different directions. But she knew she had to hang on, to ride out the storm. *Life won't stop for you.* To hell with them all—Ashe, Ross, Jules... *Get yourself together and move on.*

Raine's first thought was that Catherine Cole was gorgeous. Of average height, she had a neat, trim body with delectable curves, a fantastic mane of fiery red hair, and a face that could, if displayed to full advantage, stop men in their tracks. Unfortunately, none of these God-given assets came together. Her hair was captured in a rubber band at the nape of her neck and coiled in a bun. Her makeup was all wrong and her clothing was ill fitting and uncoordinated. She was New Image's dream client.

After introductions and pleasantries were exchanged, Catherine said shyly, "I'm so glad you could come." Her dark brown eyes were filled with sympathy. "I'm sorry about your brother."

"Thank you," Raine responded softly. "But the doctor insisted that I come here today, promising to call if I'm needed."

"You just can't imagine how much I appreciate your rallying to my plea for help. In just a matter of days, I'll be flying to New York to meet with my publisher." She paused, chewing on her lower lip nervously. "That's when I'm supposed to appear on the 'Today' show and 'Good Morning America.' And I'm scared to death."

Raine smiled. "Don't be. When New Image gets through with you, you won't even recognize yourself."

"I won't?"

Raine laughed. "Please, don't look like that's a fate worse than death." Raine's lips were still twitching as she eased herself down beside Catherine on the couch. "I promise your makeover will be painless, and when you arrive in the Big Apple you'll be a knockout."

Catherine's face brightened. "Do you really think so?"

"I know so."

"I still can't believe that I'm being flown to New York to appear on those talk shows." Her eyes were sparkling with excitement. "And while I'm there, my editor and I are going to plan my publicity tour for my next book that's due out later this year."

"Believe me," Raine said, "I can make you absolutely stunning. You're already beautiful, but you're not using your beauty to full advantage."

Catherine's face cleared, becoming animated once again. "You make me feel so much better. My husband tried to get me to call New Image after I sold *If Tomorrow Comes*, said he'd send me to Dallas for a week, if you'd be willing to take me on as a client."

Raine shook her head in dismay at Catherine's lack of self-confidence. "First thing we need to do is bolster your confidence in yourself, make you see how lovely you can be simply by using the correct makeup and colors to your advantage.''

Catherine appeared suddenly dazed, as though the thought was too much to comprehend. ''You mean you're actually going to do something with me personally today? I thought for sure I'd have to go to Dallas.''

Raine stood up with a smile. ''Well, this is unusual, I'll admit, but under the circumstances, I won't be in Dallas for a while yet, so I'll go as far as I can here. Then later you can going to Dallas for the nutrition and exercise programs. I highly recommend them.''

Catherine's eyes shone. ''Oh, I wouldn't dream of not coming to Dallas.'' She paused and frowned. ''But what about my wardrobe? I need help desperately with that, too. And now.''

Raine smiled, her eyes scanning the room, then stopping at an open door leading into what looked like a large bath, equipped with a dressing room. Her eyes lit up. ''If we have time today, following the makeup session, we'll go through your closet,'' she said enthusiastically. ''If not today, then tomorrow, if possible. Of course, it all depends on how my brother's doing.''

''Oh, please,'' Catherine pleaded, ''don't think I'm being pushy. I'm just grateful for any help you can give me.''

''Well, then, what do you say we get started? I think I've spotted the perfect place for us to work.''

Suddenly Catherine looked disconcerted. ''Oh, golly, I'm sorry, I didn't think to offer you anything to drink when you came in. It's just that when I saw you standing there I got so excited my mind went blank. Would you care for a cup of coffee or some Coke?''

Raine waved her hand. ''Think nothing of it. But, no, thank you, I wouldn't care for a thing right now. I'm fine.'' She paused and began walking toward her briefcase and carryall bag that she had left by the door. ''Thank goodness my assistant had enough foresight to send my materials, or else I couldn't have helped you today."

"Sounds like a smart lady," Catherine mused.

"Oh, she's that and much more. Without her, New Image wouldn't be where it is today."

Catherine looked skeptical. "I doubt that. Everyone knows that with your beauty and brains you could do it alone."

"No," Raine said mildly. "I could never have done it alone."

Catherine arched an eyebrow. "You can't fool me. I've read those articles about you in *Cosmopolitan* and *Woman's World*. They told how you started with nothing and worked your way to the top. That's why I was so surprised, but obviously delighted, that you're going to work with me personally. Just wait until I tell my husband."

Raine hid another smile. "Well, if we don't settle down and get to work," she said, skillfully dismissing her compliments, "there won't be anything to tell your husband or show him."

"Sorry." Catherine looked guilty, though no less enthusiastic. "It's just that I'm excited, but ready to work," she added, a grin lighting up her face.

And work they did. For the next three hours, they didn't look up. Raine began by placing the different swatches of colored material against Catherine's face, the cool colors on one side and warm on the other.

Next Raine used the drape indicator, holding each of the cool-colored swatches against Catherine's face. Immediately, Catherine looked washed out, yellow, accenting the dark circles under her eyes, and calling attention to each blemish and flaw. After going through the color combinations for the warm colors, Raine knew this vivid redhead definitely belonged to the warm family.

Then she used another series of indicator colors, consisting of the seasons autumn and spring, which make up the warm family. As Raine went through each season, it quickly became obvious that Catherine was an autumn. The rich, warm tones of the harvest season were exactly right for her. They gave her a beautiful healthy glow.

By the time Raine finished with the makeup and color demonstrations, it was getting late. She was afraid to stay any longer. Good-byes were said hurriedly. When Raine backed the car out of the driveway, she was exhausted, but feeling better than she had since Todd's accident. Not once had she thought of Ashe. And since she had not received a call from the hospital, she had every reason to believe that Todd was still holding his own.

Clinging to that hope, Raine was not prepared for Todd's empty room, or a concerned Dr. Anders as he stood at the nurses' station, Todd's chart in hand.

"Oh, there you are, Ms. Michaels," he said, a grave note in his voice. "I was just about to have the nurse call you."

Raine had to force the words through her frozen lips. "Where's...Todd?" Fear was hammering violently at her insides.

"I'm sorry, but we had to take him back to intensive care. He began bleeding internally a short time ago and we have to give him blood."

Raine's face had completely lost its color. "Why didn't you call me?" she asked tersely.

"It all happened so fast, and there wasn't a thing you could have done—and there still isn't."

Raine closed her eyes for a moment and sucked air through her lungs. "How...how much blood will he need?" She couldn't go on.

Dr. Anders's lips tightened. "More than we have at the present time, I'm afraid. As you know, your brother has a rare blood type." He paused, his expression grim. "And I'm sorry to say the blood bank is out; there's none to be had."

Raine looked incredulous. "What!" Unconsciously, she clutched the doctor's sleeve, feeling his muscles contract underneath. "But surely you have ways of tracking down the type you need," she cried, increasing the pressure on his arm.

Dr. Anders laid his hand over hers for a brief moment. "We're doing everything possible, leaving no stone unturned."

Raine bit down hard on her lower lip to stop its trembling. "Can I see him?"

Under thick bushy eyebrows, the doctor's eyes were gentle as they peered down into Raine's stricken face. "I think that can be arranged, but please, no longer than ten minutes."

It was after dark before Raine parked the car and let herself into Todd's apartment, having stayed in the waiting room for hours following her allotted time with Todd. As soon as she rested and had a bite to eat, she planned to return to the hospital. They were still waiting for blood.

As she slipped out of her dress and into a cotton caftan, she felt some of the numbness leave her body. She padded into the kitchen, where she scrounged up some cheese and crackers and began munching on them while the coffee dripped.

As she sat down at the dining-room table and tried to nibble on the crackers, she wondered again how long she would be able to cope. Her head suddenly began to swim; she closed her eyes, only to have Ashe's words of a few nights ago rise unbidden to the front of her mind. "I want to help," he'd said softly, seductively. "And I want to see more of you."

No! she cried in silent agony. She did not want his help, did not need his help. Opening her eyes, she pushed aside the food and scrambled to her feet. God! What kind of strange hold did that man have on her? Why couldn't she dismiss his pursuit of her as she had so many men in the past?

She had never felt more vulnerable or more uncertain. Her home and the life she had lived all seemed to have blurred around the edges. *Don't do this to yourself!* Suddenly realizing the coffee was ready, she made her way to the cabinet and was in the process of pouring herself a cup when the jarring chime of the doorbell stilled her hand.

Who could that be, she wondered with vexation. A neighbor checking on Todd? A friend? None too happy with the thought of company this late in the evening, she trudged reluctantly to the front door.

"Who's there?"

"It's Ashe, Raine."

With trembling fingers, she clung to the knob.

"May I come in?"

Chapter 6

Ashe," she repeated dumbly.

"Yes. Ashe."

There was a disturbing silence as she tried to subdue the butterflies in her stomach. "What...what do you want?"

"Raine, please..." His voice sounded distant.

The entire time her hands fumbled with the lock, her mind kept signaling "beware," but her heart was betraying her. With hands that seemed to be severed from her body, Raine slowly pulled back the door and stepped aside.

Ashe looked as though he had just gotten out of the shower, his hair damp and curling. He was dressed casually in a knit shirt and a pair of jeans that clung to his body, molding his hips and outlining the powerful muscles of his thighs.

Raine was intensely aware of him, aware of his eyes upon her, making her conscious of the daring dip of her neckline, the tangled disarray of her hair.

He crossed the threshold slowly and made his way into the middle of the room, his mere presence seeming to shrink the size of the room.

Raine gazed at him, her heart pounding as she pushed the door shut with the brunt of her weight, leaning heavily against it.

"I know you're wondering what brings me to your doorstep at this time of night." A strained, uneven note had crept into his voice, lowering the timbre of it.

Raine swallowed hard, feeling her heart beat in her throat, but still no words escaped her lips. Not only was she surprised to see him, but she was surprised at how haggard he looked, almost as though he hadn't slept in days. He looked as if he'd been on a three-day drunk. Perhaps he had, she thought wryly, then mentally corrected herself. Nothing could drive Ashe Elliot over the edge; he was much too sure of himself, too much in command.

Suddenly, Raine felt a tightening in her stomach. *Why was he here?* She hadn't seen or heard from him in nearly a week—of course, she hadn't wanted to, she told herself fiercely. But why was he here now? Had he come about Todd, or something else, she wondered wildly.

"Raine," he said softly, nudging her out of her thoughts. "I had to see you. I just came from the hospital and knew you'd be worried and upset."

She closed her eyes briefly and took a deep breath, trying to gain a grip on her emotions. Damn him! She didn't want his sympathy. How could he do this to her? She didn't want to be attracted to his virile good looks, his clean, manly smell. He stood for everything she didn't want in a man. Why wouldn't he leave her alone?

"Please," she whispered, her mouth dry as powder. "I think you'd better go."

He didn't speak. He came closer, stopping in front of her, a hairsbreadth away. "Don't send me away." His voice was a husky, seductive lure.

A sense of absolute finality overcame Raine as she looked up at him, making her ache with a strange excitement mixed with fear. A current was flowing between them, without words and without touch. It was the most powerful presexual experience of her life, those few seconds while she waited, her nerves tightening in unwelcome awareness.

Ashe could not move. He was utterly spellbound, finding her exquisite. Perhaps it was the all-gold outfit that pointed up the silver highlights in her hair, wisps of which escaped enticingly down the nape of her neck and in front of her ears. Her skin looked flawless, pale with a pearly sheen.

The silence stretched endlessly.

Suddenly, Ashe stepped back, shattering the moment as though it had never been. His fingers curled into a tight fist as a deep ache filled his lungs. "I didn't come here to... Oh, damn!" he muttered harshly, as he turned away and rubbed the back of his neck, afraid to touch her, afraid not to.

Raine winced, horrified at her momentary loss of control, hating herself, not understanding how she could betray herself so easily. At their previous encounter, she had found him disturbing—tonight he was both disturbing and dangerous. His clothes merely accentuated the air of unleashed power about him, the rough texture of his skin stretched tautly over his bones, so that every movement he made was sinuously defined.

"Please...just go," she whispered, her words coming out in a breathy gust. How could she have imagined she could control this situation when she couldn't even control herself?

Ashe's eyes refused to let her go. "No," he said, "not until I tell you the reason I came." The controlled violence in his tone underlined his every word.

Raine held up her head. "It doesn't matter."

He was regarding her with nerve-racking intensity. "It's about Todd."

"I know about Todd, about the blood situation." Raine expelled her breath slowly. "And as soon as I get a shower, I'm going back to the hospital."

"I've just come from there. I have the same blood type as Todd."

Raine's head snapped back. "Does that mean..." Her voice faltered, hope clawing at her chest.

"Yes," he said gently, "I just got through giving a pint of blood, and I'm going to post notices on the bulletin board at the plant first thing in the morning to see if we can get more blood locally."

Raine shifted her eyes, emotion choking her throat. She didn't want to answer him; she didn't want to become involved or expose the grief that he had inflicted, however indirectly. She hated him, and she especially abhorred him when he was gentle.

"Thank you," she said stiffly.

"Raine, look at me."

"No...I...please," she stammered, turning her back on him completely and crossing the room, stopping in front of the window. "I'm grateful for what you've done, what you're doing."

"Damn it! It's not your gratitude I want, and you know it."

She trembled. "I wish you wouldn't say that."

"Why?"

She felt his presence behind her, his cologne tantalizing her senses, making rational thinking impossible. "You're not playing fair."

"Whose rules are you basing that on?"

She swung around to face him. "You know I'm upset and confused, and I resent your playing a game with my emotions." She shivered, as a chill feathered along her spine. "I don't even know what you want with me." And she didn't, not really. She was not his type; yet the day she saw him at the hospital, something had sparked between them, some terrible chemistry had begun to work. And it was still working, yet she vowed to fight it.

"No?" His brows arched. "I thought I'd made that painfully obvious."

Raine moistened her dry lips. "We're practically strangers."

Ashe shrugged. "That can be easily remedied."

"No, it can't." She was growing desperate. "I want you to leave."

"And if I don't?"

Raine gasped. "Why are you doing this to me?"

"Why? Because I find you fascinating. Because I want to kiss you and touch you, and make love to you."

"Stop it!"

"Don't be afraid," he said softly, keeping his distance, daring himself not to move. Suddenly, he knew that she was right. He had pushed her too far, too soon, had played on her vulnerability. The situation was much too delicate. He cursed inwardly. *Back off!* he warned. *Before it's too late.* Despite his resolution, his eyes drifted downward, seeking the rich curves of her body.

"Please…"

With his eyes on her mouth, he sighed. "You're right. I shouldn't have come here." Then he paused, looking like someone who had just been hit in the stomach with a shovel. "But I was also tired and worried and in desperate need for companionship." *Your companionship,* he longed to add, but did not, for fear of upsetting her further.

"Anyway," he said, "I guess I owe you an apology. But I..." His voice played out, silenced by her whiteness, her stricken look. "Oh, what the hell!" he added, clamping his jaws together, diffusing the tense silence.

Suddenly, it was all too much. She could handle his arrogance, even his rudeness, but she couldn't handle his humbleness. She felt her defenses disappear like waves washing away sand castles.

Her lips parted as she tried to speak. But nothing was forthcoming. She just stood there, her hair hiding a portion of her face, her breasts clearly outlined beneath the thin cotton of her dress as she struggled to regain her breath, her eyes brimming with unshed tears.

And Ashe lost his head.

With a savage groan, he stepped closer, all his good intentions gone with the wind. He caught himself just in time. "Raine..."

She knew what was going to happen, but she could not move. Suddenly, his arms were around her and the kisses she had been dreading were being pressed on her mouth.

She began to struggle against the iron strength of his arms. He didn't hurt her, but he didn't let her go.

Then for a brief moment, her mouth was free. "Stop fighting yourself," he said. As though she were a puppet on a string, her eyes closed, and she opened her lips to him. She felt his grip tighten and then relax. She wrenched her head back, and the wetness on her face came from tears.

"Don't!" she pleaded. "Let me go!"

"No," he said, pulling her trembling body closer to his. "You're driving me crazy. I can't seem to leave you alone, no matter what I do. And it's tearing me to pieces." His voice was gravelly, filled with pain.

Raine shook her head from side to side, but his tongue brushing the soft mound of her breasts, visible above the low-cut rim of her bodice, was an intoxicating inducement.

The warm, moist caress was like an abrasion to skin already sensitive to his nearness, and Raine's legs turned to jelly as he continued his exploration.

Ashe lowered his head and kissed her nipple through the dress, then opened her palm against his mouth. The two gestures completely disarmed her, brought her close to tears.

"It's the shock," she mumbled incoherently. "Shock does such strange things. Afterward, these things are never easily explained. Never easily..."

Once more he put his mouth to hers softly, filled with an intense longing to be a part of her. Raine's lips, in surrender, were pliable and exquisite, as he'd known they would be. His arms tightened around her, his heart pounding as he smoothed the hair back from her face, looking through the dim light into her eyes. He'd never met a woman who was so utterly desirable, so utterly a woman.

Unconsciously, Raine placed her hands on his face, sighing so that her breath, like a soft cloud, enveloped him. The kiss deepened, her mouth softer and warmer than anything he'd ever dreamed of.

"Oh, Raine," he groaned, marveling that someone so willowy and slender could feel so voluptuous. She seemed to sink deep into his flesh.

"Ashe, please," Raine whispered, feeling the situation rapidly slipping beyond her control. But he was oblivious to her words, continuing to arouse feelings in her that she had not known she possessed. "This is wrong."

"Nothing is wrong," he murmured, plundering her lips and breasts hungrily with kisses.

Don't think, she told herself. Only feel. Let this feeling carry you through the night. Feel. *Feel.*

His own response was evident. Raine was aware of the rigid thrust of his desire, and there was something dangerously exhilarating in knowing she could arouse him like this. The thin barrier of their clothing was little protection from the muscle that swelled against her stomach. Suddenly, the precariousness of the situation hit Raine full force.

Turning her fear into reality were Ashe's next words, "Oh, Raine, how I want you, need you," he murmured desperately.

That note of urgency sharply penetrated Raine's drugged senses. Need. No! I can't need him. I don't want to need him. I don't know how or what it is to need a man. Suddenly, she panicked, her body stiffening.

"Oh, God!" Her shuddering withdrawal left him feeling as if someone had pitched him into icy water. But he refused to let her go, his arms clinging to her.

"No!" she cried, extracting herself with difficulty. "Ashe, I..." She fought for her next breath. "This has got to stop."

"Why?" he muttered harshly. "For God's sake, why?" There was a look of desperation pinching his features as he fought for control.

"You know why," she said, staring at him wild-eyed. But she wasn't sure that he did. After all, she had given him the impression...

"The hell I do!" he countered violently. The lines bracketing his mouth had deepened, and Raine knew that he was hanging on to his control by a mere thread.

She shook her head before moving away from him.

"You wanted me, Raine." His voice cut into Raine like an ice pick. "Nothing you can say will change that. It's just that simple."

Simple! God, if he only knew, she cried silently. Nothing was ever that simple. There were no words to tell him that she was afraid, that she had never made love to a man, that at the age of thirty she was still a virgin. Unheard of, but true. *I don't know what it feels like to have a man's body cover mine, or what it feels like to have him inside me...*

Raine was weeping on the inside as she turned her back on Ashe, despising herself for letting him back her into this compromising situation, for penetrating her carefully erected defenses.

"Raine," he said quietly, "don't shut me out. Give us a chance."

Her shoulders slumped. "I can't," she whispered. "You don't understand."

A deep silence blanketed the room as Ashe stared at her. He wanted Raine Michaels. He wanted her in every way, with physical pain, with passion, with tenderness. He understood the fire in the loins only too well—now he accepted the ache in his heart as real. He had almost despaired, until the moment when in spite of herself she had responded. Yet she had refused him. Besides the passion in her, he knew she feared him and mistrusted him. The impulse to push must again be resisted. There was always tomorrow...

He took a tentative step toward her and stopped. "All right, Raine, you win for now." Pausing, he watched a tear slide down her cheek onto the wobbling sweetness of her upper lip. "But remember this. You belong to me. I knew it the first time I saw you, and I'll never let you go."

With those words he walked out the door, closing it quietly behind him.

For the next few days, Raine walked around in a state of befuddlement, unable to get herself to perform properly. Because work was the furthest thing from her mind, she called Val and had her get in touch with Catherine Cole so that she could fly to Dallas for a day, and Val could take her shopping and complete her wardrobe.

With her near-fatal involvement with Ashe, her own life suddenly seemed to require closer and more careful scrutiny. She sat for hours beside Todd's hospital bed, tracing that turbulent scene with Ashe, her thoughts and feelings going around and around in her head. She couldn't seem to connect with anything.

She had not seen or heard from Ashe. The night he had walked out of the apartment, she broke down and cried for hours. Finally, she had managed to pull herself together and, after slipping on a pair of pants and blouse, had driven to the hospital, hoping to outrun her torturous thoughts.

The moment she had tiptoed into the intensive care unit, she was greeted with the good news that her brother had improved slightly, pushing the prospect of surgery a little further away. The blood bank in Houston had located several pints of Todd's type of blood and flown it to Tyler immediately. Since he was better and the unit was practically empty, the nurses had allowed her to stay with him the entire night.

But her thoughts would not be laid to rest. They were a seething caldron of anger, bitterness, and humiliation, directed solely at herself. How had it happened? How could she have let him touch her in such an intimate way? It was just sex, she told herself—wanting to experiment with the unknown. She fought against him relentlessly, but nothing seemed to help. Ashe Elliot continued to hover around the edges of her every waking moment.

Now as she opened the door to Todd's apartment, after spending another day and well into the evening sitting with Todd, she froze in her tracks and blinked several times, positive her eyes were playing tricks on her—either that, or she was in the wrong apartment. Ridiculous? She wasn't *that* far gone, was she?

Again Raine shook her head as though to clear her vision. Nothing changed. A young woman was standing in the tiny kitchen, in front of the stove, humming to herself, obviously in the process of stirring something. For a split-second, Raine's senses wallowed in the delicious aroma that gently wafted to her nostrils. The spoon clutched in the woman's hand hung suspended in midair.

Raine moved deeper into the dimly lighted room and slammed the door behind her.

"Who are you?" a shrill voice demanded before Raine could push the same words through her lips.

Raine advanced farther into the room. "That was my question," she said evenly, though her heart was palpitating. She was no longer frightened, only curious.

The strange young woman chose at that moment to walk out of the kitchen and stand within inches of Raine. "Who...who gave you the key to...Todd's apartment?" This time there was no mistaking the tremor in her voice.

Raine did not hear a word she said. Rudely and without conscious thought, her eyes dipped to the woman's stomach and clung there. She was, it looked like to Raine, in the advanced stages of pregnancy. Raine was mystified rather than shocked. What was going on?

"Please...answer my question," the woman was saying. "Who gave you the key...?"

Raine drew in her breath and let it out slowly, praying for patience. *Who was she, anyway?* A friend of Todd's? Surely not. And pregnant. Who, then? A friend of a friend? Possibly. But not probable.

On closer observation, Raine saw that she was lovely. Refreshing. Young. She couldn't have been more than twenty years old, twenty-one at the most. Her wheat-colored hair covered her head in tiny ringlets, and her heavy-lashed blue eyes were wide as she stared intently at Raine. She was dressed for comfort in a pink maternity top and white walking shorts. She reminded Raine of a life-sized doll.

Breaking into the silence, Raine said, "I think I should be the one asking you how *you* got the key!" She paused, pitching her purse on the couch. "This *is* Todd Michaels's apartment, right?"

The woman nodded her head in the affirmative, without saying anything.

"Then who are you?" Raine pressed. "I have a right to be here. I'm his sister, Raine Michaels. Now, who are you?"

Suddenly, a wide grin broke across the childlike features, making her appear even younger, more like a little girl. She clapped her hands and came forward, reaching out and grasping one of Raine's hands tightly within hers, and began pumping it up and down.

"I'm Heather," she said. "Heather Roberts, Todd's fiancée."

Even though the hands on the illuminated clock beside the bed registered two o'clock, Raine was just climbing into bed. Every bone in her body ached, making her feel as though she had been used as a punching bag. She crawled in between the cool sheets, determined to think of nothing except sleep. But her mind rebeled, unwilling to shut down, replaying in detail the last few hours.

When Heather had identified herself as Todd's fiancée, Raine's head had reeled. She had been struck speechless.

"What!" she'd screeched.

Fiancée! Pregnant fiancée! No, it couldn't be! Raine told herself frantically, hysteria bubbling beneath her calm façade. It just couldn't be true. But, oh, God, she knew that it was. This woman-child standing before her had no reason to lie. Why? Why hadn't Todd told her? Where had Heather been all this time? Why hadn't she been at Todd's bedside? None of it made any sense.

"Raine... It's all right if I call you Raine, isn't it, especially since we're soon to be sisters-in-law?" Heather asked, looking up at her with round innocent eyes. "I take it Todd never told you about me, about us," she added shyly.

Raine staggered to the couch and lowered her trembling body onto it. Then she peered up at Heather's face and whispered, "No...no, he never told me."

Heather began to fidget nervously, running a hand through her tangled curls. "I begged him to tell you, especially since the baby's due in a couple of months, but he said he wasn't ready and for me not to badger him, that he'd tell you in his own good time. Even his boss, Ashe Elliot, tried..."

Heather's voice faltered and finally played out when she saw every ounce of color drain from Raine's face. "What's...what's the matter?" she stammered. "Did I say something wrong?"

Todd, how could you do this to me? Raine screamed inwardly, unable to believe that this was happening. Did everyone know about Heather but her, his own sister? And Ashe. What of him? Why hadn't he told her? Damn him! He could have spared her this shock. Don't think about that now. Don't think about *him* now. Her insides churned in revolt. She felt sick.

"Are you sure you're all right?" Heather inquired hesitantly, her voice sounding hyper, squeaky. "You don't look so good," she added bluntly.

Shifting her gaze away from Heather, Raine stood up, digging for strength she didn't know she possessed, forcing herself to play this nightmare out to the bitter end. "Don't worry," she said, "I'm fine."

After noticing that the strained, pinched look had disappeared from Heather's face, Raine said the first thing that came to mind. "Were you planning to get married?"

"Oh, yes," Heather answered quickly. "But not until Todd had enough money to buy us a house. He said he didn't want to raise a baby in a cramped apartment." She sighed as she walked hesitantly to the couch and sat down beside Raine. "Somehow, though, there just doesn't seem o be any way to save money.'' Her face quickly brightened, only to become suddenly subdued as she prattled on. 'Ashe Elliot—I mentioned him a while ago—he's a dear. Well, anyway, he wanted to help us, but Todd wouldn't even talk to him. I still have hope...''

For once Raine didn't flinch when Ashe's name was mentioned. But inwardly she cringed. It was apparent, she thought cynically, that Heather had Ashe pegged as a larger-than-life hero.

Suddenly, Heather's lower lip began to tremble. ''Do you know where Todd is?''

Oh, God, the question Raine had been dreading. Thinking quickly, she countered with a question of her own, postponing the inevitable. ''Where have you been?''

''Well,'' Heather mused, temporarily diverted, ''I've been to Mississippi to visit my aunt, the only living relative I have, who's awfully sick with a bad lung infection. I had to beg Todd, though, to let me go before the baby was born.''

''But to travel that far by yourself with the baby so nearly due!'' Raine was flabbergasted and her sense of frustration was building by the second. Damn! Heather was just a child, but Todd should have known better!

Heather giggled, showing off a bottom row of slightly crooked teeth, but even that flaw failed to detract from her youthful beauty.

Raine usually found people easy to read, but this girl was such an odd mixture of maturity and innocence, alternating between poise and childishness. Was it an act? No, she was positive of that. Heather was such a baffling combination of practicality and abandon that Raine could see why her brother had fallen for her.

''I know how to get just about anything I want out of Todd.'' Heather paused knowingly and giggled again, her face turning a bright red.

I just bet you do, Raine thought, despising, yet envying, Heather's naïveté. Had she ever been this innocent? She didn't think so. She was born knowing more than Heather did now. And she hated to be the one to make Heather grow up. For it was an iron-clad cinch that Heather knew nothing of Todd's accident. How in heaven's name was she going to tell her?

Suddenly, Heather jumped up as if she'd been shot, severing Raine's concentration. "Oh, no!" she yelped. "I forgot about the sauce. Don't you smell it?" Before Raine could react, Heather was gone. Seconds later she heard her banging around in the kitchen.

Reluctantly, Raine followed her into the kitchen. "I didn't smell it either, I'm sorry," she said. "Is there anything I can do to help?"

Heather was nearing tears as she stood in front of the sink, water gushing from the faucet. "There's nothing anyone can do now," she wailed. "It...it was spaghetti sauce, and Todd's favorite. And I can't imagine where Todd is and why you're here and he isn't." She sniffed loudly.

"Heather..." Raine began.

She acted as though Raine hadn't spoken her name. "Todd always calls me when I'm gone, but since I hadn't heard from him and couldn't get any answer here, I decided to come back early and surprise him." She paused with a shrug, sniffing back the tears. "Some surprise, huh!"

"Heather," Raine said again, "why don't you come into the living room and sit down?"

Raine could have sworn that she would have to fight for everything that God had given Heather at birth, but this time she was wrong. Heather knew. She might as well have said, "Sit still, Heather; we're going to play Russian roulette and you're the victim." Heather looked shell-shocked.

"What happened?" she croaked, her eyes rounded, fear turning them a darker shade of blue.

"Come on," Raine urged soothingly, "let's sit down." Heather followed. Her steps were slow and trudging, which Raine knew had nothing to do with her pregnancy.

Raine sat rigid, afraid to tell her the truth, yet afraid not to.

"He's dead, isn't he?" Heather asked suddenly, her voice low, distant.

Raine gasped aloud, though Heather's words were as calmly spoken as if she'd said that the sun was shining.

"No," Raine said softly, drawing her hand into her lap and covering it with her own. "No, he's not dead, but he's been hurt, hurt badly."

Heather went to pieces. Her loud anguished sobs echoed around the room, piercing Raine's heart with each pitiful cry.

"No...no," she kept murmuring over and over while clutching at Raine.

"Shh!" Raine pleaded, suddenly afraid the shock and upheaval would harm both mother and baby. Tears were scalding her own cheeks as she rocked Heather in her arms.

After a moment Heather pulled back and whispered between gulping sobs, "I knew this was going to happen. I..." Her voice gave in to another vicious sob of pain.

Raine was becoming more alarmed by the second. She fought hard to keep herself from panicking. *Oh, God, I'm not this strong. I can't handle this.* But she had no choice. There was no one else.

"Heather...please, stop...listen to me!" Raine cupped her wobbly chin in her hand and forced Heather to look at her. "Todd is going to live. You must believe that. Do you understand what I'm saying?"

Heather nodded slightly as Raine removed her hand. "Tell me what happened."

Raine told her. When the ordeal was over, Raine felt as though her life's blood had been drained from her body.

"When...when can I see him?" Heather asked, mopping at her face with the tissue Raine had thrust in her hand.

Raine's heart turned over at the pitiful, woeful note in Heather's voice. She's nothing but a child herself, Raine thought despairingly. "First thing in the morning, I promise."

After that, Heather finally settled down, and they talked for hours, about everything. Raine was grateful for Heather's chatter. It seemed to ease the tension through its lack of content, like a wordless song. Raine found out how she had met Todd. It was at a party of a mutual friend. It had been love at first sight, Heather said, and Raine believed her. Raine also found out that Heather had no one she could depend on except Todd. Her parents were dead and there were no brothers or sisters, only her aunt, who could offer no help.

Heather was like a happy child. She seemed to delight in almost anything. Raine envied her for that. Even though she was terribly upset about Todd and at times she would break down and cry again, she was still one of the most upbeat persons Raine had ever known. Finally, calling it a night, Raine felt as though she had known Heather all her life and loved her dearly, yet the added responsibility loomed heavy and frightening.

Now as Raine rolled over and looked at the clock once more, she noticed her face was wet, wet with tears. Funny, she thought, she didn't know she had any tears left. After wiping them on the edge of the sheet, she got up and tiptoed down the short hall and peeped into Todd's room, where Heather lay sleeping.

Raine stood and watched her steady breathing, the way her arm cradled her stomach, for a long minute before dragging herself back to bed.

"It's just not fair," she whimpered aloud, staring at the ceiling, wondering how she was going to handle it all. Then a little voice whispered, *Who said life was fair?*

Chapter 7

She could not identify the noise. Whatever it was kept digging into her subconscious until she finally rolled over with a muttered groan. She then covered her head with the pillow, but still no relief came. The grating noise did not go away.

Raine groped blindly for the alarm clock, positive it was the culprit. But after slamming around on the bedside table and knocking the clock to the floor, she realized the sound was coming from the telephone in the living room.

It continued ringing with dogged determination. Smothering a string of curse words, Raine flung back the cover and hit the floor, afraid that the jarring sound, if allowed to continue, would wake up Heather.

"Hello," she said breathlessly, lowering herself into the nearest chair.

"Raine, honey, don't tell me you were still in bed?"

"Oh, hi, Val." Raine's breath was still coming in small spurts as she tried to make herself coherent. She frowned. "What time is it, anyway?"

"Well, it's after nine o'clock," Val replied. "Gee, I'm sorry I got you out of bed. But I had no idea I'd even catch you at the apartment, much less wake you up."

"Thank goodness you did." Raine sighed. "We should have been at the hospital way before now."

"Who's *we?*"

Raine cursed her slip of the tongue. She was not ready to tell Val or anyone else about Heather and the baby. Not yet. Not until she had come to terms with it herself.

"I'll tell you about it later," Raine answered lightly.

There was a slight pause. "Are you sure you're okay? You sound—oh, I don't know...detached, strange. Has something else happened to Todd that you're not telling me?"

Raine sighed as she searched for a more comfortable position in the chair. "As a matter of fact, yes. We've passed through another crisis. The hospital couldn't get enough of Todd's blood type, but hopefully that's all been squared away now."

This time it was Val's sigh that filtered through the long-distance line. "I was hoping my news would cheer you up, but now I'm not so sure. It'll probably just throw you into a deeper depression."

Raine laughed. "Let's hope not. Anything good you can tell me will be an improvement over the past few days. What's up? I was going to call you this morning and find out how your day went with Catherine Cole and to find out if by any chance Ross or Jules had called."

"That's what I'm calling about. Jules, that is. It's my good news. He wants to meet with you tomorrow afternoon at two o'clock in his office."

"That is good news!" Raine exclaimed. "And it proves that I got my message across to Ross."

"Well, it appears that you did, because now Jules is eager to talk to you." Val paused. "Is that going to present a problem now that Todd has had another setback? It's terribly short notice, I know, but Jules is leaving at the end of the week to go out of the country, and this is the only time he can see you.''

Raine's hesitation was brief. "That's fine. I'll make arrangements for Todd to be looked after while I'm gone.''

"Good deal,'' Val responded, sounding relieved. "Also, there's a meeting to follow with your banker, if that's agreeable.''

"Great. I'll try to take the late-afternoon flight.''

Val's voice was full of excitement. "Oh, Raine, I'll be so glad to see you. You won't believe the progress they've made on the building. It's beginning to look like a boutique instead of a hollow shell. It seems like you've been gone a month not a week.''

An unexpected lump rose to the back of Raine's throat. "Me, too,'' she whispered unsteadily.

"I'll see you tomorrow.''

The moment she hung up the receiver and looked up, Heather was standing in the doorway, her eyes wide and uncertain.

"I...I heard the phone. Was it...?''

"No,'' Raine assured her gently, "it wasn't the hospital.''

Heather raised her slumped shoulders as though new life had been pumped into them. "When can we go see him?''

Raine smiled sweetly. "As soon as we both get dressed.'' Her tread was light as she made her way back to the bedroom, after watching Heather scoot down the hall to her room. For the first time in days, she felt good, and she wasn't going to let anything spoil that.

The memories of the next hour would remain nestled in the corner of Raine's heart for the rest of her life. When she and Heather opened the door to Todd's room, having learned that he had been transferred back to 507 earlier that morning, he was lying with his back to the door. He was fidgeting, looking as though he was searching for a comfortable position for the hand that was gouged by the intravenous needle.

It was obvious he hadn't heard the door open. But something must have alerted him that he was no longer alone, for he very gingerly rolled over.

His drug-glazed eyes widened before finding and clinging to Heather. He blinked several times, and then a whimpering sound passed through his swollen lips. He made an effort to raise himself.

Raine stood transfixed. It was as if she was watching a tragic play from afar. Her heart swelled with both love and pity when she heard Heather's answering whimper.

"He...Heather..." Todd's hoarse cry suddenly filled the room.

Like a bolt out of the blue, Heather shot around the edge of the bed and eased her cumbersome body down, so that she was kneeling beside his bed. "Oh, my darling...my darling...my darling," she whispered.

Still Raine could not move, nor could she utter a word. Tears dripped from her eyes in a steady stream, washing her face. The only time she moved was to open her purse frantically and dig through its contents for a Kleenex. Not bothering to think about her makeup, she wiped at the tears, struggling to stop the flow. She was afraid that once the dam broke and she began crying, she would not be able to quit.

Looking up, she saw that Heather was holding Todd's hand to her cheek, showering his palm with tiny kisses. And for the first time since the accident, Todd seemed alert. Then she knew she hadn't been mistaken; her brother was trying to shape his lips into a smile.

"Thank God," Raine whispered aloud.

Suddenly, Todd's eyes shifted, searching. "Sis...is that you?" His voice was barely above a whisper and rough like sandpaper, his eyes fluttering shut.

Raine crossed to the bed and reached for his other hand. "Yes it's me."

Todd's eyes blinked and opened once again. "I...I...should... have told you..."

Raine shook her head. "Shh! It's all right. Save your strength; we'll talk later."

Todd nodded before putting a gentle squeeze on her hand and then letting it go. So as not to burst into tears again in front of them, Raine forced aside another huge lump in her throat and turned to Heather, "I'll be out in the waiting room if you need me."

By the time she reached the cool quiet of the empty lounge, she had managed to pull herself together, although her mouth was as dry as a bone and her head throbbed below her right temple. Chewing on her lower lip, Raine stared out the window into the bright sunlight, her thoughts, like a whirlwind, whipping through her mind.

Now that Todd was better, she must turn her attention to Heather and the baby. With Todd unable to care for the them, the responsibility was hers. Another in a long line of many, she thought dejectedly. Normally, she would have been able to take all this in stride if it weren't for Ashe. She was appalled with her continued obsession with him. She didn't understand it, nor could she accept it. But it was there, steadily hammering away at her thoughts and weighing heavily on her heart. The fact that she hated herself for that weakness did not make things any easier. Suddenly, her head twisted on her slender neck as if to avoid a blow.

You're a fool, Raine Michaels! You're nothing but a challenge to him. Why can't you accept that? Once he's had you in his bed, he won't want you anymore.

How long she stood there she didn't know. But eventually she was able to ward off the hysterics by emptying her mind of all thoughts and by promising herself that Ashe Elliot or any other man would never usurp her hard-won independence.

"How about some company?"

Raine was brought back to reality with a jolt. Slowly, she turned around and lifted her eyes to encounter his handsome face, now so very close to her own.

"You!" she exclaimed, seeing in flesh and blood the epitome of all her troubles. His dark features twisted into a wry smile.

"I'm still not welcome, I gather," he remarked, his drawl giving the words an unwanted attraction. As he towered over her, Raine saw the tiny lines based at the corner of each eye, and she felt a quickening of her pulses. He was the most sexually disturbing man she had ever known, as well as the most unpredictable.

She turned away. *Why doesn't he leave me alone?*

"I can't believe you don't have an effective comeback to put me in my place."

Raine suddenly found herself fighting against the urge to give up the struggle against him. How much easier it would be if she would simply give in to this attraction, she thought weakly, only to squash the unworthy notion quickly.

"I..." She looked up, saw the gently mocking light in his eyes and his smiling mouth, and she couldn't think what it was she'd been about to say.

"That's better," he said lightly, leaning toward her.

"What is?" Her eyes were glued to the muscles of his chest and watched as his stomach tightened beneath the fine gray silk of his shirt.

"Seeing you smile."

"Oh," she said, his words throwing her completely off balance. That wasn't at all what she'd expected him to say.

He chuckled and then his eyes darkened, becoming serious. "You've been crying." It was more of a statement than a question. Then, adding to her confusion, his roughened thumb reached out and gently grazed her cheek.

Raine froze for a timeless moment.

"A tear; it was trapped on your eyelash," he said huskily, his eyes refusing to release hers.

Such a light, innocent touch, yet so intimate. Every inch of her flesh surged to life, becoming hypersensitive. She was having trouble breathing. It was uncanny. A touch and they went off like a skyrocket together.

"It's Todd, isn't it?"

"Yes." It came out as a gasp, and she raged at herself to regain her self-control. She wet her lips with the tip of her tongue. "I mean, no."

Ashe's brows drew together in a frown, but he kept his silence, waiting for her to continue while drinking in the sight of her. Had it been a week since he'd seen her? He closed his eyes for a moment, his jaw rigid as a spasm of desire raged through him.

When he opened his eyes again, they fell to her breasts and their movement under the luxurious blouse. He breathed in her perfume, his senses more sharpened by the second. She smelled to him of fresh things, of water and scented soap.

His loins stirred painfully.

Suddenly, he was desperate to put things back on an even keel, afraid that if he didn't he would haul her into his arms right there in front of God and everybody and to hell with the consequences.

"What do you mean, yes and no?" he asked urgently.

Raine raised her eyes and met his probing ones. "I just found out about Heather."

He suppressed a sigh. "I was afraid you didn't know."

"Well, you were right," she confessed heavily.

"Several times I started to ask you if you'd heard from Heather. But when you never mentioned her, I didn't know what to do." He tipped his head to one side. "I wanted to tell you…"

"I wish you had. It would have made the shock easier to handle."

"It wasn't my place, you know."

"I know."

"How did you find out?"

Her lashes swept up. "The hard way. I walked into Todd's apartment last night and Heather was standing in the kitchen demanding to know who I was."

"God, Raine, that's a damned shame."

"Yes, isn't it?" she said flatly.

"Knowing Heather, I don't have to ask how she took the news of the accident."

"You're right. She went to pieces. It took me until two o'clock this morning to glue the pieces back together."

That explains the dark circles under her eyes, he thought with a heartfelt sigh. But rather than detract from her fragile beauty, they enhanced it. A barrage of emotions ricocheted through him, and it was only the strongest sense of self-discipline that kept him from reaching out and drawing her into his arms.

Instead, he impulsively tucked a strand of hair behind her ear, his fingers lingering. "I'm sorry you had to go through that alone," he muttered thickly.

Raine went stiff, the provocative touch sending the blood rushing heatedly through her veins. "I managed," she said, stepping back.

Then, abruptly, his mood shifted, seeing the panic in her eyes. He had the urge to throttle her. "Dammit, Raine!" he said angrily. "Why won't you let me help? All you have to do is ask!"

"No…I…"

"Raine, I warned you that no matter how many stumbling blocks you placed in my way, I wasn't giving up." He paused, capturing her gaze and holding it steadfast. "And I haven't changed my mind."

Suddenly, it seemed there was no one else in the world but the two of them. Even the abrasive noises of the hospital corridors went unnoticed as their eyes held and the mysterious current crackled between them.

Raine felt as if she were tumbling forward very slowly, like Alice down the rabbit hole. There was nothing in existence but his eyes, and her breath caught suddenly in her lungs.

"I want to see you tonight," he mumbled in a strangled tone.

No! she moaned in silent misery. She couldn't let herself be lured into seeing him again with his smooth, soft words. She must cling to her vow to be strong.

"Raine," he persisted.

She looked away with a jerk. "Ashe, I can't."

"Damn your bullheadedness!" he ground out harshly. "Would it make you feel better if I begged?"

There was a moment of frigid silence.

Ashe beg? Unheard of! Ludicrous! What did he want from her? An affair? Or did he have an ulterior motive? But even more disturbing, what did she want from him?

"No, of course I don't want you to beg," she said unsteadily.

Ashe took a step closer, then stopped, his eyes narrowed into a lazy measuring look. He kept his silence while he thrust his hands in his pockets, watching her. This action tightened the material across his well-muscled thighs, drawing her attention to his arousal, now strong and unyielding.

It brought to mind the intimacy they had shared at his house. She felt the trap closing...

"Raine."

Her eyes closed briefly as she searched for the right words. "I'm...leaving for Dallas this afternoon, but..."

It was obvious he never heard the "but," for dark color swept up to his hairline and he said, "Raine, what are you trying to do to me?"

"But I'll be back in a couple of days," she added in a throaty whisper.

An abrupt tension suddenly penetrated the air.

Ashe looked surprised, then guarded, and then he smiled, the beautiful smile that had the power to grab her heart and run with it.

Making no pretense of misunderstanding her, he breathed achingly. "I don't know whether I'm more tempted to turn you over my knee or kiss you until you're senseless."

Raine linked and unlinked her fingers. What had she done? She could almost reach out and grasp a handful of the tension that still hung heavily in the air.

"Ashe..." She could not get past the lump in her throat.

"I'll see you when you get back," he said, his gaze traveling over the fragile planes of her face. "And that's a promise," he added softly before turning and walking away.

Watching him, Raine saw the sound structure of her life slowly crumbling, and the sad part about it was that she didn't know how to stop it.

Dallas. Such a cosmopolitan city, up and coming with the best of the larger cities. Raine loved it. To her, it was synonymous with work, and she was always at her best when she was working. And today was no exception.

Maybe it was because she'd been in her own bed and gotten a decent night's sleep for a change, even though she'd had to fight off thoughts of Ashe and the promise of tomorrow. But she knew that if she was to get anything worthwhile accomplished, she could not afford to dwell on the dangerous game she was playing. Too much was at stake.

She had taken the last flight out of Tyler and caught a cab straight to the office after calling Val and telling her to meet her there. Ross, she'd learned after talking with him, had a business engagement he could not postpone, so she and Val had enjoyed a snack from the closest pizza parlor and had worked until after ten o'clock.

Now this morning she was back at it. And the day was proving to be a busy one, even though she had gotten started at the ungodly hour of seven o'clock. But she had to gear up for the meetings with Jules Burns and her banker, and preceding those was a luncheon date with Ross.

For the first time in days, she felt free to concentrate on her work. She had spoken with Heather just before she left home. Heather had assured her that everything was fine and that she, Heather, was capable of taking care of things. Raine hadn't been too sure of that, but she'd had no choice. She'd had to come to Dallas. Her mounting responsibilities were a sobering reminder, not to mention that she needed to put distance between her and Ashe Elliot.

As she sat down at her desk with a freshly brewed cup of coffee, she reached for a stack of notes and files six inches high on her blotter. Though Val had handled things extremely well without her, problems and questions that only she could deal with had piled up, and they all seemed to need attending to immediately.

The top folder contained the list of new clients and their comments about New Image and dozens of other items she had to see about for the boutique. As she looked through those, Raine felt the tightness inside her began to ease. This was where she belonged. This was where she was the happiest, doing the thing she loved best—making women beautiful and successful. She didn't need a man to make her life complete. Did she? Then, realizing where her thoughts were taking her, she shook her head abruptly and once more concentrated on the work before her.

The only time she looked up was when Val's chirpy voice bade her a good morning. After acknowledging her presence with a smile, Raine dug back into the task at hand. Now that she had the other pressing items out of the way, she could concentrate on the designs for Jules's consideration.

She had been working on perfecting them for months, yet she was still not satisfied, although Ross was. He had been enthusiastic in his approval. But today was her last chance to make them even better. They had to be as perfect as she could make them.

Having freed her mind of all thoughts of Ashe, her imagination soared. Images came to her: bold patterns in vivid color, exotic combinations and fantastic designs too complicated for today's woman, but containing some single ideas she could modify and put to use—and those were the ones she was using to alter the styles already on paper. Sketches flowed from her pencil as fast as her hand could move, followed by new ones, only then to have to choose the best for the collection she would take to Jules.

The hours passed in silent absorption, in the same circle of contentment Raine had felt when she had created her first design. She had longed for the day when the women who came to New Image for a makeover could shop on the premises for a new wardrobe in their seasonal color without having to leave the building.

The opening of the boutique would make that possible, but her line of clothing combined with the stunning lines she was already planning to stock were sure to be an unbeatable combination, assuring her of instant success. And wasn't that what she'd always wanted? Nothing had changed, had it?

Suddenly, the buzzer sounded next to her ear, severing her concentration. Without looking up, she slammed her finger down on the button and asked, "What is it, Val?"

"Ross just called and asked that you meet him at the Top of the Hyatt in twenty minutes."

Raine frowned, laying down her pencil. "Is it that time already?" Where had the morning gone, she wondered in dismay.

"Afraid so." Val laughed. "I don't think you've looked up since you walked in this morning, have you?"

Raine laughed. "No, but I've sure gotten a lot accomplished. Shortly, we'll find out if it's going to pay off."

"Well, I for one will keep my fingers crossed," Val declared before the intercom went silent.

A short time later, Raine was ready to go. She looked her best, she knew, in a soft fuchsia two-piece silk suit with a matching blouse. With a sigh, she grabbed the handle on her briefcase and marched to the door, thinking, This is it; for heaven's sake, don't blow it!

Ross Thomas was smiling as Raine came through the door of the restaurant. He was his usually impeccable self, with his carefully brushed silver hair, keen eyes, and a well-exercised body set off in an expensive suit.

"Hello, my dear." He greeted her with a cool kiss on the cheek. "You're looking much better than I expected after your harrowing experience." He touched her elbow lightly as they followed the maître d' to a corner table overlooking the Dallas skyline. "In fact, you're more beautiful than ever."

"Just goes to show you what a good makeup job can do," Raine said with a smile while sitting opposite him in the booth.

Ross leaned closer, his eyes narrowing. Then he grinned. "Well, now that you mentioned it, I can see..."

Raine lifted her hand in front of her face. "Stop right there. No fair probing. Take what you see at face value or forget it," she quipped, suddenly enjoying the light, shared banter. She was relieved to see that apparently he had forgiven her for forcing his hand on changing the meeting with Jules.

The waiter brought wine for Raine, Scotch for Ross, and a dish filled with toasted cereal and nuts. Ross slid it aside. "Execrable dish. The view, however, is fine. Tell me first about Todd. I take it he's better, or you wouldn't have been able to leave Tyler."

Raine gazed at him a moment, trying to decide if there was any hidden sarcasm behind his words. Finally, deciding it was her own paranoia causing her to read more into it than was there, she said with feeling, "You're right, he is better."

He smiled and lifted his glass. "That's good news. So without sounding crass or unfeeling, you're free to concentrate on meeting with Jules. And if everything turns out like I hope, all your worries will be over."

Raine's mouth turned down at the corners, and she turned away. If only that were possible. But, unfortunately, that was not the case, not with Heather and the baby weighing heavily on her mind. For a few hours, in her office, she had managed to put those burdens aside, but she knew now she had been chasing rainbows.

"...I can't wait to see your latest designs," Ross was saying, beckoning the waiter for another drink. "And I'm still finding it a miracle that Jules agreed to see you so soon. He certainly didn't give me any indication of that when I told him you couldn't make the last meeting."

"I am, too, but Jules isn't all that bad. He's just your typical moody, temperamental designer who wants to have his cake and eat it, too, yet he knows when to back down." She smiled confidently. "But, remember, he's seen several of my designs already and, even though he wouldn't admit it at the time, he thought they were good."

Ross's voice was vibrant and warm. "Well, it doesn't matter now. At least we've gotten him to agree to consider helping you, and that's our biggest plus yet. I can't wait to see what changes you've made in the sketches. Are you pleased with them?"

Her eyes sparkled. "They're good, really good."

"You're something else, you know that? And as soon as you've tied up the deal with Jules, I want to take you out tonight and celebrate." He raised his glass once again, leaning toward her.

"Ross, no," she began, a shadow dimming her features, and she didn't lift her glass in an answering salute. Although it warmed her heart that Ross was as excited as she was about her work, she could not let him think that everything was back to normal, that everything was rosy. She had to tell him about Heather and the baby.

"What's wrong, Raine?" Ross looked disconcerted. "Did I say something wrong?"

Raine hesitated. "No, it's not you. It's me. I..." Her words played out as the waiter appeared to take their orders.

"What will you have?" Ross asked politely, though his face bore a hint of anger. Raine knew he was none too happy with her.

For a moment, Raine concentrated on the menu. Then, looking at Ross, she said, "The shrimp salad with the house dressing will be fine."

"Make that two," Ross said tonelessly, handing the waiter the menu.

Once they were alone, Ross turned back to Raine, his brows knitted. "Now, tell me, what don't I understand?"

After a short pause, Raine said, "Todd, I just found out, has a fiancée."

Ross looked puzzled. "So."

Involuntarily, Raine smiled. "You've heard the old saying: keep a woman barefoot and pregnant. Haven't you?"

He frowned. "Yes, but I still don't—"

"She's pregnant, Ross!"

"What!"

"You heard me. Pregnant. Seven months, to be exact. And a mere child to boot, with no money, no family, no nothing except Todd, who has no money, no nothing, except me."

Ross looked appalled. "Are you telling me you're going to assume responsibility for that woman and child?"

Raine was prevented from answering by the arrival of their food. Quickly, she made an effort to take a bite of the chilled salad, realizing that she hadn't eaten any breakfast.

After a moment, Ross broke the silence. "Well, are you?" His voice was tight with control.

Raine didn't pretend not to follow his line of questioning. "What choice do I have? She's just a child, and if Todd is responsible—"

"That's just it," Ross cut in swiftly. "How do you know he is?"

"I thought about that, too, but if you could have heard Heather—that's her name—and then seen the two of them together, there would be no doubt in your mind."

Ross released a long sigh, pushing his half-eaten food aside, and reached for his drink. "What are you going to do?" There was an exasperated edge to his voice.

"Ask Ed Giles at the bank for more money, over and above what I need to finish the boutique and to pay a manufacturer to make my designs—if Jules agrees to help, that is."

A grimace flittered across Ross's face. "I've told you before I'll be glad to loan you—"

"No. Please don't even say it. This is something I have to do alone." She paused with a half smile and reached over and laid her hand on his. "But, thanks, anyway."

His eyes softened. "You know I'd marry you in a minute if only you'd say the word. You're just so damned independent. But maybe that's why I—"

"Please...not now," Raine whispered. "I..."

"I know," Ross said, patting her hand before taking another gulp of his drink, "you don't love me." Then he grinned, lightening the mood. "But you can't blame a man for trying, and I won't give up."

Suddenly, she shifted her gaze and her heart constricted. She was remembering another man who had spoken those same words to her, and so far he had kept his promise. She shivered.

"What's the matter?" Ross demanded, concerned. "Are you cold?"

"No. If anything, I'm just tired."

The lines around his mouth hardened visibly. "How much longer do you intend to stay with your brother?"

"As I told you before, as long as I'm needed." She paused. "Now that Todd is better, I'm sure the investigating board will hammer him with questions. I wouldn't dare leave him to face that alone."

"I take it they still feel he's responsible."

"As far as I know, they do," Raine said bitterly.

Seeing the determined thrust of her chin, Ross knew a moment of extreme unease. "You intend to fight them tooth and toenail, don't you?"

She doubled her fist into a tight ball. "I'm going to try, but I don't know how much good it will do."

Ross sighed. "How do you know he is innocent?"

It was a loaded question, and he got the reaction he feared he would. Raine's eyes turned stormy, making him catch his breath. God, she was lovely when she was mad, he thought.

"Because I know my brother," she snapped. "He would never deliberately disobey an order. It's got to have been a mechanical failure and they just don't want to admit it."

Ross sighed again, a bitter twist to his lips, knowing he was bringing further wrath down upon his shoulders by asking this question; but he plunged forward, nevertheless. "When do you intend to quit playing nursemaid to your brother, getting him out of trouble? He's been nothing but a leech since Nam. Why..."

Fury colored her face a bright red. "How dare you!" she spat softly, but ruthlessly. "Don't you ever speak that way about Todd again!" She felt tears sting her eyelids. "You don't know what you're saying."

"Hey, calm down," he said, a strained smile on his face. "All right, maybe I did step out of line," he added by way of an apology, "but I hate to see you with so much responsibility."

Thankfully, Raine felt the tension ease within her. The last thing she wanted was to fight with Ross, but neither could she allow him to attack her brother.

Ross smiled. "Am I forgiven?"

"Only if you promise to mind both your mouth and your manners in the future," she said briskly.

"Would you believe me if I told you my lips were sealed forever?"

"No."

He laughed and shook his head as he signed the charge slip. Then, looking at her, he said, "If I'm not mistaken, we have a very important meeting to attend."

"We?" she asked with a laugh.

Ross didn't bat an eyelash. "Of course. You didn't think I was going to let you go alone, did you?"

A short time later, walking out of the restaurant, Raine looked through the window at the bright sky, not a cloud in sight. Her steps were buoyant with hope.

With sleep eluding him, Ashe left early for the plant. After a hard rain the night before, the air smelled clean and fresh. The early quiet of the streets was like a healing balm as he drove from his house, everything hushed and still, like a fine work of art about to burst into life. Only the avid joggers were out, their shoes slapping at the pavement. As they passed, Ashe returned their exuberant greetings with a wave of his hand, sharing with them that private moment suspended in sunlight. While others slept, they savored the beauty of the morning.

Today Raine was due in from Dallas, he thought, parking his car and taking the stairs to his office. But would she come back, he wondered. Or would she make it a point to stay away longer in order to keep from fulfilling her promise to him?

Ah, that promise. It had kept him awake the entire night, tossing and turning. Images of her kept projecting themselves across his mind: the way she looked yesterday at the hospital; the sunlight casting her in a golden glow; the haunting shadow in her eyes. He was consumed by the need to stand her before him and then tenderly take off her clothes, freeing her body for his hands, his lips. God! He was in bad shape.

Maybe Mac was right. Maybe he did need to get away and tie one on. Would he then come to his senses? No, he thought not—not until he'd topped Raine Michaels's silky body with his own and made her his.

But for now he had to get to work. The final report, via Colonel Jackson, was due today, and then later the two of them were to go to the hospital and hopefully question Todd. He dreaded the whole ordeal.

Besides that, he was due in the engine room to discuss another change on Black Cobra. Barring any complications, his "baby" would be ready for its first test flight with him in command of the throttle. He experienced an exhilarating jolt at the thought.

Several hours later, he found himself still bent over the engine, time forgotten. He hadn't even looked up when his assistant, Jake Everette, appeared in the doorway.

"Hey, Ashe," he shouted, "You're wanted on the phone."

Ashe raised his head, a scowl on his face. "Is it Jackson?" he shouted back.

Jake shook his head and motioned for Ashe to come there.

With a muttered curse, Ashe threw down his tool and crossed the room in giant strides. "What's up?" he demanded, coming up to Jake.

"Don't know." He scratched his head. "But whoever it is said it was real important."

Uttering another string of expletives for having interrupted his work, Ashe bounded up the stairs and grabbed the phone.

"Elliot here."

After a moment of listening, his features paled. "Christ!" he muttered. "Yes, of course I'll take care of it."

Then, slamming down the receiver, he turned to his assistant and said tersely, "Cover for me with Jackson. I won't be back today."

Raine not only breathed a sigh of relief, but she felt as though she was walking on air. Jules Burns loved her designs and had promised his help. After several long hours of tedious negotiating, she and Jules had finally come to terms.

She couldn't have been happier. And not once had her promise to Ashe crossed her mind, nor had his face rose up to haunt her. Now that, she thought, was a step in the right direction. For once, everything seemed to be falling in the right place.

The room was still buzzing with people. Jules had demanded his assistants be present, as well as several of his top models. He'd said he wanted them to meet her.

Now, amid all the confusion, Ross sat down in a chair beside Raine. "Well, my dear, we did it. Or, more to the point, you did it. And I'm so proud of you."

Raine's heart swelled with pride. "Thank you, but without your influence with Jules it wouldn't have been possible. And thanks seems such an inadequate word."

"Sure you can't stay and celebrate?" His voice was filled with disappointment.

"I'm sorry, Ross, I really must get back and see about Todd and Heather." She smiled. "If Todd is still better, I'll be back at the first of next week."

Suddenly, Raine felt a tentative hand on her shoulder. She whirled around. It was Maggie, Jules's secretary.

"I'm sorry to interrupt," she said, "but there's a man outside who said he must see you. Now."

Raine frowned, looking at Ross, clearly puzzled. "I can't imagine who it is," she said, standing up.

The moment she walked through the door, she froze. "Ashe! What brings you here?" Then her hand flew to her heart. "It's Todd, isn't it?" she whispered.

Ashe covered the distance between them, his jaw clenched. "No...it's Heather. There are complications. They may have to take the baby."

Chapter 8

Raine sat stoically, staring straight ahead as the Lincoln ate up the miles between Dallas and Tyler. She could not cry; finally, the bottomless well within her had run dry. It was as though it was all a bad dream, just another in a long succession of many.

The only thing that seemed real to her was Ashe's big, brawny body, which filled the seat to capacity. She felt crowded with him so near. It was as though he took up too much space, making her aware of his every movement, no matter how slight. Yet, for reasons she didn't care to pursue, she was glad that she wasn't alone, that he was with her.

Amazingly, when Ashe had told her about Heather, she hadn't come unglued, at least not to an extent that anyone could see, but on the inside every nerve in her body had tightened and then had begun clamoring for relief.

But Ashe had known; he had seen the signs of panic leap into her eyes and had taken over with soothing calm. She had let him, even though she was vaguely aware that Ross was hurt that she hadn't turned to him for comfort and help. At the time, she had been desperate to leave, to get to Heather, and Ashe was her quickest way to Tyler. Even though Heather had swept into her already cluttered life unexpectedly, she had managed to carve a place in Raine's heart.

From the second Ashe's competent hands had nosed the car south onto the interstate, she had begun playing the "what if" game. What if she was too late? What if they had taken the baby and it was too premature to live? What if this sudden turn of events set Todd's recovery back another notch? What if, what if, what if...

Suddenly realizing she would go completely crazy if she didn't get control of her thoughts, she turned and stared out the window, shifting her mind to her accomplishments of the day. But it didn't work. No matter how hard she tried, the fear would not let go. Nor could she block out the bleak thought that she would never again be in charge of her life. Ashe, by his magnetic presence, was drawing her in with bonds more powerful than chains, and she could not risk that.

A forceful sigh escaped through her lips as she let her head rest against the back of the cushioned seat, listening to the purr of the engine.

Suddenly, Ashe's low voice nudged her back to the moment at hand. She turned troubled eyes in his direction. "I'm sorry," he was saying, "really sorry about this."

"I know, and I haven't thanked you for coming after me." There was a waver in her voice.

Ashe longed to put his face against hers and hold her, skin touching skin, absorbing the pain slashing at her insides. Instead, he ground his teeth together and wrapped his hand tighter around the steering wheel and confessed, "I hated to have to do this to you, but I didn't know what else to do."

Raine relaxed, turning slightly toward him so when he took his eyes off the road for a split second, he could see the crest of her nipples pointing upward under her blouse, just the right size, round and firm and pointing gently. His fingers bore down harder on the steering wheel.

"You did the right thing," Raine said softly, staring at his profile, noticing how clear his skin looked, not rough as she'd first thought, but soft-looking and blemish-free, like a newborn baby's. She itched to reach out to prove to herself that she was right, or to realize what she was seeing was merely an illusion. Suddenly, she winced, ashamed of those thoughts. But it was as if a fire had been started somewhere within her, and even though she was conscious of it, her body had commenced an independent reaction to it and it continued to spread throughout her system.

"Why don't you close your eyes and try to sleep? I know you're exhausted. I promise I'll wake you when we get to the city limits of Tyler." He was concerned. The purplish shadows beneath her eyes made her appear ethereal, as though a giant puff of wind could pick her up and carry her away. Again, Ashe had to fight the urge to wrap his arm around her slender shoulders and pull her against his hard body.

He groaned inwardly, feeling the perspiration collecting on his forehead even though the air-conditioning was on cold. He had been looking forward so much to their promised evening together. Dammit! He knew he was being selfish as the image of Heather's pale, frightened face rose up to haunt him. But he'd been so close to luring Raine into his arms, and now once again he had been thwarted. What concerned him at this point was that he didn't know how much longer he could keep on going this way.

Raine couldn't sleep. After a moment of forcing her eyes shut, they popped back open. Suddenly, she felt the urge to talk.

"Please...tell me what happened."

Ashe wiped at the moisture on his forehead with the back of his hand. "There's not much to tell, really. I was in the plant bending over an engine when I got a phone call from Dr. Anders saying that Heather had gone into premature labor. I shot out of my office like something was after me and went straight to the emergency room." He paused, maneuvering the car smoothly around an old pickup truck creeping along in the fast lane. "Heather was crying for both you and Todd. Dr. Anders was in the emergency room when she came in and told her doctor that he'd ask me to get in touch with you. I decided then it would be easier all around if I went to get you."

Raine suddenly pushed the panic button. "Todd doesn't know, does he?"

Ashe's piercing gaze moved quickly to her face. "No, of course not. But I don't know how much longer it can be kept from him, because he's sure to miss Heather. There's been a remarkable improvement in him just since you've been gone."

"Well, at least that's good news."

"Of course," he added, "Dr. Anders cautioned that although he is improving steadily, he still has a long way to go."

"I hope you remember that when you and the colonel start badgering him." She made an effort to keep the censure out of her voice, as she wasn't prepared for another major confrontation. But she couldn't let this opportunity pass without letting him know that she was aware of his intentions.

Ashe let out a long breath, relaxing the explosive pressure behind his rigid muscles. "I've told you before, and I'll tell you again, I have no intention of playing a vigilante or letting Colonel Jackson do so either." Suddenly, his expression relented outwardly as he saw that Raine was perilously close to tears. "I promise you can be present when we question Todd. Is that a fair deal?"

Raine wanted an excuse to lash out at him, to keep reminding herself that he was out to do Todd in, that he was pursuing her for God only knew what reasons, but she couldn't. In his gentleness, she could not label him the enemy, not when he had the power to make her insides melt with just one look, one touch. And whether she wanted to admit it or not, she needed his strength. She needed *him*. But with each throb of need, something within her seemed to slip, like a cloth sliding off a table, exposing its flawed surface.

"Well, is it?" he asked, the warm sound of his voice bringing her sharply out of her reverie.

"Yes," she said in a small voice, knowing she was just adding another nail to her coffin.

The hospital was a hubbub of activity by the time they arrived. It was the dinner hour, and they had to make their way around the carts ladened with trays of food. The smell, saturating the air, almost made Raine sick.

Heather, they were told, had been moved to the same floor as Todd. By the time they opened the door and silently stepped into the dimly lit room, Raine was a bundle of nerves.

Like Todd, Heather had an intravenous tube hanging from a metal post beside her bed. She was alone, curled up in a fetal position. Ashe stood just inside the door while Raine tiptoed to the side of the bed.

As though she sensed that she was no longer alone, Heather's eyes opened, then shut, then opened again.

"Oh, Raine," she whispered, her voice sounding scratchy and weak. "I was afraid you wouldn't come."

Raine sat down beside Heather, her mouth as dry as sawdust, hot tears stinging her eyes. Then her hand moved up to Heather's forehead and gently pushed back the tumbled curls. "You know better than that," she admonished. "You knew I'd come as soon as I heard."

A sob rattled Heather's body as the tears ran in rivulets down her pale cheeks. "My baby!" she wailed. "My baby!"

"Shh! Don't cry," Raine begged, feeling stricken on the inside. "Shh! Everything's, going to be all right." Suddenly, she felt Ashe's presence beside her, felt his comforting hand on her shoulder. He didn't say a word, but he was there and she reveled in it.

Raine's soothing words seemed to have calmed Heather somewhat. Her eyes fluttered shut, while her fingers spread like a fan over her still swollen stomach. "I'm...I'm so tired."

Heather's pitiful moan tore at Raine's heart. She tilted her chin as though to keep it above water. Dear Lord, how much more could she take?

Raine did not move for the longest time, nor did Ashe. The only sound in the room was their uneven breathing and Heather's shallow panting.

Satisfied that Heather was indeed asleep, Raine stood up and walked to the window. Momentarily, she heard the door open behind her. Swinging around, she encountered Dr. Anders's steadfast gaze. Before Raine could say a word, however, the doctor motioned for her and Ashe to follow him. It was obvious that he did not want to disturb Heather's peaceful slumber.

Raine's brows were knitted with worry as they quietly left the room. Once in the corridor, Raine turned pleading eyes on the doctor. "Will you..." She paused, as if uncertain of how to continue. Then, after a moment she plunged on forcefully, "Will they have to take the baby?"

Lines of fatigue were carefully etched in Dr. Anders's face. "Not yet," he confessed. But when he saw the light spring up in Raine's eyes, he held up his hand in caution.

"I've spoken to Heather's obstetrician and he tells me it's going to be a touch-and-go situation for the next several hours. Heather is pre-eclamptic." Then, seeing a perplexed look on Raine's face, he explained further. "In layman's terms it means that her blood pressure shot up dangerously high. This condition in itself is extremely threatening to both mother and baby, but coupled with Heather's weakness and general neglect of herself, it has made the situation much more volatile."

Raine felt caught in a vicious circle, and the strain was beginning to show.

"What are their chances?" Ashe asked, speaking for the first time, his eyes locked on Raine's face, his concern mounting by the second. She looked about ready to fall on her face.

There was a short silence while the doctor seriously considered how to answer the question. As Raine waited, the feeling of anxiety expanded in her chest.

Finally, Dr. Anders spoke, though his words were well chosen. "Good, if we can get the fluid level down and the blood pressure stabilized. But if we do get things under control and she carries the baby to full term, she'll have to change her way of living. Nothing but the right foods—absolutely no salt—and plenty of rest will be the order of the day from now on until she delivers. But I'm sure Dr. Bryant will explain everything to her. She's in very capable hands."

"I...understand," Raine replied. There was a touch of panic in her voice that she failed to mask. "I just can't bear the thought of anything happening to her or the baby, not to mention the effect if would have on Todd."

"Why don't we cross that bridge when we come to it?" Ashe chimed in, smiling encouragingly.

For a moment, they stared at one another, Raine noticing the warmth in his eyes that was as potent as any brandy. She caught her breath while resisting the temptation to thrust herself into his arms, aching to transfer the responsibility of the pain and despair she was feeling to his strong shoulders. *Forget that!* she told herself ruthlessly. *It can never be!*

Nevertheless, it required herculean effort to pull her eyes away from his and concentrate on what was being said.

The doctor shifted his feet and coughed discreetly, suddenly claiming their attention once again.

"Isn't that right, Doctor?" Ashe was saying, though none too steadily.

"He's right, Ms. Michaels," Dr. Anders said. "In a few hours we should know something." He paused, his gaze encompassing them both. "Will you be here?"

Raine spoke up immediately. "Yes, of course. I'm not budging until I know, one way or the other. I'll more than likely be in Todd's room; if not, then you can find me across the hall." She pointed her head toward the waiting room, adjacent to where they were standing.

"And I'll be with her," Ashe added, his lips taking on a stubborn twist, making it clear to Raine that he was not leaving.

"Good." The doctor sounded relieved. "I'll talk to you later, then."

Raine placed a tentative hand on his green-coated arm. "Thanks...thanks for everything," she whispered.

He squeezed her hand lightly before nodding his head toward Ashe and then took off in a hurried stride down the hall, his shoulders hunched.

The hours crept by, like sand through an hourglass. But somehow Raine endured, never once losing her composure. At Ashe's insistence, she forced down half of a sandwich and a cup of coffee. From that point on, there was no telling how much coffee she consumed.

Although she looked in on Todd several times, he was always asleep, and for that she was thankful, because she had no intention of telling him about Heather, and he was alert enough now to know something was wrong.

Still they waited. Raine prowled the room like a caged animal. She could not stay put in one place for long. Ashe, though outwardly calm, looked tired and haggard.

Yet his eyes tracked her every movement. And though she hated herself for it, each time his eyes remained fixed on her, a warm weakness invaded her body. It was as though he was beckoning to her without words, *I'm here. Let me hold you, lean on me.* She held her distance, fear holding her with chains of steel.

If she could have read Ashe's thoughts, she would have had cause for alarm. He longed to hold her, all right, to squeeze her, bite chunks out of her warm, sweet-smelling flesh, while whispering in the velvet fold of her ear, *Bear with me. I've never prepared myself for this. You see, you're something I thought would never happen to me.*

But he, too, kept his distance, unable to deal with these emotions that were hammering relentlessly at his insides.

It was eleven o'clock when the doctor came through the door of the waiting room.

Raine's eyes went unerringly to Ashe as fear halted her pacing. He covered the short distance between them and together they moved toward the doctor. Dr. Anders looked jubilant as he laid a hand on Raine's shoulder.

Raine felt as though her lungs would explode as she answered the smile on his face with one of her own. "Doctor?" The fierce constriction in her throat made speech nearly impossible.

Ashe's heart soared with relief and thanksgiving as he watched the scene being played out in front of him. His delight was almost painful as he saw Raine's facial expression change from one of despair to one of joy, her smile flashing like sunlight through a passing storm.

"I told Dr. Bryant I wanted to be the one to tell you two, but I guess you've already figured out that the news is good," Dr. Anders said, his voice firm but low. "I'm indeed happy to tell you the crisis has passed. We aren't going to have to take the baby, after all."

Raine stood mute, staring up at him while giving in to the warm bubble of relief that swelled within her.

"She's resting now," the doctor added. "It will be in the morning before you can see her."

Then, without warning, it happened. Later she couldn't recall how it came to be. She was in his arms, crushed against his solid warm chest.

She clung to him as though she would never let him go.

Over her head, Dr. Anders's face blossomed into a wide grin and he winked at Ashe before silently disappearing from the room.

It was when she felt a mat of wiry hair graze her cheek that she realized where she was. Still she did not move; his arms were like a haven from which she never wanted to escape. But then cold reality began to seep in and she made an effort to regain her composure. Taking a long shuddering breath, she turned in his arms, tilting her head backward, her eyes colliding with his.

"I'm sorry," she apologized, red-faced. "It's just that I felt so helpless...so..."

Gentle hands were busy smoothing her soft curls. "I know. You have nothing to apologize for, believe me."

Keeping her head averted, she gently disentangled herself from his arms and stepped back. There was a moment of awkward silence as they both fought to calm their racing hearts.

Then, suddenly, Raine's teeth began to chatter. It started from deep within, her insides feeling bruised and battered.

She sucked her lower lip between her teeth as her head rolled forward like a weakened flower stem threatening to break. Her arms crossed in front of her breasts trying to ward off the chill that continued to pelt her body.

Ashe reacted instantly. "Dammit!" he muttered as an arm reached out and circled her shoulders, drawing her once more next to the lean contours of his body.

"Come on, I'm getting you out of here," he said through stiff lips. She was having a delayed reaction, and worry was forming an icy knot of dread in the pit of his stomach.

But Raine couldn't seem to move. The muscles in her legs felt like sharp knives. She was dead weight against him.

"Do you want me to carry you?" he asked urgently.

It was those words that penetrated her muddled senses, causing another twist of panic within her. God! No way could she let him carry her out of the hospital!

While shaking her head to the contrary, she took a step forward. The rest was easy. However, Ashe's arm remained locked around her like a vise as they stepped out into the damp night air. It had been raining; there were pools of water everywhere. Raine sucked in the fresh-scented air, pulling it through her lungs with relish as Ashe saw her comfortably settled in the car.

She was aware of his eyes on her from time to time as they sped through the deserted, slick streets. But she dared not look at him. Her emotions were already riding next to her skin. Oh, God, one more look, one more touch, and she would not be responsible for her actions.

Out of the corner of his eye, Ashe's eyes raked her profile. He stifled an oath. Her features were molded into a tight, pale mask. Was she regretting the moment in his arms? No doubt, he cursed bitterly. Suddenly, as he turned his eyes back to the street in front of him, it dawned on him that he cared—really cared—about this woman. Not love.

That was a word that was no longer a part of his vocabulary, but he did care.

However, this admission brought him no comfort. He scorned himself. *Face it, Elliot, she despises you, despises everything you stand for.* He drew a harsh breath. So where did that leave him?

Shaking off that thought and once again becoming a party to the constrained silence, he eased the car next to the curb and killed the engine. Wordlessly, Ashe uncurled himself from behind the wheel and, after opening Raine's door, extracted the key from her fumbling fingers. By the time he opened the door to Todd's apartment, Raine was shaking again. Somehow, though, she managed to program her rubbery legs to cross the room. She turned on a lamp, and instantly the room was bathed in a soft, golden glow.

Raine turned and stared at Ashe, who was standing just inside the door, a closed expression on his face. Their eyes met and locked.

A tension electrified the air.

Raine tried to speak, to thank him for bringing her home, for keeping the vigil with her, but not one word got past her swollen throat.

Ashe moved closer and then stopped. "Will you be all right?" His voice was husky, uncertain.

"Yes...yes. I'll be fine."

"Are you sure?"

"I'm sure."

"I guess that's all."

Still they looked at one another.

"I'll be going."

Raine moved then, almost closing the distance between them. She had been trying to display her self-confidence, but she had failed, and suddenly the thought of being left alone was abhorrent. Would he truly abandon her?

Ashe remained welded to the carpet. They stood two feet apart and waited. For the first time he could remember, he was at a loss as to what he should do. His head was spinning. Dare he touch her? Dare he answer the desire that had beaten through every word and gesture the entire evening?

"Raine?" He spoke as though in pain.

Again the words would not come. But she could not turn away either. The inner battle increased her trembling. She stood aloof, feeling like an intruder in her own body, wanting to reach out to him.

She never knew if she had or not. But it didn't matter. Nothing mattered as they came together like two halves of a soul. His arms, as they locked her close, were like velvet chains around her quivering limbs. Raine had never dreamed of such fire, such sweetness; she could never have imagined it.

Ashe was overwhelmed by the intensity of her response, couldn't believe this was actually happening to him, that she was letting him hold her of her own free will. He thought he had died and gone to heaven.

He put his hand on her hair, to know its softness, its depth. Her hair was like summer, like sunshine, like golden apples, like shimmering water. He wanted to bask in those magic qualities, lose himself inside the liquid fire he could feel bubbling inside her.

Suddenly, Raine stirred. Fear jolted through Ashe and his arms tightened around her.

"Ashe..." Her voice was muffled against his chest.

He bent his head, her breath whispering against his ear. "Shh! Dear heart," he murmured thickly. "Don't talk, just feel, feel how much I need you, want you."

With that confession, red-hot hunger drove him to mold her soft, trembling lips to his.

Raine moaned as breaths mingled and tears meshed. It was as though they floated in a fog. Nothing seemed real.

Suddenly, Heather receded as a peripheral character in a play; Todd became a background figure in a painting. Even her work seemed unimportant in the vast silence of their shrouded world. All that mattered was her happiness at being with him, cut off from the balance of civilization.

Ashe was on the brink of madness as he tasted the sweetness of her lips, smelled her perfumed flesh.

He pulled away from her, his breathing raw, and looked down at her, gently lifting her chin, forcing her to meet his eyes.

"Raine..." His voice was raspy, a question in his eyes.

She did not hesitate or pretend to misunderstand him. "Yes."

His heart began pumping wildly. "Oh, Raine," he groaned, the tip of his tongue moving on her lips, and she opened her mouth, her whole body hot.

At that moment, she could believe him. Her body felt radiantly alive. He hadn't planned this, any more than she had. But she was falling; she could feel herself pitching forward and knew she could not stop now. There was a real and inescapable finality to all this.

But a hyper little voice warned that she was embarking on an impossible path, that she was being crazy and irresponsible, that this was madness, that this was unforgivable. She was complicating her life beyond any semblance of sanity. Raine ignored the voice. No amount of reason could lessen the burning need that drove her to banish all lingering doubts and yield to the delights he offered. Yes, she thought, this was what she wanted. It was what she had wanted for hours, for weeks, though she admitted it to herself only now for the first time. She ached to be touched by him, to feel him expand inside her, to become a part of another. Just this once, her heart whispered. She longed to seize all the pleasure this moment offered. Regret would come soon enough, but for now there were only the two of them.

"Ashe," she murmured thickly, lifting her hand to touch his cheek, innocently straining against him.

"God, Raine! Please don't move. I feel as if my skin's going to crack and I'll come pouring out."

Raine caught her breath, excitement freezing her movement, feeling exhilaration shoot through her. To think she had the power to affect him like this! But would he still feel that way...

Her silent thought was never finished. Suddenly, Ashe swept her up in his arms and demanded urgently, "Where?"

In a jerking motion, Raine pointed in the direction of her bedroom. Shouldering the door shut, he set her down on her feet and said, in a low voice, "Don't move."

Ashe left her standing in total darkness until she heard the swishing of the curtains and saw the inky blackness give way to the sky, once again alive with the cold, platinum pinpricks that were the stars.

She waited, and when his tall silhouette stood with her beside the bed, she kept swallowing, watching him as he first eased her jacket from her shoulders, then slowly, deliberately, unbuttoned her blouse and slid it down her arms, letting it fall into a pool at her feet. He then unzipped her skirt and it fell past her hips, to the floor.

His eyes burned down into hers. She had never experienced such heady, eruptive turmoil before, and it left her helpless, mindless, totally at his mercy.

He unfastened her bra and looked at her breasts, before covering them lightly with his hands.

"You're beautiful," he said, brushing his mouth against hers.

"Oh, Ashe," she whimpered, still helplessly spellbound.

He let out a great sighing breath as his hands moved down to her waist and slid down under the elastic rims of her slip and pants, down inside over her buttocks as he made a soft, satisfied sound and stepped back.

She was so exquisite it stopped his breath. Now that she was naked, the secret generosity of the flesh was all laid bare, the small, unexpected softness that would give so readily to accommodate his own hard angularity.

Treating her as though she were a fragile piece of glass, he brought her against him, kissing her slowly, hungrily, before pulling away, leaving her feeling bereft as his arms released her.

"Ashe?"

"It's all right, dear heart. It's just that I want nothing between us but the air we breathe."

Unable to remove her gaze, she watched while he took off his clothes, watching his tanned skin emerge, thinking how much better he looked without clothes. But when his pants were off and he removed his underwear, she stared, then quickly looked away.

For a moment she felt frightened. But then he lowered her with him onto the bed and pressed her close against him. The closeness was wonderful, better than anything she'd ever known.

"Oh, Raine, if you only knew what you do to me," he whispered before his mouth covered hers in that sensitive, loving way. Then his mouth was on her breasts, tugging gently on one nipple, then the other, and something in the very middle of her body seemed to give way. She was aware of his hand on her thigh, moving up. She stiffened, anticipating being hurt. But then she ceased to care, because he was kissing her mouth again, then her breast, so when his hand moved against her, she quivered at the unexpected pleasure of the sensation, opening herself to him, wanting more.

"So beautiful," he murmured. "Does it feel good?"

"Oh, yes," she whispered. "Yes."

His hand rubbed at her rhythmically so that she wanted to move somehow, desiring him to touch her all over, her senses dizzy from the motion of his hands. His tongue was painting spirals in her mouth, making speech impossible.

"You've got me on a high," he murmured, spending what seemed like eons lingering over her ears, throat, shoulders, and breasts.

"I can hear you vibrate," he added. "So alive, so achingly real. I love your breasts. They're firm, but soft and round. I like your navel. Round, too, and your hard hips and right there beside the bone, it's soft as moonlight. And here. I like the way your thighs curve right here and the best here, here..."

"Ashe, please...now!" She couldn't take any more. She wanted him. She wanted to feel him inside her...to know at last what it was to be loved by a man.

Ashe needed no second invitation. He was like a man possessed as he tenderly, indulgently moved her legs apart, then knelt between them. Then, ever so slowly, exquisitely, he began the descent into her.

Raine was enraptured, impatient to know all of him. Arching herself against him, she was unprepared for the stinging, tearing pain and she cried out.

He froze. "God, Raine!"

"Please...don't stop," she gasped.

"You're not a virgin?" he whispered, horrified.

"Yes...of course." Her virginity was so much on her mind that it never occurred to Raine that he wouldn't know.

"Oh, God, dear God."

"Please, please, Ashe...keep on...go on...don't worry if it hurts...I want it," she said urgently as she touched him in the dark with her hands to show him she meant her words.

He ground his teeth and began moving inside her, each movement reaching an apex of incredible pleasure. She moved up against him, unaware of what she was doing, aware only that he was plunging deeply into her body.

"Beautiful, oh, yes," she heard herself whisper, her eyes shuddering closed as the feeling tossed her into the center of a whirlpool and sucked her down, down, down, taking her away so she was barely aware of his continued movement, his final completing thrusts.

She was aware only of *feeling*. Something reaching all the way through her, penetrating everything....

Chapter 9

He could feel the length of her nestled softly against him. The sheets, he noted, were cool, but her flesh was as hot as fresh bread. He was no cynical pilot now, just a man in love with a woman and in bed with her for the first time.

Suddenly, he went stiff. Sweet Jesus, he thought, staggered as if he'd been struck in the chest. *I'm in love with her!* Sweet Jesus! How the hell had that happened, he wondered, tenderly covering her with the sheet, watching her as she slept. How the *hell* had that happened?

Raine awakened slowly, knowing before she opened her eyes that she had slept long and deeply. She felt content and warm, like a rose petal kissed by the sun. Then she stretched her limbs, only to make a face as a throbbing jolt of pain shot through her. What was wrong? Why was she sore? Then she remembered. Ashe. The memory of all the divine things he had done to her, until, with their bodies still fused, he had fallen asleep in her arms, made her give a long sigh of pleasure.

Regrets? None. Tomorrow? More than likely. But she
wouldn't think about that now. *Relish the moment*. What
they had shared had been the most wonderful experience of
her life, infinitely worth waiting for. It made her feel like a
new woman, mentally and physically complete. She had
never felt better.

After a minute or two, she turned toward him. His eyes
were open, watching her, his leg still pinning her under him.

"Good morning," he said, propping his head on his elbow. He wasn't smiling. She couldn't tell what he was
thinking.

"Good morning," she responded softly, hating to intrude upon the spell of enchantment that surrounded them.

He looked at her thoughtfully, his eyes darkening. "You
should have told me, you know."

Her heart sank. "Would it have made any difference?"
She pulled away, creating a small distance between them,
fear beginning to nibble at the edge of her awareness.

His face taut with concern he asked, "Did I hurt you
badly?"

"Only for a moment." Her voice held a tremor. "But I
didn't want you to stop. It was...wonderful."

The silence that followed was filled only with heartbeats.

Raine's thoughts were going haywire. God! What must he
be thinking of her? Had she let him down, not satisfied
him? Wasn't it true that men preferred their bed partners to
be skilled in the ways of making love? Suddenly, her heart
felt like a piece of lead. Had she come up lacking?

He sighed. "Back to your question of a moment ago."
His voice grew hoarse. "No, it wouldn't have made any
difference. I wanted you more than I've ever wanted anything in my life." Even as he talked, he felt the heat in his
groin rise again. Would he ever get enough of this woman?

"You're not sorry?" She felt the color rise to her cheeks. "I mean..." Her voice trailed off into nothingness as she saw the stark desire in his eyes.

"How could I be sorry?" he groaned raggedly. "You are absolutely perfect." *And I love you,* he almost said. "I'm glad I was the one to show you what it can be like between a man and a woman." He pulled her next to him again, his lips brushing hers.

"I'm so glad I pleased you," she whispered into his mouth. "I was so..."

His lips stopped her, and he pulled her against him with a feeling bordering on desperation, before rolling over and taking her with him. Instinctively, her legs closed, capturing him between her thighs. His kisses, his hands, his captivity amid her thighs made her tremble with need.

Suddenly, he shifted, easing her down onto him.

Her eyes widened as she held her breath, shivering as he seemed to expand inside her.

"Ashe! Oh, God, what..."

He chuckled at the shocked but rapt expression on her face, thinking she had never looked lovelier. "Oh, dear heart, you're just beginning to learn what it is to please a man." Then his grin disappeared as she began to move and he put his mouth to a nipple. He groaned, a hand curving on the other breast.

"I love it," she said thickly, spreading herself until the tendon in her thighs threatened to snap, their pace increasing, "love it."

"Oh, God, now. *Now!*" he moaned, holding her hard.

And then no words, no reality, just a remote cry originating somewhere in her soul and answered by another...

"I wish you'd told me, Todd," Raine said lightly, her gaze resting on her brother's face. Gradually, Todd was beginning to look more like his old self. Even the abrasions on his face and neck no longer appeared ominous. There was a silence as Todd averted his thin face, turning toward Heather, who occupied the chair next to his bed.

It had been four days since Ashe had walked out of Todd's apartment to catch the next flight to Washington, D.C. He had waited until they had stumbled out of bed and taken a long, leisurely shower together, once again exploring one another's bodies until they were dizzy with desire, to tell her he had to go out of town for an important meeting with the Defence Department and that he'd be gone over a week. Although her heart had plummeted to her toes at the unexpected news, she had kept her silence, not wanting to interrupt the feeling of magic that surrounded them.

However, the moment the door had closed behind him, that sense of magic had long since disappeared like leaves in a windstorm, leaving a feeling of raw panic in its wake. But she brushed that thought aside now, as this was the first time Todd had felt well enough to talk.

"I know I should have told you," he said gruffly, breaking into the long silence, his eyes clinging to Heather for a moment before turning to Raine. "I was such a fool for not shouting it to the world."

Heather smiled at Todd before she turned toward Raine. "We're just lucky everything has turned out the way it has." Her voice was shy. "And we owe it all to you, Raine."

They were lucky, Raine thought, refusing to take credit. They were her family; she'd had no choice. And because Heather had done exactly as the doctor ordered, she was now able to drive and spend several hours a day with Todd.

"That's right, Sis," Todd chimed in, claiming Raine's attention once again. "And I'm sorry for all the heartache I've caused you." He paused, easing his head back on the pillow, though his eyes never veered from Raine's face. "First the accident, and knowing how you felt about my flying, I'm sure you must have gone through hell. And on top of that to find out about Heather the way you did, and then the unexpected trouble with the baby, the whole ordeal was a bit much.''

"I agreee," Heather said sweetly. "And I'm sorry for my part in it."

Todd shifted his position only to wince and grab his side. When his breathing was back to normal, he spoke again. "I wanted to tell you about Heather, but I kept putting it off, just like I put off marrying her." He paused again. "It's just that I was afraid something like this would happen—" pain filled his eyes momentarily as Heather squeezed his hand "—but there just never seemed to be enough money. You know when it comes to money, I'm a disaster." He grimaced. "I've made several bad investments and my money situation is tighter now than ever. Again I want to say I'm sorry and I love you."

Raine smiled through her tears as she crossed to the bed and kissed him on the forehead. "You're forgiven, but if you ever do anything like that to me again I won't be responsible for my actions."

His lips twitched. "Which one are you referring to?"

"Both," Raine shot back with a smile. Then her face sobered. "I may not have any control over you flying, but keeping Heather a secret was dirty pool."

Heather giggled, shifting her cumbersome weight in the chair. "You just slay me," she drawled, then giggled once again.

Raine hid a smile and rolled her eyes upward. She was more and more convinced that her first assessment of Heather had been correct. She had definitely been shortchanged in the brains department. But Raine loved her the way she was and wouldn't change a hair on her head. Her innocent outlook on life was contagious.

"Well," Todd said, reaching over and caressing Heather's stomach, "you can rest assured that as soon as all this is behind me, I plan to make an honest woman out of Heather."

"I'm glad," Raine whispered, no longer fighting back the tears of joy. She was delighted that Todd had finally come to his senses and was going to marry Heather. But it had taken his learning about Heather's dilemma to wake him up to what he'd almost lost. She'd finally had to tell him; he kept asking for Heather, but by the time she did so, the danger had passed.

"Raine." Todd pulled a face. "I guess you know I'm being held responsible for the accident."

Raine's heart skipped a beat. "Yes, I do."

He was watching her closely. "Ah, so you've talked to Ashe Elliot, my boss."

Raine's face flooded with color as she lowered her gaze. How she hated this type of deceit. On the other hand, how could she admit to Todd that not only had she talked to Ashe, but that his hands and lips had tutored her body, introducing her to a world filled with magic? No. She couldn't tell him that. He would be shocked and he had come too far to risk another setback.

Composing her features to hide her raging thoughts, Raine raised her eyes to meet his. "Yes...I've seen him, but to my knowledge the report had not been completed."

"Well, report or no report, they have to put the blame on someone other than themselves, so you're looking at the sacrifice," Todd said bitterly.

"Please, don't upset yourself," Raine pleaded, noticing his heavy breathing and the white line around his mouth. "Let's just wait until the final report comes in and then go from there."

His eyes challenged her. "After listening to Ashe's side, do you think I disobeyed orders and was trying to 'hotdog it,' so to speak?"

Raine jutted her chin. "Of course I don't."

"Well, you're right," he said flatly. "I told that pompous ass, Colonel Jackson..."

"Todd, Honey!" Heather cut in. "Watch your mouth. It's not nice to call someone an 'ass.'" Her face turned red and she giggled again.

"Sorry, love," Todd said absently.

Raine didn't know whether to laugh or cry at Heather's inane outburst, but she did neither as her attention reverted back to Todd and what he was saying. "I told him there was a defect in the landing gear, but he wouldn't listen to me."

"When...when did you last talk to...Ashe?"

Todd frowned. "I guess it was about four days ago. He came by early that morning on his way out of town; said we'd talk again when he got back."

Raine's heart increased its tempo, only suddenly to settle back down. So he wasn't back yet, she thought, only then to chide herself for caring if he was back or not. Somehow, someway, she had to find the strength to stop this snowballing effect he was having on her life. She didn't know who she was anymore, and that scared her.

Todd looked to be on the defensive. "He's discussed it with you, hasn't he?"

Raine could not look him in the eye. "Yes. Yes, he has, but I told him in no uncertain terms that I thought you were innocent."

Todd's short gasp caused Raine to whip her head back around to face him. For a dreaded moment, she was afraid he might be in pain. "Did you really? I find that hard to believe."

"Why?" She felt a sharp letdown at his lack of faith in her.

"It's simple," Todd said. "I know how you hate the thought of my risking my life on a daily basis."

"That's true, I do. But being held accountable for a crash that wasn't your fault isn't my idea of the way to end your career."

Suddenly, a slow grin spread across Todd's face while his eyes shone with relief. "I would've loved to have heard that conversation. I bet you gave him hell, Sis."

Raine flushed and again averted her eyes. "Well, let's just say we had a serious discussion," she admitted with a slight smile.

"Well, in the end," Todd said, "I think Ashe will come around—he knows me. But right now, I think he's letting Jackson influence him."

Raine doubted that, but she kept her mouth shut about that, not wanting to upset Todd any further. He had already exerted more energy than he should have, and it was obvious by the fatigue showing on his face that he was exhausted.

"Let's hope they both come to their senses while at the same time finding evidence to prove that you weren't at fault."

"They have to," Todd said doggedly, his eyelids beginning to close. "My whole future—my whole life—rests on it."

Raine's heart was heavy as she watched him drift into a deep sleep, despair etched in every line of his face. She blamed Ashe, yet at the same time she could think of nothing but the way his naked limbs had felt entwined around hers.

Suddenly unable to stay one moment longer in the room, she whispered to Heather that she would see her later and made her way out of the hospital.

It was while she was walking to the car that she realized the worst was yet to come. Why hadn't she listened to the warnings of her conscience? Her heart? She felt helpless now. Numb. But soon that would pass and her senses would once again spring to life and the real fight would begin. And not with Ashe Elliot. He wasn't the enemy; she knew that now. No, her real adversary was one to whom she was bound for life.

Herself.

The remainder of the week passed slowly. Raine spent the bulk of her mornings with Todd and Heather at the hospital, and then in the afternoons she passed the time on the phone talking to Val discussing business. But as each day passed, it was becoming more difficult to conduct business from afar. She was needed physically at New Image. She knew she should return to Dallas, but she could not bring herself to do so. Oh, she kept telling herself that both Todd and Heather still needed her, and to a point they did, because it looked as though Todd might have to have surgery, after all, on his stomach. But her motive for staying was not that clearcut. Ashe Elliot held her there as though he had her bound in ropes.

Although she had not heard one word from him since that night of wild passion, thoughts of him haunted her day and night. She felt herself being destroyed inch by inch. How could she have created another monster in her life by letting Ashe become too important to her? What about her obligations, her commitments to her work?

Could this craving she felt to be with him, to be a part of him, be love? No. She would not believe that she was in love with Ashe Elliot or he with her. Their attraction toward each other was physical, and nothing else. She had to believe this, because she knew loving him would destroy her. A man who had no respect for life was incapable of loving in return. And she could not stand the thought of living the rest of her life in fear, fear that once he walked out the door he would never come back.

Yet, she admitted with aching honesty that she was not ready to give him up, that she wanted once again to feel that heady excitement she had felt in his arms. So she filled the days and the hours waiting until she heard from him.

Today brought no changes in this routine. She had just come back from the hospital and was trying to settle down and call Val. But she couldn't seem to sit still, feeling unusually restless and dissatisfied, hating herself for not ending this ridiculous charade and going back to Dallas.

Raine heaved a long sigh, deciding a tough round of exercises was what she needed. Since she had been here, she hadn't jogged her daily mile or rolled on the floor, and those were two things she did religiously at home.

It took her only a few minutes to shed her dress and pantyhose and slip into a pair of walking shorts, a knit top, and jogging shoes. She had just brushed her hair back out of the way, when the sharp clang of the phone halted her action.

"Damn!" she muttered under her breath, laying the brush down and stomping to the phone.

"Hello."

"Your voice is music to my ears."

Her insides did a flipflop. She was so stunned at hearing Ashe's voice that she was almost unable to respond.

"How are you, Ashe?" she managed to eke out.

"In health or in temper?" he asked a little dryly. "Oh, I'm all right, I guess." Suddenly, his voice was deep, throaty. "Have you missed me?"

Silence.

"That's a leading question," she said evasively, trying to ignore the erratic beat of her heart.

"Well, I've sure missed you," he muttered roughly.

New life pumped through her at his admission, but it was as though her voice was under lock and key, making speech next to impossible.

"Is Todd still getting better?" he asked in answer to her silence.

"Yes..." she hedged.

"Good. I want to see you."

His soft-spoken words ignited a need deep within her, yet she tried to ignore it, knowing that seeing him would merely prolong the agony. The receiver began to shake in her hand. "Ashe, please. The...other night was a...mistake."

"Raine, don't." There was a note of pleading in his voice. "Why are you doing this? I thought what we shared was something wonderful." He paused. "God, this has been one hell of a week, and I'm dying for the sight of you."

She felt her hands grow clammy. His voice was so wonderfully warm and expressive, and she knew in that moment he meant what he said. She was weakening.

"Raine, can you honestly tell me you don't want to see me as much as I want to see you?" he asked harshly, sounding as though he'd reached the end of his patience.

She couldn't speak. She felt as if she were suffocating. All those sleepless nights she'd dreamed of this moment, but now it was as alarming as if she'd just been offered a handful of heaven. Was the price too high?

"No, Ashe...I want to see you, too." The words spilled out before she could stifle them.

He breathed achingly. "I'll be there in fifteen minutes. Dress casual and bring a swimsuit." The line went dead.

She stood holding the receiver as though she had been struck dumb. She had made her choice. She must live with it no matter the consequences. But for now, she would look for no more dark shadows.

When the doorbell chimed, Raine had just slipped into a pair of jeans, a blue crop top, and she had stuffed her swimsuit in a tote bag along with a cotton sundress and sandals just in case of an emergency.

"Hello."

Her voice came out cracked and small. She was totally unprepared for the sight of Ashe. As he stepped into the room, a hesitant smile on his face, their eyes clung. Time stopped. It was as if the air were being slowly emptied out of the room, leaving them gasping for their next breath.

"God, Raine...I've missed you." He was fighting the temptation to grab her and squeeze her against him. It seemed as if he'd been away from her for an eternity. But something told him to go slowly, to take it easy. He realized she was nervous and that she was harboring regrets over their night of passion. He could see it in the slight uncertainty of her smile. He could understand that. He, too, was having difficulty in handling his own feelings. What they had shared was too new, too fragile to rush ahead. But it was hard. God, it was hard...

Raine's eyes had shifted downward to his mouth, the same mouth that had brazenly sought and memorized every secret part of her body, leaving its imprint there. Her heart was beating heavily, slowly, as if it had grown too large for her chest.

"If you don't stop looking at me like that," he said huskily, "I won't be responsible for my actions."

She was beautiful. The scanty top—he was convinced it was unintentional—leant a fascinating definition to her breasts. He tried not to be obvious, not to stare, noticing their rounded swell before moving lower to the trim line of her hips.

Raine swallowed, feeling overheated again. His admission was heady stuff. It made her feel drunk. She must remember to hold him at arm's length and use him cautiously, like an addictive drug.

"Are you ready?" he asked, his voice cloaked in warmth.

"You...you haven't said where we're going," she noted, covering up her confusion by reaching for her bag.

He smiled. "Hope you like a barbecue."

She raised her eyebrows. "I love it. Why?"

"Friends of mine—they're neighbors also—are throwing their annual shindig at Oak Lake near both our ranches." He laughed. "This state wouldn't be big enough to hide me if I didn't go, but even at that, I wasn't about to go with you." There was a short pause. "To tell the truth, I'd forgotten all about it until I walked into the office a little while ago and the phone rang."

"Oh," she said, feeling an unwanted twinge of disappointment.

Ashe tweaked the end of her nose, grinning lazily. "Is that all you have to say?"

She recovered quickly, flashing him a determined smile. "Fine with me. As I said before, I love a barbecue."

Why, she wondered, did she feel as though her hand had been slapped just as she opened the cookie jar?"

The party appeared to be in full swing by the time Ashe steered the Lincoln into a wooded area off a black-topped road. Raine winced as she moved her stiff muscles. They had been riding for only a couple of hours, yet she was tired of sitting and glad they had arrived.

For the most part, the trip had gone smoothly. They had kept the conversation—what little there was of it—on an impersonal basis. He had amused her with tales about Mac and Alice, who were hosting the barbecue, as though he had been determined to keep things on the light side. But at times when she felt his eyes on her, the tension had built to a screaming pitch. However, neither had acknowledged it, for fear of breaking the tender thread that held them together.

Now as he shoved the gear into Park, he turned toward her and smiled, causing her heart to leap around crazily.

"We're here," he quipped inanely, his eyes dipping to her mouth.

"I know." Her voice was choked.

He moved closer.

"Shouldn't...shouldn't we be getting out?"

"There's no hurry."

"Are you sure?"

"I'm sure."

"What are we waiting for?"

His breath was melting her skin. "I think you know."

She opened her mouth to speak, but the words were suppressed as he took his mouth to hers, with his body, his whole self. She was tingling with anticipation as though it was the first time he'd ever kissed her. He nipped slowly, then mouth to mouth, and then hard, holding her tightly against him.

"Ashe, please...someone will see us," she whispered, when she was finally able to dislodge her mouth.

The silence was heavy as Ashe fought to breathe. Then suddenly he grinned, though his eyes were serious. "Just because you got off this time—"

"Hey, you two! Y'all gonna stay in the damned car forever?"

Raine jerked her head up and around at the sound of the loud voice. Her heart was knocking against her ribs.

Ashe chuckled. "Don't be alarmed; it's only Mac. Come on." He then proceeded to grab her hand and shuffle her out the left side of the car behind him.

Raine waited, the color remaining high in her cheeks, while a tall, red-haired man vigorously pumped Ashe's hand.

"Mmm, not bad, not bad, my friend. In fact, she's a real beauty." He sidled up to Raine. "Mickey McAdams," he said, taking her hand in a hard-gripping handshake that would rival the one he gave Ashe.

"Raine Michaels," she said, smiling. "It's a pleasure to meet you, Mickey."

"Hell, Raine," he snorted, "call me Mac. All my friends do, and any friend of Ashe's—" he paused and slapped Ashe on the back "—is a friend of mine. Anyway, I hate the name Mickey. Sounds like a goddamned monkey's name." He winked at Raine. "Guess we'd better be headin' toward the camp. Alice'll have my head if I let anything happen to all that meat."

Raine laughed. Mickey McAdams was loud, but instantly likable. She fell in step between the two men, conscious of Ashe's light, possessive touch on her arm, as they made their way down a wooded path and then into a clearing.

Suddenly she stopped, catching her breath. "Oh, Ashe, it's beautiful," she said, turning to face him, her eyes sparkling."

Oak Lake. She could see now how it came by its name. Its blue water was surrounded by a heavy growth of oak trees. The trees stretched their rugged trunks upward until their lush foliage seemed to brush the sky. From where she stood, Raine could see the soft, sandy earth that bordered the lake, giving it a beachlike appearance. She itched to run barefoot through it.

"We have our gathering here every year," Mac said. "I'm proud you like it."

"Like it! That's an understatement."

"Ashe, this is a lady after my own heart." He grabbed Raine's hand and placed it in the crook of his arm. "Now, to introduce you to my better half and my two wild hellions. Ashe, tend to the meat, will ya?"

Over Mac's head, Ashe shrugged his shoulders and grinned, as if to say, *Don't worry, he's really harmless.*

Alice McAdams reminded Raine very much of Val, except that she was much older and much larger. But she had the same quick wit and endearing personality. Raine liked her on sight.

"Welcome," she said, after introductions were made, excitement pouring from her eyes as she clung to Raine's hand. Then, dropping it, she turned and hollered toward the lake. Several heads were bobbing up and down in the water. "Amy, Josh, y'all come over here. Uncle Ashe is here!"

Raine laughed as the two kids, whooping and hollering, bounded out of the water, shouting in unison, "Where's Uncle Ashe?"

"Whoa, you two!" Alice demanded, stopping them in mid-stride. "I want you to say hello to Uncle Ashe's friend, Ms. Michaels."

"Hi-ya!" the boisterous Josh said on the run, dragging his pudgy-legged little sister behind him, searching for Ashe.

Alice shook her head apologetically. "I hope you'll pardon their manners. But when Ashe is around, they don't have time for anyone else."

Raine watched as they clambered up to Ashe and hurled their arms around him. She was seeing yet another facet of his personality. Ashe and children? If she hadn't seen it with her own eyes, she would never have believed it. Would this man never cease to amaze her?

For the next hour Raine was kept busy meeting the other guests who were in attendance—all pilots, she learned, and their wives. After a while, the names began to run together.

Alice laughed, keeping Raine under her ample wing. "Don't worry, hon, no one expects you to remember their names."

Raine tried to hide her dismay, not because she couldn't keep the names straight, but because she was out of her element. She had nothing in common with these women. She lived in a different world.

Shaking her head to diffuse her thoughts, Raine pitched in and helped Alice make a huge salad while the men clustered around the grill, drinking beer and exchanging stories about the latest antics in the air.

Ashe's golden body seemed to stand out as he stood to the side with his Nike-clad foot propped up on a can. He looked delicious in a pair of cut-off jeans and short T-shirt. Then, as though on cue, she watched in spellbound fascination as Ashe threw back his head and laughed at one of the men's hair-raising tales.

She shivered, the light fading from her eyes. Suddenly, her thoughts turned to Todd and her father. *What am I doing here? I don't belong...*

"What's the matter?" Alice asked softly. She and Raine were slightly off to themselves, so no one else could hear their conversation.

"Nothing," Raine hedged, averting her gaze.

"Huh!" Alice challenged, "I wasn't born yesterday."

Raine was taken aback at her bluntness. Then she smiled, only it never reached her eyes. "You're right, something is wrong."

"And I bet I know what it is, too. You don't cotton to Ashe's flying, do you?"

Raine frowned and rubbed a hand over her forehead. "Is it that obvious?"

"No, not to everyone. It's just that I've seen that look so many times, that look of sheer terror." Her eyes were gentle with concern as they rested on Raine.

Raine sucked in her cheeks. "You're right, I hate the thought of him climbing into a plane."

After a moment, Alice said softly, "Believe me, you'll adjust."

Raine's lips were colorless. "Have you?"

Alice hesitated slightly. "Yes, for the most part. Of course, there are still times when Mac takes off in the plane, headed for what I know is a dangerous assignment, that a feeling of dread creeps into my stomach."

Raine shook her head violently. "I could never endure that."

Alice looked shocked. "Surely you don't mean that?"

Raine didn't mince any words. "Oh, I mean it, all right."

After a moment of uneasy silence, Alice changed the subject. "I don't recall ever seeing Ashe this relaxed."

Raine flushed, while attacking the lettuce. "Oh, really." She tried to appear unconcerned, but her heart was fluttering at this unexpected compliment.

"Yes, really," Alice responded. "As well and as long as we've known Ashe, he's never introduced us to any of his women."

His women. She suddenly went cold. "I don't know what to say."

"You could say you cared."

Raine paled, the knife stopping in midair. "Look, Alice, I..."

Alice held up her hand. "I'm sorry. Don't pay any attention to this interfering busybody." She smiled wanly. "I've been living with Mac too long. He's famous for letting his mouth overload his 'you know what'—" she grinned broadly "—and I've picked up the nasty habit." She paused. "It's just that we love Ashe, and since Laura..."

It was as though a bell went off in Raine's head. "Who's Laura?"

An incredulous expression crossed Alice's face. "You mean you don't know?"

"No. Should I?"

"Why, why..." Alice spluttered.

"Go on."

"Well," Alice began uncomfortably, "Laura is Ashe's...ex-wife."

Raine never got a chance to respond, even if she could have. Suddenly, Ashe slid his arms around her from behind and pulled her against him.

"My, but we look serious."

Without turning around, Raine said, "Alice and I have been getting acquainted." She was positive he could hear the tremor in her voice.

"Well, if it's all right with Alice, I've come to kidnap you." He ruffled Alice's curly head. "What'd you say? I want my best girl to sample the water before chow time."

Alice smiled. "By all means. We're about finished here anyway."

Ashe massaged the back of Raine's neck for a moment, before whispering in her ear, "You see that light spot just a little way out?" His hand left her neck and pointed toward the water. She nodded. "That's a bar. See it?"

Again she nodded.

He laughed. "Last one to it is a slowpoke."

She ran, her feet almost snared in the soft earth, longing to be by herself, to think. Snatching the tote bag from off a picnic table, she dashed into the thickness of the underbrush, working her way through until she was in an open glade, completely shut off from the water. Bees buzzed lazily around a honeysuckle vine that had rooted in a decaying stump, and birds swung across the blue bit of sky just above like tinky, airborne gliders. The sun gave a warmth like a caress in the quietness. But she was oblivious to it all.

Her mind was in a state of turmoil. Why had it upset her to find out that Ashe had once been married? Was it because he'd made such a big deal out of telling her how "immune" to marriage he was? Or was it the fact that he hadn't told her the real issue? The questions buzzed around her head, but she had no answers. *Don't think about it now. Don't let the past rob you of today.* After all, there was tomorrow. She could think about it then, couldn't she? Anyway, hadn't she promised herself, *no dark shadows?*

Suddenly, she felt the same old excitement pummel through her. A deer bed just to the right of her had recently been occupied. The grass had been flattened and was only now springing back into its original position. She could imagine the tawny body of the deer, nose to the wind, ears alert, as it rested. She put on the swimsuit quickly, knowing that by this time Ashe would have beaten her. Ashe. She envisioned the smile on his face and it was like an electric charge to her body.

As she left her private haven, she could hear screams of delight from Amy and Josh. When she crossed to the water, she saw Ashe tossing a ball to them.

He looked up and saw her. "Here comes Slowpoke," he drawled. "Now let's see who can swim first to the sandbar."

She ran to the water, feeling its coolness on her feet, before lapping upward to lie against her waist. Then she was swimming, knowing that Ashe was still behind her. She swam easily, conscious only of the cool water around her, until finally her feet found the firm footing of the bar and she crawled up, almost breathless. She saw Ashe's brown arm reach up beside her.

His eyes were laughing. "So," he said, "you beat me. Fairly, too, I guess." He shook the glistening drops from his face and head and eyed her critically. "How did a city girl like you learn to swim so well?"

Raine grinned saucily. "I'll never tell."

His breath almost stopped. Was she actually flirting with him? "Them's fightin' words, girl." His grin matched hers. "I'll make you tell," he teased. "Can't stand the thought of there being any secrets between us." His grin widened.

The laugh lines around her eyes instantly disappeared. "Ashe...why didn't you tell me that...that you had been married?" There, she'd said it. So much for her good intentions, she thought. But it was as if the words had wings; they had flown from her mouth.

The silence developed an icy edge.

"Damn Alice!" He clamped his lips together in a thin line.

She looked at him without flinching. "Care to tell me about it?"

"No, I don't." His dark face was inscrutable. The expression in his eyes as he looked at her sent a shiver down her spine. "It was a long time ago."

"I see." She stood up. "Come on," she said coolly, "let's join the others."

Ashe said nothing. Furious and hurt, and knowing she had no rational reason to feel either emotion, Raine stood at the wider side of the bar and bent forward to dive.

Instantly, she knew she had made a mistake. In the split-second before her fingertips cut through the silver of the water, she saw the shallowness surrounding the bar, the light streak of danger, and then the bottom was too close to her eyes. She shut them, knowing that she would strike...and then a heavy, velvet blackness closed over her. There was no sandbar, no lake, no sky above...there was nothing at all.

Just the silent, everlasting blackness....

Chapter 10

Ashe turned his head when he saw Raine stand up to dive. He wanted to speak, to tell her to wait, to tell her he was sorry for snapping at her, for marring the beautiful day, but the words had not come in time. It was as if his jaws had locked, bidding him to be silent. He hated discussing his past, his marriage, with anyone, and especially with Raine, because he was afraid she would never understand. Wasn't it true that everyone had cellars inside them—things in their past they tried to bury and ignore? Well, he was no exception. His past was bleak and sordid. With Raine he wanted to start anew. Was that too much to ask?

Raine cut the water cleanly, her fingers like two darts. She would have to make a shallow dive, he thought suddenly. Anyway, the water wasn't too deep around the bar. But surely she had realized that, as good a swimmer as she was. He would wait, he decided, until she surfaced; then he would take off and beat her in. There would be no more "serious" discussions to cloud the day. He had acted like a fool, he knew, but he planned to rectify that and woo her until her bright laughter filled the air.

He saw under the water the moving bit of blue that was Raine's suit. Holding her breath, the rascal, waiting for him to come after her. He stood up, brushing the sand from his trunks. Now, he thought, he would go in and swim in ahead of her. The spot of blue color was almost motionless now, and as he watched he saw Raine's body turn slowly in the water. Her hair lay like an outspread golden fan, and one arm was stretched out, as if reaching.

His heart jumped and then pounded like a sledgehammer. Something was wrong! She was so still!

He cut the water and reached for her. In a moment he was towing her to the bar. Gently, he laid her on it, face turned to the side, pillowed upon one dripping arm. Not Raine, he thought desperately. Oh, no, not Raine!

Kneeling astride her slim body, he began the respiration count, feeling the trembling of his hands as he placed them on the wet fabric of her suit.

"One...two. One...two. One...two."

Dimly he hears shouts from the bank. Alice and Mac and the others apparently knew something was wrong. But he paid no attention, his lips moving as he continued to count. Raine's body was soft beneath his fingers. It must not be too late! She couldn't die! He wouldn't let her. He must make her live, breathe!

The sun was a hot hand upon him as he worked. Perspiration dripped from his face, ran down his arms, and fell between his spread fingers. A soft sound came from between Raine's lips, but he knew that it was only caused by his efforts in trying to force air into her lungs and out...

The ache in his arms was like a twisting knife blade now, but he must not stop! "Count, damn you, count! Count!" he repeated to himself. God, if it hadn't been for him and his bullheadedness, Raine would be living and breathing now, not lying so still beneath his hands.

Mechanically he kept on with the count. The sweat poured from him, its saltiness running into his mouth. A sob caught in his throat. Was it too late? Suddenly, he knew that if Raine didn't live, he didn't want to live either. She had been the turning point in his life. With her, life had gradually begun to be precious to him, to mean something. She could not die. She must not!

Doggedly, he kept up the count, the movement. What if his aching arms failed, he asked himself in panic. What if he could not go on any longer?

The fingers of one hand cramped and he forced them to open in spite of the pain. It seemed years had gone by since he had lifted Raine out of the water.

Then miraculously her flesh moved beneath his hands. He held his breath, still keeping up his monotonous counting. It came again, a gentle rise of the back. She was starting to breathe. He gauged his timing with her shallow breaths, his heart choking him in his anxiety, and kept on. Stronger, her breath came and went and finally, after an eon of time, he took his hands away and watched her breathe on her own.

"Raine! Raine!" The two words must have come from his lips, although he had no recollection of speaking. A low moan came from between Raine's white lips and she opened her eyes, looking into his.

She moved slightly. "Lie still, dear heart," he said. "You're with me. You're all right. Just lie still."

"Ashe?"

"I'm here. Rest now," he whispered, cradling her lax body next to his, his eyes raised to the heavens.

She opened her eyes on a totally strange room. She blinked, trying to remember what had happened, how she'd gotten there. Soft light bloomed behind louvered shutters, and something faint stirred the flimsy drapes. She'd slept, for the first time in a long while, as sweetly and soundly as a newborn baby.

But somewhere along the line she'd also become as weak as a baby. It was all she could do just to raise her head from the smooth pillows. She felt curiously boneless and soft, as if her insides had broken open and shattered into a million pieces.

Suddenly, a muted sound jarred her eyes open. She winced against the pain as she rolled her head toward the noise.

The soft glow of a lamp in the corner of the room relieved the darkness enough so that she could make out the figure sitting close to her bed. Ashe. Blood rushed to her head as she saw his taut, pale face, bringing the horror of what happened back before her eyes in full technicolor.

"Ashe...?" She was disoriented, confused.

"Oh, Raine," Ashe whispered, taking her hand in his and turning the palm next to his lips. "Thank God, you're finally awake!"

"Ashe," she said again, "I hit my head."

"I know, my love, but you're all right now."

She smiled, her eyes dreamy. "How funny for you to say 'my love.' You of all people."

His words poured out as if they were afraid of being stopped. "Forgive me for not starting back to the bank when you did. Forgive me for so many things...for not knowing you were in trouble sooner, for being cross and moody..."

He had bent forward in his earnestness, his features twisted in agony, and her lips were near his own. He yearned to kiss the sweet curve of them, but something held him back. Gut-wrenching fear. Fear of rejection held him motionless.

"Ashe, don't," Raine whispered, seeing the guilt and pain mirrored on his face—so unlike his usual arrogant, confident self. Suddenly, she longed to ease the pain, reassure him. "I'm all right, just a little sore. It was an accident, pure and simple."

He rubbed the back of his neck wearily. "We both know that's not true, but we'll let it go for now."

Raine's eyes looked beyond him, scanning the room. "Where am I?" she asked hesitantly.

Ashe's face gentled. "My ranch."

"Really?"

He smiled indulgently, glad to see the color returning to her wan features. "Yes, really."

"But how..." She paused, licking her parched, dried lips. "I don't understand."

His eyes became dark once again. "It's a long story. We'll talk about it later," he said evasively.

"How long have I been asleep?"

"A long time." He looked down at his watch. "It's after ten o'clock."

She was shocked. "That late?"

"That late. But sleep was the best thing for you. Now, why don't you let me get you something to eat."

She made a face. "I'm not hungry."

"Oh, yes, you are." He grinned confidently. "Especially when you taste the delicious chicken-and-rice soup I've spent hours slaving over just for you." He reached out and tucked a loose tendril of hair behind her ear.

Raine's heart soared at the intimate contact.

He peered down at her for a moment longer and then added, "How about if I bring you a small bowl of it?"

"Oh, all right, if you insist."

"I insist. I'll be back shortly."

Effortlessly, he untangled his long legs and strode to the door. There he paused and turned, flashing her that heart-stopping smile. "Don't go away," he said huskily. "I'll be right back."

It was then that she knew. She loved him. Somewhere between Tyler and Oak Lake, between darkness and dawn, she'd fallen helplessly, hopelessly in love with Ashe Elliot.

She didn't know how long she lay without moving, still as a stone. She could feel the world spinning on its axis. Oh, God, how had it happened? How had it sneaked up on her like a thief in the night? She wasn't prepared for it; nothing in the world could have prepared her for this moment. It was so sudden, so violent, this feeling, this desire flowing through her like warm honey. Love. Dear Lord! How could she love a man she didn't know?

She couldn't answer that question, but she loved him nevertheless. And with that certainty came another: he would destroy her. No, loving him would destroy her. She had fallen in love with a man who was afraid to give himself, a man who was as different from her in personality and values as daylight was to dark.

Everything worked against them—nothing for them. They were from two different worlds. Their careers were incompatible, their life-styles in total conflict, but most of all, they were pursuing different goals in life. In the event she ever married, she wanted security and roots, something that she'd never had, not strife and fear. Ashe wanted none of these. To him life was just one long joyride, until that fateful day when his luck finally ran out.

Oh, she knew he wanted her; it was evident in every move he made, each time he touched her. But in the end, he would take her and use her—she would be just another face in a long line of many—and soon, because she loved him, he would become bored, and then he would cast her aside. And that would be the end of her. Hadn't he told her from the outset that he was immune to falling in love, to marriage? And if she continued with this farce, she would have forsaken everything near and dear to her for a few stolen days and nights in his arms.

Yet, with all this sound reasoning behind her, she was unwilling to give him up.

Ashe didn't realize he was shaking until he tried to dip the hot soup into a bowl. Suddenly, the hot thick liquid splattered over his hand.

"Dammit to hell!" he mumbled, just barely managing to hold on to the bowl and keep it from crashing to the floor.

After having cleaned up the mess, he leaned heavily against the cabinet, jerked a cigarette out of his shirt pocket, and fired it up, noticing that once again his hands were trembling.

He knew what was wrong with him—a delayed reaction to Raine's near drowning. He couldn't let it go, couldn't block the details out of his mind. Even now they rose up to the forefront of his mind and taunted him....

After Raine had spoken to him, her eyes had fluttered downward and she had gone from him again. But her breast had risen with her rhythmic breathing. Then Mac had come from behind him, splashing through the water, his clothes plastered darkly to his body.

"What's happened?" He had gasped out his words.

"Raine made a dive. It was too shallow and she must have hit her head."

"Good God Almighty!" Mac blurted out, kneeling on the sand, his face white.

"She's all right," Ashe said. "She's breathing, but we've got to have warm blankets and stimulants of some kind."

He looked off into the distance. "The Nelson place is the nearest. Get up there quick, Mac, and see if they have a boat or anything that we can get Raine ashore in. We can't take the risk of putting her into the cool water again. Get blankets and some hot coffee in a Thermos bottle if you can. Call Dr. Crane and tell him to meet us at my place."

The journey to his ranch was slow and painful. Ashe winced at every jolt in the road as if it cut his own body, but Raine rode securely in the backseat.

When at last they had turned into the road leading up to his house, the doctor was parked in front.

They sat in the sunny kitchen, Mac, Alice, the children and himself, while the doctor made his examination.

"Will Raine be all right, Uncle Ashe?" Josh asked, his eyes wide with fear that had spread through the quiet room.

He ruffled the boy's head. "Of course," he whispered.

Miraculously, it was so. Dr. Crane came out of the bedroom, a smile on his thin face. "She's all right," he said. "Your worries are over. She can even get up in another hour and stay up. Other than the knock on her head, which may give her a slight headache, she's as good as new." He shook his head. "But she's lucky, I have to tell you, plain lucky."

However, when Raine showed no signs of waking up anytime soon, Mac took his family and left. Ashe pulled a chair up beside her bed and hardly moved, while guilt and remorse played havoc with his heart.

It was the chiming of the grandfather clock in the den that roused him from his deep thoughts. With another scalding oath, he crushed what was left of his cigarette, realizing that Raine was probably wondering what had happened to him.

But when he pushed back the door of her room with the toe of his boot, she had fallen back to sleep. He made no noise on the carpeted floor as he carried the tray ladened with soup, crackers, and a blueberry muffin to the bedside table, where he eased it down.

Suddenly, Raine raised golden-tipped lashes and stared at him, seeing him through different eyes, the eyes of love. It was a strange, terrifying feeling.

"Raine?" His voice was hoarse with panic as he saw the pained expression cross her face. "Are you feeling sick?"

"No." Nervousness made her speak more sharply than she'd intended.

The expression in his eyes was quizzical now. "What is it, then?"

She looked away, conscious of the blush staining her cheeks. She'd been staring at him as though he was a stranger.

"I...was just thinking that I should be getting back to Tyler, to Todd...and Heather."

His face tensed.

She couldn't meet his eyes.

The silence stretched endlessly.

"Will you take me?"

"No," he said simply. "I've decided to kidnap you for a couple of days."

His answer caught her totally off guard. Her flush deepened. "You're not serious, are you?"

"You bet," he replied, before changing the subject abruptly. "Here, taste this." He sat down on the bed and held out the bowl.

She shook her head. "Please. I'm not hungry."

"You need to eat." He watched her carefully. "I'd hate to have to feed you."

Meekly, she took the bowl and reached for the spoon, irritated to find that her hand was unsteady. A delicious, sweet aroma floated through the air. She took a tentative sip; it tasted good, mouth-watering good.

"Thank you," she said, not leaving a drop. "I'm beginning to feel like my old self."

"Good." He took the bowl from her and set it on the tray. "Now...all we have to do is decide what we're going to do tomorrow."

Her mind raced desperately. "I really should insist that you take me back."

He was watching her, his face unreadable.

"Would it make any difference if I told you I wanted you to stay, that I want to take care of you, see the fatigue leave your eyes, the color return to your cheeks?" His voice was low, mesmerizing.

For several seconds she fought a silent battle with herself. "What about Todd?"

"Todd's doing fine, and so is Heather. I called to make sure, knowing you'd be worried, and I told Heather you wouldn't be back for a couple of days."

"You didn't tell her about the accident, did you?"

"No, of course not." he said softly, his eyes boring into hers. "I told her you were going to take a couple of days of R and R."

"What...what did Heather say..." Her sentence faded out. She was suddenly embarrassed.

Ashe's eyes were veiled with silent laughter. "She told us to have a good time."

Raine felt vaguely uneasy, yet excited, as if everything was speeding up and she was powerless to slow it down. "After all the trouble I've caused you, ruining the barbecue, alarming your friends, are you sure you want to be saddled with me any longer?"

"Shh! Don't ever let me hear you talk like that again." His voice was unsteady. "What's a barbecue compared to your life?"

"And I haven't said thank you for saving mine, either." She leaned back against the pillow. It was nice to let someone take care of her for a change. She hadn't realized it, but she'd grown tired, bone-achingly tired, of coping on her own. And even though she knew she was still chasing a rainbow she could never capture, she would treasure these hours, spend each moment as a miser, knowing it would be her last.

He smiled and rose to his feet.

She noticed again the elegant grace of his movements, never predictable, but as much a part of him as his hair or his skin.

"It was rough going there for a while. I thought you'd never open your eyes." He had thought it best not to mention the artificial respiration and the doctor, and Mac had agreed with him. Better that Raine didn't know how close she had come to the death that had been reaching for her.

Now, as he turned back to her, a painful silence filled the room.

He moved as though in slow motion toward the bed, hating to leave her. His face was shadowed in the dim light. He leaned down and grazed a cheek with his finger. "I need to go, to let you sleep off those good groceries."

She nodded, her throat too full to speak, wanting more of his hands, refusing to admit it. "Good night, Ashe."

"Good night, Raine." He lingered another moment, wanting her, knowing she wanted him. Not yet, he cautioned. We have time. "I'll show you the ranch tomorrow and we'll have a picnic."

She smiled, watching him walk out the door and close it softly behind him.

Raine arose in aching discomfort. But she was lucky, she thought, to be able to rise at all. If it hadn't been for Ashe—

the image of his dark face came to her as a gift. Forgotten was the disagreement over her intrusion into his past. She remembered only the feel of his gentle hands, the concern in his face, his voice.

But in spite of the stiffness, she was eager for the day ahead. Totally ignoring any thoughts to the contrary, she very gingerly rolled out of bed and, grabbing her tote bag, made her way to the bathroom.

After a hot shower, she dressed very slowly, slipping into her jeans and top, which were draped neatly over the back of a chair. Once she had laced up her sneakers, she put on her makeup and brushed her hair, sweeping it up and securing it with a barrette.

Thinking that she would be the only one up at six o'clock in the morning, she wandered down the hall and into the den, noticing the strong smell of bacon in the air. To her surprise Ashe was sitting out on the deck, sipping on a cup of coffee. She walked to the French doors and opened them, feeling the cool breeze fan her face.

"Good morning," he said, getting up and pulling out a chair for her. "How do you feel?"

"Fine," she said lightly. "But I'll admit, I couldn't run a mile."

His eyes on her were warm and compelling as he sat back down across from her. "Next time you decide to be a mermaid and scare me to death, I'll beat you."

She laughed, feeling the old familiar fluttery sensation in her stomach when he looked at her like that, making her more aware of how much she had wanted him last night.

"I'll be good, I promise," she said at last. "But the doctor said I was fine, and you know it."

His voice was easier. "Well, I just want to make sure you're up to our picnic." Without asking, he poured her a cup of coffee out of the pot sitting on a wicker tea cart to his left.

"When do we get started?" she asked, taking the coffee with a thankful nod.

Her childlike eagerness brought an indulgent smile to his lips. "Well, as soon as we have breakfast and I pack us a lunch."

"Count me out for breakfast," she said. "I'm still full from that delicious soup you made me eat."

"Are you sure?" he asked, his eyes clinging to hers. She had never looked lovelier, he thought. Even the bruised shadows under her eyes weren't a distraction. Her hair piled high on her head lent a patrician quality to her, emphasizing her seeming fragility. He wanted to make love to her until their bodies cried out to stop.

Suddenly, the tension in the room became explosive.

Raine felt as though her heart had been given an electric charge. But she couldn't move, or speak.

Ashe cleared his throat, shattering the moment. "I'd best get to the food before it gets cold," he said, thick-throated.

Trying to gather her wits about her, Raine took in her surroundings. The shapes and colors of the glorious summer morning were indisputable as the sun beamed down from the heavens, bathing everything in its magical glow. There were birds singing in the trees, wild flowers scattered about, flaunting their splendid colors, and in the distance she could see the horses roaming the corrals, and a hangar with a small aircraft was visible in the gleaming sunlight.

Suddenly, her excitement paled as it dawned upon her once again that she was doing herself a grave injustice by staying here, pretending that everything was fine, that just because she loved him things would work out. *Fool! Nothing has changed. He'll always belong to the great beyond, never to you.*

"Well, what do you think?" Ashe asked, lowering himself back down into the chair, and placing a steaming plate of hot food on the table.

Raine shook her head and blinked, trying to clear it. "I think it's beautiful," she said, watching him eat.

He lowered his fork and looked beyond her with lazy, admiring eyes. "I always feel I've just stepped into paradise whenever I come here."

"But not enough to give it up?" she asked impulsively.

He whipped around, the muscle beside his eye twitching in the smooth mask of his face. "Give up what?"

How dare you play dumb with me! she longed to scream. But she pushed the words aside as if they burned her, determined that two could play this game, and said instead, "Flying."

Imperceptibly, Ashe's face changed as if a thin cloud had passed over the sun. He was silent as he lit a cigarette and drew on it, staring at her intently through the pale blue haze. "I can't," he said simply.

She shivered at the knife-edged words spoken in his pleasant voice. "Why?" she asked, unable to control her tongue.

His eyes sparred with hers for several seconds. Then he looked away. "You already know the answer to that," he said miserably, knowing that he was slowly but surely severing the thin thread that held them together.

"Please, tell me again."

"It's what I am," he said with forced patience.

She hammered on. "But you could change that. You could expand the ranch, go into it full-time."

"I don't want to. It's that simple. I'm not a rancher. I'm a pilot. There's nothing else I want to do."

She touched his hand. "Even when it could get you killed?" Why was she punishing herself this way, she wondered miserably. Especially now? Oh, God, especially now.

"That goes with the territory." What he'd said came out flippant, brutal, and the moment he said it he was sorry. But it was too late; the damage had been done.

His words, spoken almost in a monotone, were a thin blade cutting through the silence, sliding coldly into Raine. Her lower lip began to tremble.

With a deep groan, Ashe reached for her hand and laced his fingers with hers, forcing her to meet his gaze. "I'm sorry," he whispered. "I didn't mean for it to come out like that. It's just that I've fought this same battle so many times..."

Raine withdrew her hand and pushed a wisp of hair out of her face. "With your...wife."

He tensed. "Yes. Nothing I did pleased her."

If it had been possible, Raine would have turned a shade paler. "I'm sorry, too," she whispered.

"Oh, Raine," he said brokenly, reaching for her hand again, "you don't ever have to be sorry for anything. Believe me, I understand why you feel the way you do, but I..." He stopped and jumped up. "Oh, hell, I just can't explain. I..." Again he faltered.

Suddenly, Raine knew she had to try to understand what made this man tick, what impelled him, what drove him toward his own self-destruction. By doing so, maybe she could release some of the terror that flowed through her veins like poison.

"You want to do the best, don't you?" she asked softly. "You want to drive yourself always to the maximum performance." She was groping and it showed.

But he took the olive branch, and though his expression was guarded, his voice was without rancor. "There will always be someone better than me."

"But you're twice as knowledgeable about airplanes," she responded, forcing the words through her lips.

Ashe hesitated, both shocked and thrilled that she was making an effort to understand him. He knew what it must be costing her both mentally and physically to do so and he had to make an effort to meet her halfway.

"Specifications, yes. But what makes one fly and another falter, no."

"And that's where the supreme challenge comes in."

"It's a mystery and a challenge," he said, warming to the subject. "At the farthest edges when you're up there with a plane that's never really been tested, it is a mystery. And when I sit in that cockpit, it's almost as though I don't fly the plane, but fly myself instead."

She sat in silence, mulling over his words, wanting desperately to say she understood. But she couldn't, not now, maybe not ever. But at least she had overcome one major hurdle; she had listened.

"Raine." His eyes were on her, warm and compelling.

She threw her head back, her skin red-gold in the brightness, the cool air kissing her throat. She heard Ashe suck in his breath and at the same moment she felt weak with the heavy pull of wanting him.

"Yes," she whispered.

"I was just thinking that instead of talking I'd much rather take you to the most beautiful spot on earth and make love to you."

A slow smile lit her face. "Oh, Ashe...I thought you'd never ask."

They walked for an hour through the partially cleared forest that was a part of Ashe's property. Her hand was clasped tightly within his, sharing with him the joy of their isolation. They enjoyed the slowness of the hike, dreams dancing in their heads of what would happen later. They rarely spoke, except when Ashe inquired if she was getting tired. Each time she shook her head negatively, and they continued to move through the silence, broken only by the chirping music of the birds.

Just as the sun began to make its presence known with a vengeance, Ashe said, "I don't know about you, but I'm famished. Thank, God, it's only a few more yards to go."

"Your secret spot must really be something."

He grinned. "It is."

Shortly, Ashe came to a stop. "There!" he exclaimed.

Raine's eyes widened as she took in a grassy area protected on three sides by a greater thickness of trees and underbrush. Nearby, a creek hummed over rocks and spilled into a clear pool before narrowing again and winding out of sight through the trees.

"Remind you of anything?" Ashe asked.

Raine grinned mischievously. "The old swimming hole."

He laughed and raised his eyebrows. "Well?"

"I think we ought to try it."

He laughed again. "You're something." Dropping his duffel bag on the soft grass, he seemed not to notice the flush on her face and the sparkle in her eyes. "Now? Before we eat?"

Raine's eyes gleamed. "I don't see why not. After all, we didn't finish what we started yesterday."

"Who am I to argue? Ladies first."

Laughing, she disappeared behind a cluster of bushes. As soon as she pulled off her top and jeans and felt the sun burning on her bare skin, she was swept with a dizzying surge of desire and anticipation, and leaned against the tree to steady herself. *I didn't know,* she thought. *I didn't know love could be like this.* But deep in the thicket, cut off from the world, protected by the sunlight, she knew that all their days together had led to this one, and that Ashe knew it, too.

Her light-headedness passed. Raine left her clothes on a low-hanging limb and, in silk panties and bra, slipped from the cluster of trees to the grassy surface surrounding the pool.

She did not see Ashe, but rather than give herself time to think twice, she took a tentative step into the clear water. She gasped in shock at the chilling cold. And after wading waist-high, she knew she had had enough. "No way," she gasped aloud, every muscle cringing into a tight defensive knot. Grasping a low-hanging branch, she pulled herself out of the water and, standing in the sun, turned to look for Ashe.

Across the pool, the water broke into a long wake. Raine heard him shout as the cold struck him, and she watched him swim toward her with powerful strokes, bursting through the water to grab the same branch she had used.

"I'll race you back!" he panted.

"Forget it!" she said, her teeth chattering.

"You got that right!"

They both laughed through numb lips as Ashe staggered from the water. "Do we have any towels?"

Raine shook her head. "I think that's something we forgot."

"Damn! Stay put, I'll see what I can find."

She relaxed against a warm rock. The hot sun dried her almost instantly, but her skin was still covered with goose bumps as she stared apprehensively at the deceptive, sun-sparkled pool.

"One small towel," Ashe said, returning. "Wrapped around the bottle of wine. Not the best, but beggars can't be choosers." He looked down at her. His muscles quivered, but he stood still, gazing at her, unable to move or think. The sight of her never failed to fill him with need, with a desperate desire to put his hands on her, to know that she was real and accessible to him.

"God," he murmured in a strangled tone. "You're lovely."

Raine's thoughts stirred as she looked at him. Brushing a wispy strand of hair from her eyes, she made a move to stand up.

"No," Ashe whispered, falling to his knees. He began to dry her arms with the towel.

"The sun..." Raine murmured.

"Let me." Taking the towel, he gently stroked her neck and shoulders. Her skin began to tingle everywhere he touched. Suddenly, from Ashe's wet head, a drop of water fell like a sliver of ice on her breast and she flinched.

There was a wicked gleam in his eyes. "Sorry..." Then thrusting the towel aside, he bent over and put his tongue to the spot on her breast. Something inside Raine twisted wildly and the twisting continued as the sunlight engulfed them, as if it had replaced the blood in their veins.

"Raine," Ashe murmured. "My sweet, sweet Raine." He unhooked her bra and slipped her panties down her slender legs while Raine leisurely removed his white briefs.

Their bed was the fragrant grass. She turned to him and he came into her arms, cool from the breeze nipping at their damp skin. Pressing against him, she felt the tautness and strength of him as Ashe brought his open mouth down to hers. The kiss blossomed, like the sweet-smelling honeysuckle vines around them, feeding their desire.

Raine's arms kept Ashe close. "This was on my mind," she whispered, her lips against his, "before I went into the water. I wanted you..."

"And I wanted you..." he muttered hoarsely.

And then, seeking the delicate folds of her softness, he felt her legs part for him and he thrust into her, into the darkness of her body, and he glided with the sunlight through the heavens while Raine cried his name in the magic summer air....

Chapter 11

Legs wrapped tightly together, toes touching, they smiled at each other. It had to break. They were going to have to speak, yet neither wanted to break the spell. Raine was content to lie quietly, her head on his shoulder, lips meeting in tiny, sipping kisses.

Ashe moved his palm slowly up the curve of her hip to her breasts. Ah, her breasts. They delighted him. He could, with his mouth and hands, tease her flattened nipples erect, make then change color and shape. They were softer than his dreams. He rested his cheeks against them, breathing slowly, deeply, while his body absorbed her sweetness.

Raine caressed his back, his shoulders and muscled arms, and stopped with her fingertips on the dark hair of his chest. Her hands told him things words never could in a dialogue of shifting messages, changing rhythms. She raised herself on one elbow, looking down into his eyes. "I feel so greedy," she whispered.

"No, my darling," he said, and smiled at her, passion burning through his veins. "Alive, happy, part of me..."

He lowered his mouth to hers, kissing her, drinking in the sweet vision before him. She closed her eyes, flattened her hands, and sent them on a luxurious tour of all the parts of his body she could reach.

"Oh, God, Raine, I love you," he said, on each nipple, taking them lightly into his mouth.

Raine's arms tightened around him as she was filled with a joy that knew no bounds, warming her after she had been so cold. The joy stayed with her as Ashe's mouth moved from her breasts to her stomach.

"You taste like ripe peaches," he murmured, his mouth on her soft skin. "And wild flowers and pine trees."

His eyes moved over her, his hands smoothing, stroking, a part of her, surrounding her, and she felt herself pressed against the moist earth, open to his mouth, his tongue, as they whispered against her.

His touch, soft, insistent, leaped through Raine's body; a low groan escaped her mouth as she underwent a paroxysm of physical joy. A wild cry rippled from her throat—*I love you, part of me*—the feeling so exquisite, so piercing. Her throat emitted sad, softer sounds, her body arching, feeling drunk, impossibly high, receiving the sense of his flesh through his mouth and fingertips. And then suddenly the whole world opened before her in a blaze of light, then slowly faded away.

They lay together, and kissed. The sun sparkled bravely on their bodies as they whispered aloud thoughts of dressing, eating, walking back—but instead their eyes melted together, letting their bodies awaken in a long embrace.

His arms enfolded her so tightly her breasts were crushed against his chest, her face buried in the curve of his neck and shoulder. Stirring, she showered his neck and chest with warm, moist kisses. "Your skin feels so good," she murmured. "Hard and warm—and I can feel your heartbeat here—" She kissed the hollow at the base of his throat and then his mouth, open and as demanding as hers. She smiled at him, his lips forming her name.

"...I want you. I want you, please," he moaned. His hands slid over her hips and Raine shifted slightly. He looked again at her face, slipping his hands beneath her, raising her up, and then in slow motion buried himself inside her. The sharing of the day became the sharing of their bodies until Ashe heard her cry out and, still cocooned in their throbbing warmth, he let himself go, his cry meeting hers.

They lay still, their lips touching, until Ashe whispered contentedly, "We have to talk."

"Mmm..."

Ashe raised himself on one elbow and looked at her. "What kind of answer is that?"

Raine laughed softly and stretched. "I was just thinking of all the things I want to talk about. But not now. Tomorrow."

"Tomorrow we'll be going back...back to civilization."

"Oh." She wanted to forget.

"Raine. Tell me you love me."

She touched his lips with her fingers while trying to control her racing heart. "I'm...afraid to. It even frightens me to think it. I was so settled; I never thought of myself as falling in love. It's as if, when I'm with you, when I think about you, I become someone else. I move further away from the person I was and from my obligations. And I get scared: who am I now, and what do I want and how can I dream of you and long for you and still feel the way I do about your flying, and when I feel so bound to my obligations, to Todd and my work?

That was the closest she had come to talking about the forces that drove their lives in the "real world." "And," she added, trying to speak lightly, "I haven't loved...I mean, fallen in love...ever. I've never known what it's like to give of myself to another person." She paused. "I like it, but it's confusing. It's all so new—and so perfect. Now."

Ashe leaned over her. "Thank you." He kissed her slowly, lingeringly. "As long as it's true, the words can wait."

Raine ran her fingers down his throat, to his chest. "If we can just be together..."

"One day at a time, my darling," he whispered. "One day at a time."

The day came to an end all too soon. Late afternoon found them strolling, hand in hand, toward the house. The sky, once a flaming crimson, orange, and amber, was fading to a violet, smokey gray. They had snacked and loved away the afternoon, though not necessarily in that order.

Relaxed, sated, filled with a soft, glowing happiness, Raine refused to think about the future, knowing that nothing had been settled, merely postponed. She still had her own fears to overcome, but at the moment nothing was important except Ashe and what they had shared. Tomorrow was filled with promise, and even though no commitments had been made, she knew where there was love, there was hope. And with that she would have to be content. For now...

They saw her at the exact same moment. She was standing on the edge of the deck, a hand raised to her forehead.

Raine felt Ashe stiffen beside her, his grip on her hand tightened. His steps faltered, then once again speeded up. Turning, she peered up at him while trying to match his uneven gait. "Ashe, who is that?"

"It's Hannah, my housekeeper."

"Do you think something's wrong?"

Ashe's lips were turned down at the corners. "More than likely; I left a note when I made our picnic lunch, telling her where I'd be."

Todd? Heather? Had something happened to them? Raine began to conjure up all sorts of terrible things in her mind, panic shadowing her every step.

"Relax," Ashe said softly, reading her mind. "It's probably nothing, just my office calling about some little nit-picking something. But Hannah is easily intimidated."

It was then that Hannah saw them and stepped off the deck.

"Come on," Ashe demanded, "let's meet her halfway."

"Thank God, Mr. Ashe," an out-of-breath Hannah said, her ample breasts heaving as she grabbed Ashe's outstretched hand. "I..."

"Calm down, Hannah," Ashe said, "and tell me what's wrong." His voice held urgency, yet was calm.

Tears were streaming down her lined face. "Oh, Mr. Ashe," she whimpered, "something terrible's happened." She turned pleading eyes toward Raine as though to say *help me*. But Raine wasn't capable of helping; her heart was lodged in her throat and all she could do was stare wild-eyed at the housekeeper.

"Dammit, it, Hannah!"

"It's...it's Mr. McAdams."

"For chrissakes, what about Mac?" Ashe had a grip on her upper arm and was prepared to shake her if necessary.

"He's...there's been an accident..."

"And?"

"He's dead, Mr. Ashe!" she cried. "He's dead!"

Rain.

The liquid fell from the sky in a steady drizzle. But Raine

was oblivious to it all, as were the others gathered at the graveside service for Mickey McAdams. Her thoughts were centered on Ashe.

The moment Hannah had delivered the heartbreaking news, the following hours had become a living nightmare. Ashe had been inconsolable. They had left immediately, driving through the twilight to the McAdamses' ranch. Ashe had sat behind the wheel as if he was carved in stone. Nothing about him resembled the warm, charismatic, loving Ashe of the afternoon.

Hannah had been unable to give them any details, other than the fact that Mac's plane had crashed in Mexico and that he'd been killed instantly.

Raine had managed somehow to put her own icy fears aside. She had to be strong for Ashe, even though the tears she had seen trickle down his face had nearly been her undoing.

When they had reached the house and Alice had run into Ashe's arms, once again Raine felt herself slowly dismantling on the inside, reliving in her mind the time when the news had come about her father—her staring at the front door as if she no longer owned it or controlled it—and outside the door a man stood, informing her with her mother, drunk, listening in the wings, that her father's body had been "burned beyond recognition." And on the heels of that thought had come another: the news of Todd's crash and his near brush with death.

Then suddenly when she had thought she couldn't handle the pain, she had only to take one look at Ashe's white face to know that she had no choice. She couldn't add to his burden by falling apart now.

Since that night, when he had brought her home in the wee hours of the morning, she had not laid eyes on him until now. But she knew his obligations had rested with Alice and the children and she understood. She loved him more because of it.

Suddenly, the rain became heavier, drawing her attention back to the solemn words of the preacher. She raised her head, her tears mingling with the rain. Man and heaven wept...

How anguished Ashe looked, she thought as he paid his last tribute to his lifelong friend.

His suit was dark like his hair. The only relief to the darkness was the stark white collar of his shirt. He looked incredibly, extravagantly, totally magnificent: the width of his shoulders, the tapered cut of his jacket, the thighs beneath his slacks hard and long. It was all she could do to stay put. She longed to go to him, to hold him close and comfort him.

But she knew that was impossible. He was still holding himself aloof from her, had made no effort to seek her out. Every taut line of his body and tense angle of his face told her this. She kept her distance and held her silence, knowing that when he was free, he would come to her.

And she would be waiting.

She wandered aimlessly around Todd's apartment. She could not seem to settle down and she knew why. Instead of walking the floor like a caged animal, she should be on her way to Dallas. Several days ago when she'd talked to Val, Val had told her how badly she was needed. She knew she had stayed away about as long as she could. Val had brought her up to date on what was happening with the boutique. The shelves and racks were soon to be installed, she'd said, and the merchandise was beginning to arrive. She had to return soon if she intended to open her boutique on time. And there was still the unanswered question of extra financing...

But none of this seemed to matter. Only Ashe mattered. Her thoughts and heart were filled with nothing but him. Where was all this going to lead, she asked herself. An affair? Was that what she wanted? At this point, she honestly didn't know. It was all too new, this feeling of being a part of another human being.

And the loneliness. She felt it now more acutely than ever before. She wished now she had let Todd and Heather talk her into staying longer at the hospital, even though Todd had bombarded her with questions concerning her relationship with Ashe the minute she had come back from the funeral.

As she forced herself to sit down on the couch with a cup of coffee, she recalled every word of their conversation....

"Hey, Sis," he'd said, "what's this I hear about you cavorting with the enemy?" Even though he'd smiled, his eyes were serious. She'd known ever since she'd returned from Ashe's ranch that he'd been dying to ask her about him, but knowing how upset she'd been over Mac's death, he'd refrained from saying anything.

A guilty flush had stained her cheeks. "I've been wanting to tell you, but..."

"Believe me, I understand," Todd replied gently. "These things just happen and we have no control over them."

Raine's eyes widened. This couldn't be her brother talking, not the Todd she had always known who thought only of himself, never of her.

"Todd, it just happened," she whispered, including both her brother and Heather in her confession. "And even though I'm uncertain about our future, I can't seem to let him go."

"But how you're going to handle his flying is what I'd like to know. Since Dad died we both know you're hung up—"

"I...know," she whispered. "That's why I'm not thinking beyond today."

"Well, in my book Ashe is one helluva guy, and I'm certain it's not him who's the pain in my ass, but Jackson. Apparently the verdict is still out, or Jackson would've been on me like a dog on a june bug."

In spite of the seriousness of the situation, Raine couldn't suppress her smile. And neither could Heather. Her girlish laughter rang out from the corner of the room where she sat looking at a baby-care book.

But then another twinge of guilt shot through Raine. "Ashe hadn't mentioned the report and I haven't asked him," she confessed. "I will, though," she added quickly, "as soon as I get the chance. No matter what you think, I'm not abandoning you, or the fight to get your name cleared. But I'd be a fool not to admit that things have become a bit more complicated than I'd anticipated."

"Don't worry about it, Sis," Todd said sincerely, beckoning for Heather to come to the bed. "Of course, I want my name cleared, but I have no intention of flying ever again."

"Oh, Todd," Raine cried, her heart suddenly bursting with joy. "I'm so glad." If only Ashe would say those magic words to her...

Todd grinned. "Somehow I knew you'd approve."

"Oh, I approve, all right, but only if that's what you really want. I know what flying means to you."

"Not anymore," Todd said with confidence, reaching for Heather's hand. "Heather and the baby have taken first place in my life now."

Raine smiled through her tears. "Oh, Todd, that's wonderful news."

"But what about you?" he asked. "I know you're needed in Dallas. You've neglected your business for so long now. Of course, I blame—"

"Don't," Raine cut in. "No apologies. I did what I had to do, because I love you. And just remember, I still intend to help you."

Suddenly, Todd's eyes lost their brightness and his lips pressed firmly together. "I hate like hell to have to depend on you for money."

"Todd—"

"No, Sis, please don't interrupt. As I was saying, I don't know how long it's going to be before I can get another job, and with the baby coming and all..." He paused. "Dr. Anders told me this morning that I'd have to have months of physical therapy on this damned leg. I'll practically have to learn to walk all over again." He paused again, changing his position on the bed. "And if the board rules against me, I'm not sure how long Ashe will carry me on the company's insurance."

Raine moved closer to the bed, her chin jutting out with determination. "As I've already told you, but obviously you weren't listening, brother dear, I intend to see that neither of you wants for a thing. Now, please put that worry out of your mind, all right?"

A grin relieved his tense features. "All right, I surrender. You always were too bossy for your own good. However, I do intend to pay you back, someday, somehow."

A sharp pain in her leg suddenly jolted Raine back to the present. Drat! Her foot had gone to sleep. With a grimace she stood up and tried to walk. Needing to refresh her cup of coffee, she forced herself to hobble toward the kitchen. She had just reached the cabinet and set her cup down when the doorbell rang.

Ashe. Instinct told her it was Ashe. Excitement shot through her like quicksilver. *I knew he'd come,* her heart sang. Even though they had been apart only a few days, it seemed like an eternity.

On legs that still weren't steady, she crossed to the door and yanked it open. Her eyes did not miss a single thing about him. For an endless moment, she concentrated on his drawn, haggard face. He looked as though he hadn't slept in weeks instead of days. His eyes were sunk back in his head and there were dark circles under his eyes.

They stared in silence.

"Am I welcome?" Ashe asked, his voice subdued.

It made her ache inside to look at him. "Oh, Ashe," she whispered, "how could you doubt it?"

His voice was harsh with emotion. "Well, I certainly wouldn't have blamed you if you'd slammed the door in my face."

She stepped back. "Please, come in."

Lines of worry ruled his forehead as he crossed to the middle of the room and turned toward her. "I don't deserve you, that's for sure," he said heavily. "Oh, God, how I've wanted you with me, but I was afraid..." He paused, as if weighing his next words carefully. "I was afraid—*selfish* is a better word—to put you through the pain again. Oh, hell, what I'm trying to say is that something snapped within me, and for a while I couldn't seem to deal with it." His voice cracked. "You see, I loved Mac..."

She sailed into his arms like a warm south wind, sweet-smelling and soft, her smooth cheek pressed against his. "Oh, Ashe. I'm sorry, so sorry."

He cradled her in his arms. "I know, I know," he whispered, unconscious of anything at all but the woman he held with such fierce, awesome love. After those nights and days and hours and minutes and seconds without her, he felt he had come home. Her gentle voice wrapped around him and brought the pieces back together again. Ashe buried his face deep in the silk curtain of her hair and abandoned himself to heaven.

"And I understand, really I do," she said, clinging to him with all her might. Time had no meaning; there was nothing but this lovely closeness. Then after a moment, she pulled back. "How's Alice?"

The haunted look came back to his eyes. "Better, thank God, but for a while there I wasn't too sure she was going to make it."

Wordlessly, she reached up and touched his face, wishing she could absorb his pain.

For the longest time they stood in silence, holding the look as each sought an end to the torment. Then he drew her close again and whispered, "My darling, my darling," his fingers slowly threading through her hair to bring her lips to his. The kiss went on and on.

"Oh Ashe, I missed you so much," Raine said possessively.

This time it was Ashe who suddenly pulled away, gulping for air.

"Ashe?"

"Raine, I want you so much," he said thickly. "I've about reached the point of no return."

She acted impulsively. Her hand dipped down and surrounded the steely hardness, covered only by the thin material of his slacks. She felt him throb against the palm of her hand.

"Oh, God, Raine, oh, God," he groaned urgently, his eyes brilliant as they gazed down at her.

Horrified at her boldness, Raine felt her face turn fire-engine red.

Suddenly, his eyes took on a teasing gleam. "You're priceless, you know that," he said with a belly laugh.

Her lashes veiled her eyes, unable to meet his gaze.

"Come here," he demanded huskily, the teasing gone from his voice. It had dropped to a raw hoarseness. "God, how I've ached to hold you like this."

She melted into him. Contentment and love flowed through her, making her feel dizzy and light-headed.

"And I ached for you."

His hold tightened. Then suddenly he swept her up and carried her toward the bedroom in a blur of impatience. Ashe let her slowly slide down his body until her feet touched the carpet, reveling in the curves brushing the hardened planes of his belly and thighs.

Then, with feverish fingers, they undressed one another. Naked, they fell to the bed, touching everywhere.

"I want you to love me. I want you inside me, Ashe," she begged.

"Mine," he whispered fervently. "Forever mine."

At first he held back, but she drew him to her, and he gave more as she loved him with her hips and her buttocks, until he gave himself completely.

She felt all of him as he filled her totally. Her fingers walked up his spine as she wrapped her legs around him.

Ashe was thrusting up in mindless delight, very fast.

And she moved with him, her nails digging into his shoulders, into the skin of his powerful buttocks. He exploded into her with such force that no part of her was left untouched.

And in response to her cry, he felt himself hang on the edge of his own blazing rapture and then together their coiling excitement crested and they began the ecstatic plunge downward, free and trembling, gradually coming to earth.

"Ashe," she said drowsily, "I love you."

He cradled her in his arm, their faces together, and they slept.

That night of love set the precedent for the next several days. Raine thought she had never been so happy. Tucked away in the corner of her heart were her insecurities, her fears, her questions. But she refused to give in to those thoughts or let them detract from her coveted time with Ashe. *Remember, Raine, relish the moment!*

She did just that. During the day while Ashe was at the plant, she spent time at the hospital with Todd, who was now learning to get around with a walker. And twice she took Heather shopping to buy necessary items for the baby. Another day she spent in Dallas, frantically trying to make up for all the time she had been away.

But the nights belonged to Ashe. She was learning the true meaning of the word magic; the love beating within her became inseparable from the beating of his heart. And Ashe found it impossible to get through a day without talking to her on the telephone or sending her a flower, a note, anything to keep the fragile lines of communication open between them.

Today was no exception to the rule. It was Saturday and they had driven to his ranch and had just finished a leisurely dinner and were lying in bed. They had eaten on the deck and made love in the hammock beneath the stars and then, in the white light of the full moon, slipped naked into the Jacuzzi, letting the gush of hot water massage their muscles until they were weak. Then after climbing out, they had run laughing through the warm night air to Ashe's bed.

"I'm worthless, absolutely worthless," Raine said languidly, her head on his shoulder. She didn't want to move. "I don't think I could make a decision now even if my life depended on it." She laughed softly. "I have no energy left."

"Mmm, that's too bad," Ashe murmured, "because I was about to ask you to make one."

Her lethargy vanished. "Oh? And what is that?"

"I want you to promise me something."

"Anything," she said, her voice purring with contentment.

He kissed her forehead tenderly. "Promise me you'll come to the airstrip the day after tomorrow and watch me take Black Cobra up for it's first trial run. Next to having met and fallen in love with you, this will be the biggest moment of my life. It's the culmination of my years of hard work and sacrifice."

Raine lay still. The old crippling fear was squeezing her heart. *No!* she cried silently. *I can't stand the thought of him flying that plane. Not now! Oh, God, not now. Not when everything's so perfect.*

The panic-stricken look mirrored on her face stabbed at Ashe's heart. He silently cursed his lack of finesse in telling her, but, dammit, he'd had to do it. And there was no easy way. He wanted her to share his life, every part of it. Yet she was so against his flying. He had vowed to help her overcome her fears with loving tenderness, and if he failed...well, he wouldn't think about that now; the thought was too painful. For right now, he had to figure out a way to unlock that frozen look that was pinching her lovely features.

"Raine."

Suddenly, she faced him, tears edging her lashes. "Ashe, please, I can't stand it or the thought of anything happening to you."

He reached out, eased his hand through the silky strands of her hair and buried her face into his chest, halting her flow of words. "Shh! Don't even talk like that, don't even think it. Believe me, I know how you feel and I also know we have a lot to talk about, but please just think about it. You don't have to give me an answer now. But I want you there to share my glory with me; it won't mean as much without you."

"Oh, God, Ashe, I don't know," she cried. "You don't realize what you're asking. You fly and I wait, and all I ask is that you come back—and I can't even count on that." The fear coming out of her voice burned his ear.

"Nothing is going to happen to me."

Her face was drawn and a vein in her neck was taut as she pulled away. "I don't know," she whispered, "I honestly don't know. I need time alone to think."

He refused to give up. "All right," he said, "but when you're thinking, know that I have no choice. The choice was made a long time ago. I have a job to do and I'll do it."

"And I know I can't stop you."

"No, you can't." His voice had not changed, but the muscles in his neck were quivering. "But no matter what you decide, I'll never stop loving you."

There was a long, stifling silence.

At last, Ashe said softly, "Let's get dressed and I'll take you home."

Later, alone in Todd's apartment, Raine stood staring out the window into the silent darkness, unable to sleep, her mind and heart in a turmoil. Her "high" had suddenly come to an end. *You should have known. Life is no fairy tale.* But she had been looking at it through a pair of blinders, seeing only what she wanted to see, accepting the fragile truce between them as though it was built on stone instead of sand. A few words, one breath of reality, and it had simply crumbled away.

So what now? Was she prepared to let him go? *No,* her heart cried. Of that she was sure. The thought of giving him up, never feeling his warm lips on hers, his hands on her body, made her blood run cold. She wanted to spend the rest of her life with him. Even though he hadn't mentioned marriage, she knew it was only a matter of time until he did.

And because she couldn't let him go, she was being forced to make a decision she didn't want to make. But she had no choice, did she? She knew that if she and Ashe were to have a future, she had to try, God help her, she had to try.

Could she do it? Could she actually watch her beloved place his life in danger? She honestly did not know.

Chapter 12

Even as she parked the car on the grounds of the Elliot Aircraft Corporation, Raine could not believe she was actually going to watch Ashe test the high-tech plane.

Oh, the whole world knew about it, heralded it as a major breakthrough in weapons technology. The papers had been crammed full of it and the televisions had buzzed, though the air force had vehemently tried to play it down, afraid the publicity would raise more questions about the United States being a warmonger nation. But there had been a leak and the media had gotten wind of it and had a field day reporting it.

However, Raine was quick to notice security was airtight. No snoopy reporters or television cameras were in evidence. But she'd had no trouble. Obviously, in the hope that she would come, Ashe had notified security and she was cleared immediately.

The sun was warm on her skin as she followed the instructions given by one of the security men at the gate and cautiously made her way toward the main office building. She had no idea where the testing strip was or even if she would be allowed there. She hoped not, she told herself grimly. If she had to watch, she'd rather it be from an observation tower or through a monitor, as her knees were already knocking together and her mouth was so dry she couldn't swallow.

She had not seen Ashe or talked with him since he had left her three days ago. She knew why he had stayed away, but she missed him nevertheless. He was forcing her to make the decision on her own. And it had not been easy. At times, she'd thought she would lose her mind. She had taken long drives, and had walked for miles, and she'd even sought Todd's advice, which, of course, he hadn't given. But in the end, as Ashe had said, it had to be her decision.

More often than not, she'd labeled herself crazy for putting herself through this kind of agony. No matter how much reassurance Ashe had given her, she still hated the danger, the waiting, the uncertainty of his fate when he strapped himself inside a plane.

So she'd asked herself why she didn't just pack her bags and go home, back to her own "little world." There she had been happy; she had been content.

And then she'd met Ashe, who taught her a whole new language, the language of love. Nothing—absolutely nothing—could take the place of being in love. It was wonderful! It was unique! And it was truly hers for the first time in her life.

Under no circumstances could she give up Ashe. Her love for him and the satisfaction she found in his arms went beyond her imagination.

And she was positive that when he asked her to marry him, he would tell her that he would give up flying. He knew how important that was to her. Anyway, hadn't his dream, his goal, been realized? Wasn't Black Cobra his contribution to the world? His banner of success? Now that he'd reached the pinnacle, wouldn't he be content to run the company from his desk and let younger men do the dangerous work? Of course he would. Then together they could build a life surrounded by lovely children and a beautiful home. No more horrifying dreams, no more waiting. It was meant to be. She would have it no other way.

And because of this, she had let herself be swayed, although the feeling of stark terror within her had not diminished. It was as strong and paralyzing as ever. Forcing down the hot bile that rose unbidden up the back of her throat, she opened the door to the office. It was empty.

Suddenly, she heard a movement behind her. Turning, she came face to face with a tall, bespectacled, blond-haired man. Without pausing, he smiled and extended a hand. "Hello," he said, lightly shaking Raine's hand before letting it go. "I'm Jake Everette, Ashe's assistant, general flunky, or whatever." He grinned broadly. "And you have to be Raine Michaels."

"Yes. Yes, I am."

His light brown eyes held a curious gleam. "Ashe told me to keep an eye out for you, said you might be coming. In fact, to put it bluntly, he threatened to fire me if I failed to spot you the minute you arrived."

Raine smiled, though somewhat bleakly. "Well, I'm here," she mumbled, still having difficulty controlling her quivering limbs. Where was Ashe?

Jake Everette could feel the nervousness emanating from this woman. Her lovely face was devoid of color. He could see now exactly why his boss was so smitten with her. She was a looker, but was she petrified! He could almost see the fear oozing from her pores.

Suddenly realizing she was becoming uncomfortable under his stare, Jake cleared his throat, smiled again, and gestured toward the door. "We have to go back outside and across to the next building. Ashe wanted you join us in the tower and watch the test on the big-screen monitor."

Once Raine had stepped back into the glaring sunlight, she dug around in her purse for her sunglasses. Now that she was no longer fighting the harsh glare, she was able to concentrate on her surroundings.

Elliot Aircraft was a huge plant. Hangars and buildings of all sizes and shapes dotted the complex. Then it dawned on her that for an operation of this size, the grounds were oddly deserted. Where was everyone? The only people she saw scurrying around were either in military uniforms or men with security tags clipped to their shirts. And now that she thought about it, the parking lots were practically empty.

Looking up at Jake Everette, she asked, "Where is everyone?"

"We're only working a skeleton crew today because of the trial run on Cobra."

"That makes sense," Raine responded distantly, trying desperately to keep her mind from thinking about Ashe—where he was or what he was doing at that precise moment.

"You'll have to get Ashe to take you on a tour." He paused, lifting his brows in question. "He hasn't already, has he—shown you around, I mean?"

She shook her head. "No. Actually, this is the first time I've ever been here."

"Well, he has quite an operation here. And if the Cobra tests out like it's supposed to, Ashe and company will be fixed for life. We'll have more contracts than we can possibly fill."

He paused to reach out and open the door to a beige metal building. After climbing the stairs they entered a room that was a beehive of activity. Technicians and military personnel were scurrying around like mice, knowing they were about to be a part of something of paramount importance. In spite of her fears and reservations, she couldn't help but feel a glow of pride for Ashe and what he'd accomplished. If only...

"Ms. Michaels," Everette said, gently nudging her elbow, "if you'll follow me, I'll get you situated."

"Ashe. Is he by any chance here?" Her eyes were searching the room.

"Afraid not," Jake replied lightly. "He's been at the hangar on the test runway since dawn this morning, running last-minute checks."

"Of course, I should've known," she said, then flushed, suddenly feeling foolish. He had more important things to do than cater to her, for heaven's sake.

Her heartbeat was increasing rapidly as she followed Everette through a network of people to a group of chairs in front of a huge monitor that was mounted and hanging from the ceiling. To the left of her were floor-to-ceiling windows taking up one wall, with a rounded table in front of them. It reminded Raine of an air-controllers' tower in a major airport.

After introducing her to several other men who happened to pass in front of them, Jake offered her a chair just to the side of the monitor. Together they peered up at the monitor. Displayed in full living color was the aircraft Black Cobra—one of a kind, the best. It seemed incredible to her that the same man whose gentle, loving hands had carried her to unknown heights of rapture was the brains behind such a dangerous-looking piece of equipment. Yet in spite of the way she felt, a small part of her felt immense pride in his accomplishments. And even though she was opposed to his flying it, she was aware of the important contribution he was making to his country.

The silence continued as both she and Jake stared at the screen for a long moment. Then Jake asked, "Well, what do you think?" He was smiling and his chest was expanded as though he had just become the proud father of twins. But then, she guessed, everyone who worked on the project must be feeling the same way. For without these dedicated men, Ashe would not have succeeded where others had failed.

"She's a beauty, isn't she?" Jake added, more to himself than to her. "Any moment now, you'll see Ashe come out of the hangar and climb aboard, and because of the sophisticated monitoring devices, you'll be able to see every move the Cobra makes."

Raine shook her head. "To me, it looks like a big glob of gray metal, awesome and menacing." She shivered. "I can't imagine how anything that complicated and cumbersome can get off the ground, much less stay up in the air."

"Huh! You just watch," Jake said proudly, his chest still protruding with pride. "The Cobra's like no other experimental machine; that baby'll fly at supersonic speed, fires heat-seeking missiles, foils radar, and generally does everything but dice carrots." His eyes had taken on a twinkle as he focused them on Raine.

His off-the-wall remark drew a smile from Raine, relaxing the tension around her mouth. "Sounds like every family ought to own two or three of them," she quipped.

Jake laughed out loud, drawing the attention of others.

"Hey, Everette," someone called, "what's going on over there? Let us in on the joke, why don't you?"

"How 'bout minding your own business, Forrest!" Jake shot back with a full-fledged grin. "You're up to your ass in work." He paused and glanced down at Raine apologetically. "Sorry for the choice of words," he said uncomfortably, then looked back at the man named Forrest. "Get back to work. You wouldn't catch on even if I told you."

Suddenly, the room buzzed with lighthearted chatter, everyone taking a breather from the tension that filtered throughout the room. Raine felt herself beginning to relax, the excitement and the carnival-like atmosphere communicating itself to her.

"It won't be long now," Jake was saying, his hand on the back of her chair, his eyes seeking the clock on the wall. "Ten minutes, to be exact." Then he smiled at her and stepped back. "If you're sure you're comfortable, there are things I need to see about."

"By all means," Raine replied. "You go ahead and do what you have to do. And thanks for everything."

Exactly ten minutes later, to the second, Raine saw Ashe, clothed in a flight suit, move out of the hangar and walk toward the Cobra, helmet in hand.

A hush suddenly fell over the premises as everyone instantly became all business. While some eyes were riveted to the ceiling, others were concentrating on operating the ground monitor, watching, waiting, tracking.

Raine's eyes clung to the screen, tears burning the back of her throat, and watched as her beloved paused to strap on his helmet, then turned to the crew that had followed him to the plane and waved his hand in salute before climbing into the cockpit.

Ashe's hands were clammy and he felt sweat drench his clothing, but other than those minor discomforts, he was oblivious to anything else. His job was to put this magnificent flying machine through its test pattern; that was all that counted.

He allowed nothing to interfere with that objective, although there was a moment back at the hangar just before he walked to the aircraft that he wondered if Raine had come and if she was perhaps at that very moment watching him. This was a proud moment for him and he had not changed his mind; he wanted Raine to share it with him, even if it was from afar.

Now, winging his way upward, the sky ahead of him was clear, pale blue, the rising sun dazzling off the glass, the glare deadened by the mask of the flying helmet. There was nothing to see.

Ashe had no interest in the stretching, endless view below him. His eyes hardly left the instrument panel, clearly noting its every function, the utter isolation allowing him the concentration he needed. And he couldn't have been more pleased; the Cobra was behaving perfectly.

He was soaring, climbing to meet his altitude, anticipation building, excitement churning. It was just a matter of moments now and he would be home free.

The moment Ashe walked out of the hangar, Raine blocked out everything and everyone around her. Ashe. Only Ashe. The appearance of his big, strong body on the screen instantly claimed her vision as well as her heart. It swelled with love and pride. He looked so eager, so much in command, so dear. *And so vulnerable.*

Then he disappeared, swinging himself up and into the aircraft. Suddenly, Raine felt as though she'd just been tossed out of a window, the bottom dropping out of her stomach, leaving in its wake blind, deafening panic, the likes of which she'd never experienced before, even in her darkest moments.

Sinking her teeth into her lower lip, she shut her eyes as the giant bird soared toward the heavens. *I can't handle this!*

I thought I could. But I was wrong. Oh, God, its tearing me to pieces. I love him too much!

A hand touched her shoulder and she jumped, her eyes popping open. "So far so good," Jake said. "It was about as perfect a takeoff as I've ever seen Ashe make. If that's any indication of how things are going to go, we've got it made." Then he sat down beside her and Raine heard him gasp. "My God, what have you done to yourself?"

Raine sat mute, only vaguely conscious of the salty taste of blood on her bottom lip.

"Hey," he said, patting her shoulder while thrusting a clean white handkerchief into her hand and waiting while she dabbed at the thin line of crimson. "Everything's going great, though I can't promise it'll stay that way. But Ashe is one helluva pilot; he's the best. Don't worry, he'll come through this smelling like a rose. You just wait and see."

Although Jake's pep talk helped, Raine's insides remained bunched up, twisted in pain as she watched Ashe nose the machine upward.

Finally, when she could speak without her voice trembling, Raine faced Jake, who had not budged from her side, his eyes still frayed with concern. "What will happen next?" she asked, hoping to convince Jake that she was indeed all right.

"Actually, he'll be doing several maneuvers," he said, glad to see that the color was returning to her face. "But the main purpose of today's flight is to get the feel of the aircraft, to take it through routine checks."

Raine's eyes were misty. "What he's doing is really important, isn't it?"

"You bet. Our country owes Ashe a debt of gratitude, no matter what the outcome."

"I know," she whispered, "and I'm trying hard to keep that in mind." She forced a smile to her lips, looking around and noticing with sudden embarrassment that several others were peering at her with curious expressions on their faces. She had to get her act together or risk making a complete fool of herself. For Ashe's sake she could not do that.

Forcing her attention back to the screen, she soon felt the brittle tension leave her bones. So far so good, she told herself. Maybe her worries were unfounded; Ashe was performing brilliantly, as was Black Cobra. It seemed as though they were a match made in heaven.

Someone handed her a cup of coffee and, sipping it, she kept her eyes on the monitor, finding that she was becoming as excited as everyone else in the room, watching Ashe handle the splendid piece of machinery with skilled perfection.

Then it happened, each terrible incident an isolated frame of horror. Just as Ashe was beginning his final approach to the runway, a loud thudding noise came over the radio at the same time that the aircraft swerved severely off course.

Raine hugged her arms to her chest, praying, fighting off the desire to cry and swear and scream. She opened her mouth, but no sound could get through her frozen throat. She watched, her battered senses reeling in shocked silence.

Suddenly, pandemonium broke out and several voices began talking at once.

"Something hit the windshield!" Ashe shouted, coming in loud and clear over the radio.

"*Jesus!*" someone said.

"Why the hell didn't we see it?" another responded wildly.

"Ashe, this is Jake! How bad is it?"

"Bad. The windshield is cracked! The cockpit is filled with fog, and I'm losing pressure fast! And I can't see a goddamned thing!"

"Ashe, your rate of descent is eight hundred feet per minute and your altitude is five hundred feet. Pull up! Abort landing approach! Do you read me?"

The screen showed Ashe immediately complying with his instructions. And then it was over as quickly as it had begun. Ashe began to climb and then circled twice, and shortly thereafter seemed to have gained control of the situation. Raine watched, with her heart still in her mouth, as he reached over and unlatched the canopy, letting it blow off.

A loud cheer, followed by foot stomping and whistling, commenced. The tower rocked while Ashe flashed the thumbs-up sign on the screen before he again made his approach for landing.

Jake turned to Raine with a wide grin splayed across his face. "Thank God! He did it! He made it!"

Raine tried again to speak, to stand up, to reach out, but nothing seemed to work on her body. It was as though she were a robot and all the power had been shut down. The room spun crazily. She felt dizzy and sick. Then she felt nothing.

Jake Everette's panic-edged "Goddamn!" never reached her ears. He caught her in his arms as she pitched forward and knew no more.

"Are you feeling better now?" Jake squatted beside her. "Here, drink this," he added softly.

Raine then realized she was lying on a short couch with her head propped up against two thick cushions. She blinked rapidly, looking past Jake, wondering where she was. But that didn't matter, not now. As she took the cup from his outstretched hand, fear shadowed her blue eyes, turning them dark and haunting. "Ashe?"

A look of sympathy softened his expression before he spoke. "He's fine. Landed the Cobra like a champ. He'll be here just as soon as he gets out of his flight suit."

Raine nodded, relief leaving her feeling weak and washed out. Then, with Jake's help, she scooted to an upright position. For a long moment she concentrated on smoothing the wrinkles from her skirt, suddenly embarrassed by her lack of control. Still keeping her eyes averted, she sipped the cold juice.

A frown drawing his brows together, Jake rose to his feet and peered down at her, his eyes still troubled. He scrutinized her closely as she set the cup on the table next to the couch.

"Where am I?"

"Ashe's office. After you fainted, I brought you here, away from the mass confusion."

Raine twisted her hands together. "I'm sorry I was such a bother, but thank you for taking care of me. I—"

He held up his hand. "Don't apologize. Believe me, I understand. For a while there, it was touch and go. We were all a little uptight."

An awkward silence fell between them and then Jake said, "If you're sure there's nothing else I can get for you, I'll be going." He crossed to the door. "It's been a pleasure meeting you." He smiled. "Hopefully, we'll meet again."

After he left, Raine laid her head back against the couch, feeling another bout of nausea coming on. She forced herself to breath deeply, hating the weak trembles.

Her body as well as her mind had taken all the abuse it could stand. Her eyes, like shutters, blinked and captured scene after scene of Ashe's narrow escape from death. As far as she was concerned, that was what it was. She didn't care what Ashe said or how light he made of the situation;

she knew for a split second when the blow was delivered to the windshield that it could have cost him his life.

Unable to sit still a minute longer, Raine slowly stood up, making sure she was no longer light-headed, and slipped into her sandals and crossed the room to stand by the window. Staring but not seeing, she suddenly staggered under the weight of the conflicting emotions raging within her.

If this was love, this explosive mixture of highs and lows, pain and terror, she wasn't sure she wanted any part of it. She longed to be herself again, not this intense, unpredictable stranger who swung from ecstasy to despair with the change of the wind. Oh, how she wished she'd never come to watch the flight. Why hadn't she gone with her instincts and stayed away? But she knew that would have accomplished nothing; in the end it merely would have postponed repairing the weak link in the chain that held them so delicately together.

The creak of the door alerted Raine that she was no longer alone. She steeled herself not to turn around, not to look at him. Could she let him go? Could she be free again? Could she live without him?

"Raine."

Her name, so sweetly spoken, gave her the answer she was seeking. She felt her defenses crumble like a straw house in the wind.

"I love you."

A cry rose from deep inside her as she whirled around and flung herself into his open arms.

"Oh, Ashe!" she cried, her heart fluttering in her chest like that of a trapped bird, tears rolling down her cheeks.

"Don't cry, please," he whispered, his mouth trailing over her cheek, along the curve of her jaw, down the slender column of her neck, sweetly perfumed and inflamed, making his head swim, his loins pulse. "I'm fine. See, you can feel that I'm in one piece. I'm just disappointed everything didn't go perfectly, but that blasted duck creaming the windshield almost ruined an otherwise perfect mission."

Raine moved back and looked up at him. "Are you sure you're not hurt?" Her eyes told him she didn't believe him.

He pulled her close again, her tears wetting his cheeks. "I'm all right," he said, then grinned sheepishly. "Well, maybe I do have a slight headache, but other than that I'm one hundred percent fit, especially now that I have you in my arms."

"Thank God," she confessed, her chin quivering as she leaned back and searched his face. "I thought I would die when...when I heard that awful sound and then I heard your voice...and then I fainted..."

"I know, I know," he crooned, rocking her like a baby. "And I'm sorry, so sorry. Jake told me and I thought I'd never get things squared away so I could get to you." He paused, tightening his hold. "You're okay now, aren't you?" His voice suddenly sounded rough.

"I'm fine, but—"

He chuckled, tipping her chin up gently, his eyes greedily touching every inch of her face. "Did anyone ever tell you that you talk too damned much?" He kissed her tenderly on the nose. "Stop worrying," he scolded hoarsely. "We have much more important things to take care of."

His hands slid over her with fervent intensity, stopping only when he boldly curved her rounded buttocks close against him. Raine was lost, felt herself melting as his lips took hers with fiery insistence. Only when they were both gasping for breath did Ashe release her.

"Oh, Raine, my beloved, Raine," he murmured, "say you'll marry me. Today. Tomorrow. Whenever." His voice grew painfully husky. "I don't want to wait a moment longer than I have to to make you mine."

Raine smiled through her tears. "Me neither," she responded deeply. "I can't wait. Now that your project is successful and out of the way, and you won't be testing planes any longer, we—"

Suddenly, every muscle in Ashe's body stiffened. Then he slowly pushed her to arm's length. His face was as cold as marble.

"Ashe?" Her lovely brows were marred by a puzzled frown.

"Where did you get that cockamamie idea?"

The sunlight lurched. Everything around them jerked out of place, then slowly settled back. The silence grew. Gently, Raine pulled her hands away and took several steps backward. "Knowing how I felt, I...I just took it for granted that you would." Her last words were almost inaudible.

"Well, I'm sorry you jumped to that conclusion." His voice cut like ice. "But nothing could be further from the truth."

Raine could feel her heart beating so loudly that it shook her whole body. *No! I won't let you do this to me!* she wanted to scream. But she said nothing; the words simply would not come.

"God, Raine," Ashe said, breaking into the stark silence. "You don't know what you're asking. Testing planes is my life."

Raine's eyes were full of hurt and anger. "Yes, I know, but *I* want to be your life. I don't want to play second fiddle to a piece of machinery. I don't want to live like my mother did."

Ashe looked at her in silence.

"All right, maybe I am selfish to some extent," she cried wildly, "but I want us to have a stable home life, have children, live like other married couples."

He was trying to show patience. "What about your work?"

His question took her by surprise. "My work? What about it?"

"Have I asked you to give it up?"

Another silence followed.

"No, but—"

"But what?" His tone was sharp, like a razor, his expression becoming colder by the second.

"That's different, and you know it," she shot back. "My work doesn't throw me into constant danger." Her voice broke. "Every time...you go up in a plane, it's the same as having a time bomb strapped inside your flight suit."

"Raine, please...listen. You're being unreasonable."

Tears were streaming down her face. She made no attempt to wipe them away, but stood still, looking past Ashe as though she could not bear to look at him.

Watching her, Ashe hurt inside with love, with anger, with frustration. "Raine—" he tried again, his voice soft "—can't you see that I've changed? Life is precious to me now, and I wouldn't think of taking unnecessary chances." He was pleading. "Those days are long gone. I love you and want you waiting for me when I come home from a hard day's work. I want to feel you next to me at night, wake up loving you every morning."

A sob broke her lips. "Oh, Ashe...I want that too, more than you'll ever know. But as long as you're flying, I'll never know if you'll walk through the front door. God, I wish I could be like Alice, like other pilots' wives. I tried, you know I did. I came here today, which was something I didn't think I could ever do. And look what happened. No. I've been through too much, seen too much pain."

Come on! he silently insisted. *Say something; do something; don't keep standing there like a goddamned statue!*

"Please...won't you try again?" He was desperate. He knew she was slipping away from him, and there was not a damned thing he could do about it.

She looked at him. "I can't," she whispered.

"Can't—or won't?"

"Can't."

"And I can't make myself into something I'm not," he said harshly. "I am what I am."

Raine's pounding heart rivaled the silence. She stared at him, battling against the excruciating pain that was ripping through her with a vengeance.

"Is that your final word?"

"No! dammit it, it's not!" His lips were curled back. "I want you for once to be honest with yourself, to face the truth. It's not my flying or the danger involved that's the real problem." His voice was harsh now, his eyes unyielding. "It's you! It's your fear of commitment, of losing your independence."

"That's absurd!" she countered furiously. Then her mind raced, her heart began beating in her throat. Was there any truth to what he said? Deep down, was she terrified of committing herself, losing her independence? *No.* Ashe was wrong. She loved him, would never stop loving him, and she wanted to spend the rest of her life with him. But she simply could not live with the fear. She had to make him understand.

Ashe saw the flicker of pain that crossed her face and his breath escaped in a small burst; he had been holding it, waiting, hoping, praying.

"I'm not afraid to love you, to give my heart to you," she whispered, "but by the same token I can't expect any less from you."

His face drained of color, his voice held no emotion. "Then I guess there's nothing left to be said."

Raine reeled as though he'd struck her. This can't be the end, she thought numbly. But it was, and she knew it. It's over, and I've lost him. *Not to be with Ashe. To wake up in the morning and not be able to think, today I'll see him; today we'll spend together; tonight we'll make love... Not to see Ashe.*

She swallowed hard, feeling her heart beat in her throat, committing every ragged detail of his face to memory. Then with a sob, she turned and, blinded by tears, pushed open the door and walked out, achingly conscious of leaving her heart behind.

Chapter 13

She's precious, Heather."

Heather giggled, her face beaming. "Isn't she, though! But, remember, we don't have to refer to her as 'she' any longer."

Raine rolled her eyes upward in mock agitation. "Finally, after a week you chose a name. I was beginning to give up, thinking that my niece was going to stay nameless."

"Well, what can I tell you except the truth?" Heather paused, disengaged the baby's mouth from a breast, and, covering the short distance to the crib, laid her gently onto the soft mattress. "It was your dear brother who practically read the pages off every baby name book I could get my hands on before ever making up his mind."

"Who do you think she looks like?" Raine asked, searching the tiny features for a sign of recognition.

"Oh, herself mostly, I think," Heather responded proudly. "But then I can never tell who a newborn looks like. To me they all look like wrinkled prunes." She paused with a laugh when she heard Raine's horrified gasp and added, "But not Christi, never Christi; she's beautiful."

"I agree wholeheartedly."

A silence fell between them as they stared down at the dainty creature who, with her fist in her mouth, lay sleeping peacefully and innocently, not a care in the world except when and where her next meal was coming from. Raine sighed inwardly. Oh, God, if only her life were that simple.

"Christi Raine Michaels—now, doesn't that have a nice ring to it?" Heather asked, breaking the short silence and raising her eyes to meet Raine's.

Raine smiled, her vision suddenly blurring with unshed tears. "You bet it does. You have no idea what it means to me to have this bundle of joy named after me."

"As I said before, you have Todd to thank for that," Heather replied. "But I was all for it, too, especially after all you've done for us," she added sweetly.

Raine leaned over and hugged her, blinking back the tears. Tears that came all too readily of late.

Heather hugged her back and then pulled away. "We miss you so much. I wish you hadn't had to go back to Dallas, but I know you couldn't afford to stay here a day longer, especially now that Todd's out of the hospital and doing so well."

"And I miss you," Raine responded with a sigh, "more than you'll ever know."

"Well, we're thankful that you were able to come and spend the day with us. I haven't forgotten the opening of the boutique is just a few days away."

"Well, I couldn't let Christi come home from the hospital without being here, now, could I?"

"Hey, you two, what's going on?" Todd demanded, coming into the room, his walker making a thumping sound

as it hit the carpet. "Sounds like the mutual admiration so-
ciety to me." A smile lit his gaunt face.

Raine dropped her arm from around Heather's shoulder
and turned to face her brother. Although still crippled, he
was doing amazingly well—so well, in fact, that he was getting restless and was clamoring for something to do to oc-
cupy his time.

Raine's gaze lingered warmly on her brother: she still
could not believe how healthy he looked in spite of his
weight loss and the paleness of his face. His eyes, though,
were clear of pain and held a sparkle. However, today he
seemed distracted, as though something was on his mind.
Raine was afraid she knew what it was, but so far they had
avoided the issue like the plague.

Smiling, she walked over and planted a kiss on his cheek.
"You're right, brother dear, we were not only admiring your
daughter, but patting ourselves on the back as well." She
looked at Heather and winked, trying to make the shadow
disappear from his eyes.

He grinned as he lowered himself onto the nearest chair,
but Raine noticed it did not reach his eyes. "Raine," he said
after a moment, his tone serious, "you haven't by any
chance talked to Ashe lately, have you?"

Raine winced inwardly. "You know I haven't," she answered. The mere mention of his name had the power to tear
her to pieces these days.

"Well, dammit, I haven't either!" he exclaimed. "And I
can't imagine why he hasn't let me know what the investigating board found." He balled his fist into a tight wad. "I
know the report is bound to be complete, and not knowing
is driving me crazy. Even though I'm not going to fly anymore, I still want the damned thing settled and behind me—
one way or the other."

Heather spoke then, her eyes on Raine, pleading. "That's why I've begged him to call Ashe. If nothing else, it'll relieve his mind, but he won't do it." She squared her shoulders. "I still think Ashe is doing everything he can to vindicate Todd, and that's why he hasn't heard." Her lower lip jutted out stubbornly.

The look Todd bestowed on Heather was filled with loving tenderness. It made Raine's heart turn over, thinking that she would never share that kind of happiness with a man. "Always the optimist—that's my girl." Then his gaze switched to Raine and he gave a tired shrug. "Who knows? She may be right. But for now, he's still paying the hospital bills," he quipped, before drawing back into his shell.

Raine felt miserable. "Oh, Todd, I wish there was something I could say or do," she cried, sharing his pain, "but there isn't. I..." A sob caught in her throat; she couldn't go on. *Why didn't Ashe get in touch with him? Surely he wouldn't...?* No. She refused to finish the thought. Ashe would never take his hostility toward her out on Todd.

Todd sighed heavily. "God, Sis, I'm sorry if I've brought up a painful subject, and I'm also sorry it didn't work out between you two. In spite of what happens with me, I still think Ashe is one helluva guy and was hoping—"

Raine made a strangling sound, aborting his sentence. "Todd...please...I don't...can't talk about Ashe right now." She turned away to hide her tears.

"Now look what you've done," Heather snapped, looking furiously at Todd.

"Raine, I didn't mean to upset you," Todd said, sounding forlorn and uncertain.

After a moment, Raine got control of herself and turned around, forcing a smile to her lips. "I'm the one who should apologize. I know you're concerned and I love you all the more for it, but—"

Heather interrupted, her eyes filled with loving sympathy. "Don't say any more. When you're ready to talk, we'll listen. And just keep in mind that we love you, too."

Raine nodded wordlessly, turning her attention away from their knowing eyes and onto Christi, watching her tiny chest go steadily up and down. She had told Todd and Heather that she wouldn't be seeing Ashe any longer. And, knowing how upset she was, they had refrained from questioning her. Until now.

"Hey," Heather cried, following another moment of strained silence, "why don't I cut the cake and uncork the bottle of champagne Raine brought and get on with the celebration of the birth of one Christi Raine Michaels?"

Raine blinked furiously and then laughed. "I second that motion." With arms entwined, the three of them made their way toward the dining room.

The uncorking of the bubbly liquid set the tone for the remainder of Raine's visit. The air was filled with laughter and warm conversation as they discussed the imminent opening of the boutique, looked at dozens of pictures of Christi, and ate until they were stuffed.

It was late afternoon when Raine said her good-byes with a promise to return soon. "Thanks for everything," she whispered, hugging each one of them and kissing Christi on the cheek.

"We're so glad you could come," Heather said again, following Raine to the car.

"Wild horses couldn't have kept me away."

As her car sped through the late-afternoon twilight, Raine thought about what a wonderful day it had been. At least for a while she had pushed aside the pain and misery that pursued her relentlessly. For that small crumb, she was eternally grateful.

Every muscle in Raine's body ached by the time she opened the door to her condo and switched on the lamp just inside the den. Her eyes were drawn immediately to the stack of paperwork that covered her desk in the far corner. Even though she had desperately needed this day away from the office, she would pay dearly for it. Not only that, but it had taken a lot out of her. Just talking about Ashe had left her drained.

She forced her weary limbs in the direction of her bedroom, oblivious to the soothing effect of the lovely room, with its glass and wicker furniture, its bright-colored cushions, and the scattering of potted plants.

Once there, she dropped her purse onto the nearest chair. After kicking off her shoes, she stripped and flung herself across the bed. *Loneliness.* It was almost overwhelming in its intensity. The moment she had walked through the door, she felt its claws sink into her once again.

Rolling over on her back, nails digging into her palms, Raine stared into the empty space above her. Eyes hot with a sudden sting, she bit down hard on her lip.

Let him go, she wept silently.

But she could not. Ashe was as much a part of her as the air she breathed.

Since their bitter parting, over a month ago, her life had been pure hell. She had tried to carry on as though the hole in her heart was not there, but it was impossible. Each day it seemed to become bigger, wider, and with it, her pain and despair grew deeper. Never had her mind known such agony.

How could she have been so mistaken, misjudged him so terribly? She had been so sure that when he finally confessed his love for her and asked her to marry him, he would want to give up flying, that the thrill would no longer be there, that loving her would be enough to satisfy him.

She should have known better. He didn't need her. He didn't need a home. He didn't need a family. All he needed was a piece of machinery and the heady excitement of living dangerously.

Oh, Ashe, she wept, *how could you do this to me?* But it was over. Finished. She had to keep telling herself this, or she would never be able to survive.

Work. She had tackled it at a grueling pace. Not only had she worked herself, but her employees as well. At one time, they had all threatened to walk out, though Raine sensed that underneath their smiles, they were serious, except Val. Instead of threatening to quit, she harped continuously to Raine to take it easy.

"You're going to have a nervous breakdown," she'd said, her eyes troubled. "I don't know what all happened while you were in Tyler or what demons are driving you, but what I do know is that if you don't slow down you won't last much longer."

For several days following Val's lecture, Raine had taken her assistant's words to heart. But it hadn't lasted. She went right back at it, as Val had said, as though demons were after her.

However, work had not been the panacea she had hoped it would be. There was nothing that would fill the void that losing Ashe had created. Not work. Not family. Not friends.

The only redeemable thing that had come out of this dark period was that she had been able to share in Todd and Heather's happiness. Three days after she had last seen Ashe, Todd was released from the hospital. She had scrambled around until she had located a larger apartment and a part-time housekeeper.

After that, she had stood as a witness along with another pilot friend of Todd's while Todd and Heather repeated their wedding vows before the minister of a small local church. It was a touching ceremony, and Raine had never seen her brother so happy. She had felt, for a moment, a piercing thrust of jealousy as she saw love for each other shining from their eyes.

Then two weeks later, Todd had called during the wee hours of the morning, informing her that he was the proud father of a seven-pound, four-ounce baby girl.

She had drawn on her new family's strength and love, helping to some extent fill the cold, aching void of emptiness she carried inside her. And, mercifully, she was learning to take one day at a time and managing to keep thoughts of Ashe from ruling her every action of every day.

Until now.

Suddenly, he was everywhere, all at once, occupying every corner of her mind. Hearing his name, talking about him, had triggered this new surge of pain. When the tears were spent, she rolled off the bed and, grabbing her robe, crossed to the French doors and opened them, the steamy night air slapping her in the face. But she ignored it as she walked out onto the patio and stood looking up at the heavens, her face covered with tears.

Face it, Raine. You can't keep on going like this! Cut the strings! Get on with your life! No more tears. No more feeling sorry for yourself. After all, didn't she have everything to be thankful for? She had her health, her family, her work, her friends. *And she wasn't pregnant.* Pain and heartache were not new to her; she had bounced back from adversity in the past. She could do so again...couldn't she?

"You look ravishing, my dear."

"Do you really think so?" Raine asked, sounding surprised as she smiled at Ross Thomas, who had just walked into her office and closed the door behind him.

"You wouldn't be fishing for a compliment, now, would you?"

Raine flushed and then saw the teasing glint in his eyes. Making a face, she decided to play along. "Now that you mention it, I was," she said lightly, then turned serious. "These past two days have been pure hell, and I wouldn't have been at all surprised if I didn't look like I'd been run over by a freight train." She laughed. "And, by the way, that's exactly what I feel like."

"Well, you could have fooled me." He took a step closer to Raine. "Other than those dark shadows under your eyes..." He paused and reached out and ran the tip of his index finger tenderly under one eye. Raine steeled herself not to flinch. Even so, Ross sensed her withdrawal. His tone, however, remained level. "I don't think I've ever seen you look better."

"It's the dress."

Ross lifted an eyebrow. "Oh?" he said innocently.

"Ross!"

He chuckled. "All right. I'll stop teasing you. I know it's one of *your* designs; I recognized it from the sketches."

Raine began to turn around slowly in the center of the room, modeling it for him. The dress was of a timeless style and simplicity: a dusty rose silk. It had a snug bodice and a wide swirling skirt, echoed by puffed sleeves.

But as elegant as the dress was, Ross knew the real attraction was Raine herself: eyes hauntingly beautiful, face flushed as she studied her own reflection, unconsciously standing straighter. Ross gazed at the delicate line of her face, disguised until now by worry or sadness, after Todd's accident and since she'd returned home. He found himself quelling the desire to pull her into his arms and tell her he loved her. But instead he murmured, "Wonderful."

"I'm glad you approve. I've already modeled it for Val and the girls and they agree with you."

"Are you going to wear it for opening day tomorrow?"

She stood still. "Don't you think I should?"

"Absolutely. And it's a shame you don't have the rest of your designs hanging on the racks."

"Well, I'm not, not really," she replied. "I'm satisfied with what I have in the boutique, and adding my own designs slowly but surely will give me something to look forward to and work toward." For a moment, her eyes lost their sparkle.

Ross didn't pretend not to notice. "Raine," he said softly, "I wish you'd tell me what's bothering you. I know you've been through hell with Todd and trying to keep his life together as well as get the boutique open, but I know there's something else." He paused, his expression anxious. "I don't want to intrude, but if there's anything I can do..." Another pause. "If it's money, you know..."

She shook her head adamantly and he got the message.

His lips thinned. "All right, but you know how I feel about you and—"

Raine smiled sweetly, coming to stand in front of him, placing her hand on his arm. "I know, and I care for you, too, but not in that way."

Unexpectedly, he leaned over and kissed her on the cheek, then raised her chin, forcing her eyes to meet his. "I've always known you didn't love me, but I kept hoping. Well, no longer. I'm not going to be a martyr or a sore loser."

He stopped, letting his last words sink in, and Raine averted her face. *He knows,* she told herself. *I haven't fooled him. Oh, God, does the whole world know how I hurt?*

"I've suspected there was someone else ever since you came home, so I have no illusions any longer." He squeezed her hand. "But, remember, if you ever need me, I'll come running. But only as a friend," he added hurriedly.

"Thanks," she whispered, giving him a hug.

After a moment, Ross's voice was light and impersonal. "How about letting me take you out to dinner and celebrate the big day tomorrow in grand style? I know there's a party planned for tomorrow night, but I thought we could get an early start."

"Thanks, but, no thanks," she said gently. "I'm exhausted and tomorrow is going to be a killer day. I think I'll go home and soak in a hot tub of water and get to bed early."

"Well, I won't say I'm not disappointed, but I certainly understand." Then, winking at her, he turned and made his way to the door. "Good luck tomorrow," he added, closing the door behind him.

Although Raine had succeeded in turning her life around, placing thoughts of Ashe under lock and key forever, there were still times when she longed to give in to her emotions and cry until she could cry no more. And tonight was one of those times.

Deciding exercise was what she needed, she quickly donned her leotard and plopped down onto the carpeted floor.

She had just thrown her legs up and over her head, her rear in the air, when the doorbell rang.

"Gosh darn it!" she spluttered contrarily, rocking to an upright position. Then, huffing and puffing, she trudged to the door and yanked it open. "Alice!"

"Hello, Raine," Alice McAdams said quietly, a smile softening her features.

Raine was appalled at how terrible she looked. There was nothing to remind her of the ample-figured woman she had come to know and like that day at the lake. This woman was skin and bones and the lines in her face were deeper and more pronounced. However, Raine would have known her anywhere. The eyes were the same; they were soft and mellow and kind, but sad, oh, so sad.

Following the moment of stunned silence, Raine said, "Oh, Alice, it's so good to see you."

They hugged. "It's good to see you, too."

"Come in, come in," Raine said, sounding rattled. "I didn't mean to keep you standing on the doorstep. It's just that I'm so surprised to see you."

"I hope I'm not intruding."

A fleeting smile broke across Raine's lips and momentarily lessened the hollowness of her own face. "Of course you're not intruding," she said. Then, unconsciously, her eyes dipped to her attire. She smiled again. "I was restless, so I decided to take a tumble or two on the floor."

Alice still seemed uneasy. "You must be wondering why I've come," she remarked, and Raine guessed her expression was quite transparent. "I was in Dallas today visiting Mac's sister, and I wanted at least to say hello before I left in the morning."

Raine took a steadying breath. Although seeing Alice again brought back painful memories, she refused to let it show. "I'm so glad you did. I've been wanting to call you, to see how you were doing, but..." She couldn't meet Alice's eyes.

Alice smiled and caught Raine's hands in a firm grip. "Don't apologize," she said, her voice raspy. "You more than did your part the night Mac...died, not to mention the flowers and the cards." She paused. "Maybe that's why I wanted to see you."

Even though it sounded good, they both knew it was not true.

Raine was convinced that Alice had something else on her mind. She could see it in her face. Her knees began to tremble as she made her way toward the couch.

Alice's eyes tracked her every movement. "Raine—"

"Please," Raine cut in, hoping to prolong the inevitable, "sit down and I'll get us something to drink."

Shortly, Raine came back with two cups of coffee. And this time there was no escape. Alice smiled her thanks and then set the cup down carefully on the table and pinned Raine with her eyes.

"I'm worried about Ashe," she said bluntly.

The tightening in Raine's chest became almost unbearable. "Alice, I don't—" she began.

"Something's terribly wrong with him."

Raine wanted to stand up, she was too fidgety to remain seated, but now, fear whispering through her mind, her legs suddenly weak, she thought better of it. "Has he been hurt?"

"No. Not in the way you mean." She sighed. "I don't know what happened between you two, and I have no intention of asking. But I love Ashe; Mac loved him like a brother, and I'm worried about him and I think there's something you should know."

On legs that weren't steady, Raine stood up, her mouth dry and tight. "What?"

Alice didn't mince any words. "He's been drinking and hasn't even been to the office at all lately." She sighed again. "I saw him just before I came to Dallas and I tried to talk to him, but I might as well have been blowing in the wind. He's all torn up on the inside—"

Raine started to interrupt, but Alice rushed on. "I wasn't going to interfere, to intrude on his misery, but then he said, 'She doesn't want me, Alice. She doesn't want me.' And then I asked him if there was anything I could do, and in that odd tone he told me, 'There isn't anything to be done. Right now I'm bleeding to death on the inside and I simply don't give a damn.' End of quote."

Raine felt as though her insides had suddenly caved in and she sat down quickly. "Oh, Alice," she wailed, "you don't understand..."

Alice gazed at her without flinching. "No. I guess I don't. But if you love him, there's nothing to understand."

The color finished draining out of Raine's face and her lips were gray. "Oh, Alice," she cried again. "I'm not like you; God knows I've tried. But can't you see? That's the problem. I love him too much." Her eyes were pleading for understanding.

Alice shook her head sadly, tears free-flowing. "No, I can't see."

"How can you say that when Mac is dead!"

Raine watched in horror as Alice's head snapped back. Raine's hand flew to her mouth. "Oh, God, Alice," she whispered urgently, "I'm sorry, so sorry. Please, I didn't mean..." Raine was openly sobbing now.

Alice recovered quickly, though her face, too, was devoid of color, but there was a sweet smile on her face. "Shh!" Alice whispered, clasping Raine's cold hands in her warm ones. "I want you to listen to me. When...when Mac got killed, I wanted to die, too, and I almost did. But then the memories kept deadening the pain, memories of all those wonderful years we had together, the laughter, the tears, the children we made, the loving tenderness we shared, and before long I found I was actually beginning to live again."

She paused and sniffed back the tears. "And I learned then that nothing, not even death, could take those memories from me. And even if I'd known what the future held for me and Mac, I would not have changed one moment of our life together. Because having Mac for a few short years was better than not having him at all.''

Raine shook visibly, and tears were drenching her face, as she laid her head back against the couch, dizzy under the hammer blow of Alice's confession.

Then for the longest of times, there was a silence as each tried to get control of her emotions. Raine felt rather than saw Alice stand up.

"I'm sorry if I've upset you, Raine," Alice whispered. "I only hope one day you'll forgive me, but whether you do or not, please remember one thing: don't be afraid to reach out and grasp with both hands what life has to offer. You may never get a second chance."

Raine still couldn't utter a word, nor could she stop crying as she followed Alice to the door. They embraced silently and Raine tried to say, "Alice—"

"No." Alice placed a finger across her trembling lips. "Don't say anything. I'm going now. My friends are waiting. Just don't forget what I've said, and I'll pray that you'll change your mind."

After closing the door behind her, Raine sagged heavily against it. *Some things never change. I love him. And I always will.* Suddenly, and for the first time, she saw a light at the end of the long, dark tunnel that was her life, and knew that without Ashe it had no meaning. And because she had been afraid to take a chance, to gamble, to trust, she had lost him. But perhaps an even bigger sin was that she had been given a handful of heaven and had failed to hang on to it.

And with that revelation came another: she would rather have him for one day than not at all.

Miraculously, Alice's prayer had been answered.

The night was so hushed, Ashe could hear his footsteps echo through the house and out onto the coolness of the deck. Tonight was the first time in days he hadn't taken a drink. After putting in a full day's work at the plant, he'd decided to come to the ranch. The minute he'd arrived he had gone straight to bed. He'd tried to sleep, Lord knew he needed it, but he'd given up. Some nights were worse than others, and this night he guessed, because he had all his facilities about him, seemed the worst of all: filled with longings and memories.

Later, deserting the deck for the kitchen, he made himself a cup of coffee, then wandered through the rooms, turning lights on, seeing Raine wherever he looked. In the bedroom, Raine, slim and lovely, exquisitely nude, lying on the bed, uncoiling with a languid, feline grace, reaching for him.

The smooth, fresh satin feel of her flesh, always cool to the touch, even after the most heated of passions. The faint, sweet flavor of her skin. The scent of her hair when he nuzzled and tasted the tender, sensitive place inside her ears.

The remembered strength of those slender, perfectly formed legs. In those deepest of all embraces she was fiercely demanding and passionately giving, putting every last scrap of energy and will into the act without reserve. Enfolding, engulfing, drawing ever deeper.

The many sensory memories kept coming and would not leave, no matter how hard the pain knotted his belly.

He stared at the phone. His hand touched it as he'd done many times in the past, then drew back. Why couldn't he get it through his thick skull that she didn't want him, that it was over?

With a muttered curse he went back to the den and sat down on the couch. His eyes landed on the thick manual he'd so carelessly thrown down when he'd come in the door.

Thank God for one small favor; the accident report on Todd Michaels was complete. Tomorrow he'd go see Todd. He couldn't put it off any longer.

He leaned his head back on the couch and closed his eyes. *Raine.* With the force of a physical pain, Ashe wanted Raine beside him. What had gone wrong? Had he asked too much of her?

Suddenly, he felt as though he'd just been hit between the eyes with a brick. *You stupid, self-centered bastard! Of course you asked too much! You asked everything of her, but weren't willing to give anything in return!* How had he been so blind? The pieces of the puzzle were beginning to fit. Wasn't it the truth that she had wounded his masculine ego by having the audacity to declare her own terms for the future? But where did he get off thinking he could dictate all the terms? Was he really that damned selfish?

Jesus!

He jumped up, weak-kneed, sweaty, and disgusted. But the disgust was with himself. He knew then what he had to do.

And with that decision, the bitter aftertaste of the betrayal began to fade from his heart.

The opening of the boutique was hailed as a success. Raine, however, had counted the seconds, the minutes, the hours until all the folderol was over and she could leave.

At present, the boutique was crowded with eager women searching through the sea of clothing for their seasonal colors. She had been congratulated, pawed, and questioned until a blinding headache had sent her scurrying to her office. All this glory was secondary. Her heart was elsewhere.

And then it was over. The day had come to an end. The last satisfied customer had left and so had the staff. And she was free. Free at last to pursue her heart's desire.

Suddenly, not wanting to waste another precious moment, she grabbed her purse, turned the lights off, and walked out the door, locking it behind her.

As soon as she stopped by her condo and packed a bag, she was going to Ashe, to beg for his forgiveness if that was what it would take to get him back. The time had come.

She pulled into the circular drive in front and hurried up the front steps, her stride bold, her purpose certain. She had just walked into the cool entryway and slammed the door behind her when she saw him.

Ashe!

Chapter 14

The sight of him made her head spin. Although she had carried him in her heart, she was totally unprepared for the living, breathing, moving image of him.

She's been proud of herself, the way she had become resourceful, tough, able to deal with what came along. But all those aspects of her self-image she had so carefully put in place were not provisions for dealing with his sudden appearance. The sight of him knocked down her carefully constructed wall as if it were made of sand.

She'd prayed for this moment, rehearsed in her mind how it would be when they met again, what she was going to say to make things right between them. Oh, God, if she could say it as easily as she could think it.

Just the turn of his dark head, so familiar, yet so unfamiliar, hit her in a rush and she felt herself choking, her throat constricting, rendering her speechless. Alice had not been exaggerating when she'd said he wasn't the same. The lean contours of his face had been honed to a brittle thinness, and it hardly seemed possible that in a little over a month a man of his strength should have become so thin. The blue eyes were dark and deep in their sockets, and even the brilliant luster of his hair seemed dulled.

"How did you get in?" she whispered in a voice she hardly recognized as her own.

He was standing now and, as their eyes met and held, time seemed suspended.

"Todd...Todd gave me the key," he said. "I hope you don't mind." Damn! This wasn't going at all as he'd planned.

The sound of his voice, so cool and formal, was almost more than Raine could bear. She advanced into the room, though careful to keep her distance, while desperately trying to restore her poise. He made no move toward her.

Raine gnawed at her lower lip. "Why...why would Todd do a thing like that?" She was having a difficult time disguising the panic that was welling up inside her.

"Todd insisted that I be the one to tell you that he'd been cleared of all wrongdoing in the accident." He shifted his feet, thinking things were falling apart around his ears. *She's so cool, so composed. Maybe you're too late...too late...too late...*

"How did you prove his innocence?" she asked. Oh, God, she didn't want to talk about Todd. Not now. *I want to talk about us.*

"We kept sending the A-7's in the air and finally the gears failed just as they had with Todd. Even though my company built it, I was never so glad when it turned out to be a mechanical failure. Only Colonel Jackson was bent out of shape because it was the plane; he was so sure it was pilot error. It made my day when that jackass had to eat crow." There was an awkward pause and then he added, "I just thought you'd want to know."

Had his words ended on a cracked note, or had she imagined it? She tried to smile, but she could not. "That's wonderful," she said. Was that the only reason he came, her heart screamed. To tell her about Todd? Oh, God, she felt any hope of reconciliation slowly fading away. He still made no move to close the gap between them, to touch her.

His breathing was raspy. She couldn't meet his eyes. The silence stretched, suddenly became crippling.

"I'm sorry," he said abruptly, backing toward the door. "I shouldn't have come here. I thought—-oh, well, it doesn't matter now what I thought—-I'd better go."

It's over, it's really and truly over. "Oh, God," she murmured aloud, turning her head in an effort to hide the tears running unchecked down her face.

Ashe's hand stilled on the door handle. He swung around. That was when he saw her shoulders quivering. He almost came unglued.

Two long strides brought him to her. He placed his hands on her upper arms and drew her back to rest against his body.

"Raine, Raine," he groaned, burying his face in the hollow of her shoulder, and she knew with sudden exhilaration that everything was going to be all right.

"I love you," she said simply, rubbing her cheek against his, all of her so remarkably soft and sweet-smelling.

Ashe felt his numb heart jump back to life. He took a long shuddering breath, almost weightless with relief and love. Then he turned her, ever so slowly, closing his mouth over hers.

"And I love you," he whispered thickly when they could breathe. But he was hungry for her and again there was a silence in the room as he drank from her lips, leaving her moist and panting.

"I'll never let you leave me again," he muttered, his words drowning inside her mouth. And then with a question in his eyes, he swept her up in his arms.

Glassy-eyed, Raine pointed toward the bedroom while burrowing against him, parting the buttons of his shirt so that she could press her lips against the exposed bones of his throat.

"Oh, my darling," Ashe groaned. Then, seconds later, he set his precious burden down on the king-sized bed. The drapes were open on the French doors, allowing the moonlight to bathe the room in a subtle glow.

They discarded their clothes hastily and found themselves naked, with Ashe's body weighing deliciously heavy on hers.

"You can't imagine how often I've dreamed of such a moment," he said, his voice heavy with passion.

"And I," she moaned, as his tongue probed her lips.

"Oh, God, we need to talk, so much to say." His words were incoherent as his tongue continued to wreak havoc with her body.

"We're not going to talk," Raine whispered. "Not now. Not now, my love."

Suddenly sliding off her, his lips hummed across each breast, sending waves of pleasure to the warm center of her before engaging in a long, slow, searching kiss that jolted her nervous system with short, electrifying impulses.

Determined to bring him the same pleasure, her lips blazed a trail down his throat, to the dark curls on his chest, his narrow waist, the smooth skin of his stomach. Sliding her hands up his thighs, she felt his fingers tug on a nipple as she ran the tip of her tongue along the warm extended flesh.

"Oh, God, Raine!" His voice was raw with hunger as she exulted in arousing him, giving him pleasure. Her hands held his buttocks, pulling him against her where small moaning sounds of wild delight rippled through her.

Then, abruptly, Ashe pulled away. Changing positions, he entered her, fiercely, insistently—one body, not two, then began moving slowly, deliberately.

"I can feel you inside me like a second heartbeat," she whispered.

"I adore you," he whispered in return, rocking with her.

It was exquisite, lethal pleasure.

She found his mouth as he moved up into her higher, then higher until she was hurrying closer to the wavering edges of an engulfing fulfillment that was more consuming, more violent than anything she'd ever known.

Together they cried out as the storm shook their bodies, flooding past the gates, and taking the gates and everything with it. She sobbed against his shoulder and he stopped moving, just holding her until they fell into a deep dreamless sleep.

The sweet dawn of morning made its presence known with the sun coloring the room a shimmering gold.

Raine opened her eyes to find him watching her, his eyes warm and tender in his dark disturbing face.

"I didn't think you were ever going to wake up," he drawled with a satisfied grin.

"Mmm." She pulled his head down so that she could touch his mouth with hers. "Is it late?"

"I don't know."

She laughed, stretching contentedly. "Then why were you so anxious for me to wake up?"

"So I could ask you to marry me," he said simply. His mouth dipped to tongue a nipple left exposed by her movement.

That intimate touch sent sparks shooting through Raine like wildfire, making her crazy for him, driving everything from her mind.

His hand slid down beneath the tangled weight of her hair. "Today. Tomorrow." He laughed. "Better yet, right now."

Caught up in his heady web of happiness, she played along. "I vote for now." Her eyes were wide open and sparkling like the clearest of diamonds.

He hugged her breathlessly and she could feel a deep chuckle rumbling in his chest. "Oh, my darling, we're going to have a marriage made in heaven."

She flashed him a beautiful smile. "I know."

"I never thought I'd ever share this kind of happiness with another living soul," he said softly, honestly.

"Me neither. I hate to admit it, but when I saw the way Todd and Heather looked at each other I turned green with envy."

He laughed again, giving her a resounding kiss before saying, "Speaking of Todd and Heather, they couldn't have been more delighted when I told them I loved you and was a fool for letting you go and that I was coming after you." He slapped her playfully on the bottom. "Of course, that was after I had told them the good news about Todd being vindicated."

Raine stared at him, her eyes suddenly turning serious, hearing only the first part of the sentence. "You mean you were coming to see me?"

His own smile faded and he nodded. "Yes, I was. I couldn't take it any longer."

"Oh, Ashe," she cried, "I was just going to stop by the house and grab my overnight bag and *I* was coming to you."

"God, what fools we've been," he whispered.

Raine reached up and touched his face, knowing that she could not live with herself until she had bared her soul to him. "Can you ever forgive me for being so stubborn and headstrong, for trying to change you, instead of loving you for what you are and the way you are? And that it—"

"Raine."

"No, please..." Her hand silenced him. "Please, my love, let me finish," she pleaded sweetly. "It no longer matters what you do as long as you love me. I've changed; I'm no longer afraid to take a chance. Loving you has given me the strength to become a pilot's wife." She paused and smiled through her tears. "Thanks to Alice, I learned how to share."

"Oh, my darling," Ashe said, his own eyes glazed with tears. "I'm the one who should say I'm sorry, beg for forgiveness for behaving like a goddamned macho idiot who thought he had to have everything his way." He paused, his mouth moving over her face as if to imprint her likeness on his lips.

"And you were right, there were times when I didn't care if I lived or died, though I never had the guts to end it all, but everything changed after I met you. Life suddenly became precious to me." He stopped talking and cleared his throat. "And because I love you, I'm willing to give up flying if—"

She cut off his flow of words with her lips and for a moment they clung together in a fierce embrace.

Then Raine pulled away. "Please," she whispered, "don't ever say it. Don't even think it." Her eyes shone with love. "Remember, I love you, not what you do, but what you are."

The sunlight dancing around the room made Ashe privy to every detail of her face, and it was completely devoid of fear and pain. For the first time, he knew she was truly free.

Yet, he also knew what it must have cost her to say those words, although there was no doubt in his mind that she meant them.

His heart expanded with love until he thought it would burst. He had never loved her more. "Thank you, my love," he murmured, "but we'll see what the future holds. Who knows, maybe I would like riding herd as much as I like flying planes." A drop of liquid fell from his eye onto her breasts. She caught her breath. "But for now, my darling, we'll take it one day at a time."

"Oh, Ashe, I love you."

"And I love you. You're my heart, my soul, my life."

"And you're mine."

As his lips closed over hers, Raine knew that she had found her heaven right here on earth.

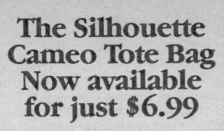

AMERICAN TRIBUTE

Where a man's dreams count for more than his parentage...

Look for these upcoming titles under the Special Edition American Tribute banner.

LOVE'S HAUNTING REFRAIN
Ada Steward #289—February 1986
For thirty years a deep dark secret kept them apart—King Stockton made his millions while his wife, Amelia, held everything together. Now could they tell their secret, could they admit their love?

THIS LONG WINTER PAST
Jeanne Stephens #295—March 1986
Detective Cody Wakefield checked out Assistant District Attorney Liann McDowell, but only in his leisure time. For it was the danger of Cody's job that caused Liann to shy away.

AM-TRIB-1

AMERICAN TRIBUTE

RIGHT BEHIND THE RAIN
Elaine Camp #301—April 1986
The difficulty of coping with her brother's death brought reporter Raleigh Torrence to the office of Evan Younger, a police psychologist. He helped her to deal with her feelings and emotions, including love.

CHEROKEE FIRE
Gena Dalton #307—May 1986
It was Sabrina Dante's silver spoon that Cherokee cowboy Jarod Redfeather couldn't trust. The two lovers came from opposite worlds, but Jarod's Indian heritage taught them to overcome their differences.

NOBODY'S FOOL
Renee Roszel #313—June 1986
Everyone bet that Martin Dante and Cara Torrence would get together. But Martin wasn't putting any money down, and Cara was out to prove that she was nobody's fool.

MISTY MORNINGS, MAGIC NIGHTS
Ada Steward #319—July 1986
The last thing Carole Stockton wanted was to fall in love with another politician, especially Donnelly Wakefield. But under a blanket of secrecy, far from the campaign spotlights, their love became a powerful force.

Silhouette Intimate Moments

COMING NEXT MONTH

AFTERSHOCKS
Catherine Coulter
Georgina was everything Dr. Elliot Mallory desired in a woman, but he couldn't let her love him and destroy her promising career. His noble side said he should walk away; his passionate side wouldn't let him.

SHINING MOMENT
Diana Holdsworth
Kate was thoroughly prepared to dislike Derek Langley, but instead she found herself swept up into a daring rescue mission behind the iron curtain, risking their lives and forging an unbreakable bond of love.

DUAL IMAGE
Nora Roberts
Ariel Kirkwood was only playing a part, yet for screenwriter Booth DeWitt the image she portrayed stirred too many bitter memories to allow him to give in to the desire he felt for the woman behind the role.

ISLANDS IN TURQUOISE
Barbara Faith
Marisa Perett had finally found a man whom she could truly love, but she had already reluctantly agreed to a sham reunion with her ex-husband for political reasons. Duty called...but so did her heart.
